"We have to talk, Emily," Will said

He pressed her down onto the sofa, then began to pace the rug, back and forth.

"What is it?"

"Look," he said, turning toward her abruptly, "in the morning I'm going to send Antonio into town to get Reverend Shumaker. We'll marry, right here in this parlor. The children can even..."

But Emily was shaking her head. "No," she said. "No, Will. We... *I can't.* I thought..."

"What *did* you think?" he asked, incredulous. "You couldn't possibly have thought we'd...behave like that and go on as before. Emily," he said, "I *want* to marry you."

She looked up into his bewildered face. "Please," she said, "try to understand, Will. This isn't my home. Someday, I'm going to have to go back to where I truly belong."

Abruptly she was on her feet, tears burning behind her eyes. How could she have thought they'd go on as before? Will was an honorable man—an honorable *Victorian* man!

Dear Reader,

Four more fabulous WOMEN WHO DARE are heading your way!

In May, you'll thrill to the time-travel tale Lynn Erickson spins in *Paradox*. When loan executive Emily Jacoby is catapulted back in time during a train wreck, she is thoroughly unnerved by the fate that awaits her. In 1893, Colorado is a harsh and rugged land. Women's rights have yet to be invented, and Will Dutcher, Emily's reluctant host, is making her question her desire to return to her own time.

In June, you'll be reminded that courage can strike at any age. Our heroine in Peg Sutherland's *Late Bloomer* discovers unplumbed depths at the age of forty. After a lifetime of living for others, she realizes that she wants something for herself—college, a career, a *life*. But when a mysterious stranger drifts into town, she discovers to her shock that she also wants *him!*

Sharon Brondos introduces us to spunky Allison Glass in our July WOMEN WHO DARE title, *The Marriage Ticket*. Allison stands up for what she believes in. And she believes in playing fair. Unfortunately, some of her community's leaders don't have the same scruples, and going head-to-head with them lands her in serious trouble.

You'll never forget Leah Temple, the heroine of August's *Another Woman*, by Margot Dalton. This riveting tale of a wife with her husband's murder on her mind will hold you spellbound...and surprised! Don't miss it!

Some of your favorite Superromance authors have also contributed to our spring and summer lineup. Look for books by Pamela Bauer, Debbi Bedford, Dawn Stewardson, Jane Silverwood, Sally Garrett, Bobby Hutchinson and Judith Arnold...to name just a few! Some wonderful Superromance reading awaits you!

Marsha Zinberg
Senior Editor

P.S. Don't forget that you can write to your favorite author

c/o Harlequin Reader Service
P.O. Box 1297
Buffalo, New York 14240
U.S.A.

LYNN ERICKSON

Paradox

Harlequin Books

TORONTO • NEW YORK • LONDON
AMSTERDAM • PARIS • SYDNEY • HAMBURG
STOCKHOLM • ATHENS • TOKYO • MILAN
MADRID • WARSAW • BUDAPEST • AUCKLAND

Published May 1993

ISBN 0-373-70549-2

PARADOX

ABOUT THE AUTHOR

"Having lived fifty miles from Rifle, Colorado, for most of our lives, we've always hoped to set a story there," says Molly Swanton, who writes as Lynn Erickson with her longtime friend Carla Peltonen. "Rifle is the oldest Western town on the train route through the Rockies, where ranching is still the predominant way of life. What better place to set a time-travel story, since Rifle still retains much of its original old Western flavor!"

Molly and Carla make their homes in Aspen, Colorado, and have been writing as a team for over fifteen years.

Books by Lynn Erickson
HARLEQUIN SUPERROMANCE
255—TANGLED DREAMS
276—A PERFECT GEM
298—FOOL'S GOLD
320—FIRECLOUD
347—SHADOW IN THE SUN
370—IN FROM THE COLD
404—WEST OF THE SUN
439—THE NORTHERN LIGHT
482—SILVER LADY
520—A WING AND A PRAYER

CHAPTER ONE

THEY SHOULD HAVE TALKED about it. Emily Jacoby sat on the Amtrak train as it approached the Moffat Tunnel and knew that she and Bill should have talked about having children from the moment their relationship grew serious.

Emily put down the travel book she'd bought last night in Denver and stared out at the white wilderness of Colorado's Rocky Mountains. The passenger car lurched a little as it climbed to the eleven-thousand-foot elevation where the train would tunnel beneath the tall, craggy mountains of the Continental Divide.

The young woman next to Emily peered past her shoulder. "Beautiful, isn't it?" she asked.

"It certainly is," Emily concurred.

"Your first time out West?"

Emily smiled. "Yes. Does it show?"

"Oh, no," the woman said, "I didn't mean it like that. It's just that you've been glued to the window since we left Denver."

"I guess I am a city slicker," Emily said. "Born and raised back East, I never really had the time to see the country."

"Train's the way to do it, then," the woman said, going back to her skiing magazine.

This *was* an adventure, Emily knew. She could have flown from Philadelphia to her new home in Seattle, but now she had the time to see things, to experience life with new eyes. Maybe it was just as well Bill had hit her with that bombshell.

"God, Emily, I wish we'd talked about this before," Bill had said three months ago at Thanksgiving. "I assumed . . . well, I guess I assumed we were of the same mind. I mean, you have your career and I . . ."

"Look," Emily had said, "I never intended to stay a loan officer at the bank forever. I *want* children, Bill. I'm twenty-seven, and maybe it's just that my biological clock is ticking away, but when we talked about marriage I thought it meant the whole nine yards."

Some Thanksgiving that had been. They'd been at her folks' house in Bryn Mawr, the posh suburb of Philadelphia, and suddenly it had become as clear as day: there would be no marriage to Bill. On the heels of that knowledge had come another surprise in Emily's well-structured world—she'd felt relief, yes, a true sense of relief that things had not worked out. She had experienced some guilt, but also a sense of lightness, the freedom of a burden lifted. The truth of it, Emily decided, delving deeper into her psyche, was that she had been really quite fed up with her life. Sick of the city, the pollution and the nine-to-five routine. Sick of her just-right car, her expensive clothes, the traffic lights and blaring horns, the sirens and ambulances wailing past her apartment window every night. Sick of two-hundred-dollar dinners for two and high heels that killed her feet. Sick of always saying the right thing and seeing the right shows, of reading the right books and ordering red wine when she really wanted a Coke.

A cozy little home with children's toys tossed all over, that's what she really wanted. And a big dog that shed a lot on the comfortable furniture. She could wear slippers all day if she wanted to. She could even drive a station wagon. If her hair wasn't perfect, so what? Parent-teacher appointments at school. Grocery carts jammed with food that wouldn't last a day with a passel of children and a hungry husband who mowed the lawn on weekends and watched football with his feet on the coffee table.

Emily needed to be needed.

Outside, the mountains rolled by. Billows and plumes of snow carried by a ferocious February wind spun off the white peaks into the clear Colorado sky. Emily felt curiously alive sitting on that train, alive and for the first time in her life keenly aware of who she was and what she wanted.

It had been a godsend when her old roommate from the university had called from Seattle at Christmas. "I love it here," Judy had said. "It's so different, Em. It's fresh, clean. It's booming, too. I mean, you wouldn't believe the difference between stuffy old Philly and Seattle. This place is *alive.*"

Emily had called her back on New Year's Day. "How's the job market there?"

"It's pretty good. Oh, maybe you won't be a high-powered loan officer right off the bat, but there are plenty of openings in the banks around here. Seattle's growing, Em," she'd said. "Take a chance. It's alive out here."

"How are the men?" Emily had asked, only half joking.

"Super. I mean *super.* These guys have fun, Em. They aren't all stuffed shirts, either. You in the market or what?"

"Well, sort of." And she'd told Judy about Bill not wanting children and about this sudden urge she had to settle down, to be needed by someone for a reason other than a bank loan.

So Emily had decided. The West it was. What did she have to lose? And now she was free, her doubts left behind in Philadelphia. Free to explore just who she really was and to set new goals, worthwhile goals.

A smile played on her lips as the train *clickety-clacked* through the Moffat Tunnel and along the side of the precipitous mountain. Below, the land was vast and white and empty, the snow dazzling and pure. The sky was so blue it hurt her eyes. In Philadelphia she'd be commuting on a crowded train or bus, and jostled on jammed streets beneath the dull winter sky. *This* was what she craved now: new sights and sounds and smells, new friends with whom she could be herself. She was starting over, ready to meet new and bold challenges head-on. At times in the past few weeks while she packed and said her goodbyes, Emily couldn't help asking herself, *Can I handle this?* But now she knew she could—she wanted this new life. Heck, if the pioneers could pack up their belongings and leave a safe, secure life in the East, then she could, too. And maybe, just maybe, there was someone out there waiting for her, someone very, very special.

"Glenwood Canyon is coming up," her neighbor said. "It's something to see."

And indeed it was. Forged by the Colorado River aeons ago, the sheer rock walls of the narrow canyon rose hundreds of feet to pierce the sky above. Below the towering cliffs, the river ran sluggishly through the ice floes of winter, twisting, winding darkly along the floor of the valley. Mountain goats clung perilously on the sides of the vertical rock faces. Emily stared, fascinated, out the window and marveled at the dangers the pioneers must have faced, forging their way west through these forbidding mountains and canyons, across the vast valleys and prairies of the high country. She picked up her travel book and found the canyon and city of Glenwood Springs on the foldout map.

As the train stopped and Emily got off to stretch her legs, sulfurous vapor steamed skyward from the world-renowned hot springs. It was cold in Glenwood Springs. Emily shivered. A raw winter wind was blowing in from the canyon to the west and dark clouds were amassing over the higher peaks. Maybe she'd even see a real western-style blizzard before reaching the high plateau country of Utah and Idaho.

She bought a cup of coffee at the hotel that serviced the Glenwood Hot Springs and roamed around the turn-of-the-century lobby. Pictures of a more peaceful, simple era graced the walls. There were photographs of the hotel itself, elegant carriages lining the circular driveway, the hot-springs pool across the muddy road and the bustling town beyond. There were daguerreotypes of miners and mule teams standing on barren mountainsides, the trees all cut for shoring up the shafts. And good grief! There was the infamous Doc Holliday, standing in front of a Glenwood Springs saloon, circa 1800. Ladies in their fin-

ery strolled the wide streets, and men in Stetsons and
suspenders lounged in front of a Mercantile store. One
photograph was of Indians, Utes, in white shirts and
vests with tall Abe Lincoln hats and long pipes. The
caption explained that the Utes first used the hot
springs as a healing winter camp before the whites
came to the mountains. Then it was princes and pres-
idents who rode the new train west in the 1890s to
partake of the beneficial waters.

"Amazing," Emily whispered, moving along the
wall, her heart feeling light. The Great American
West.

Emily's companion had left the train in Glenwood
Springs. She was a skier, apparently, heading toward
Aspen, forty miles away. But Emily had her travel
book for company and used the empty seat beside her
to prop her feet up.

The train headed out of Glenwood Springs and
through another, less precipitous, canyon. The dark
clouds of the gathering storm clung to the tops of the
mountains now, and the wind was kicking up dust
from the highway that followed the railroad tracks
along the Colorado River Valley.

West, Emily kept thinking, she was traveling
through the very heart of the American West. Every
now and then, her pulse would quicken, feeling as if
she were leaving civilization behind.

When the train gained speed on the far side of the
canyon, she opened her book and checked the map.
The next town they'd stop at would be Rifle, Colorado. Rifle. Emily pondered the name and smiled to
herself as she read about the small ranching community that, in 1890, had boasted the largest cattle

stockyards west of Chicago. Of course, with the railroad coming through a hundred years ago, she guessed
it must have been a booming town.

She closed the book and stared out the window,
images of bygone days assailing her. She could see
hardy cowpokes driving their herds across vast, sage-
brush-dotted rangeland then down into the dusty
stockyards, the wranglers sporting big handlebar
mustaches and rough leather chaps. On Saturday night
they'd get all gussied up for town—a bath, a shave, a
clean white shirt. But they'd still wear their six-
shooters and spurs. You bet.

And the businessmen of old Rifle. They'd be something to see, all right, wearing their dark suits and
shiny brocaded vests, their spiffy boots, city hats and
string ties.

But the women would be something else, Emily
knew. In old pictures she'd seen, women dressed
smartly with their tight corsets and big-bustled skirts.
Layers of petticoats and high-buttoned boots. Frilly
white blouses with cameos at the throat. And hats.
They wore anything from sunbonnets to huge, flow-
ing, feathered concoctions perched atop their pom-
padours.

It must have been an exciting time to be alive. The
country just opening up, the possibilities unlimited. A
simpler life, of course, but one fraught with challenge. How the pioneers of the American West would
have scorned modern-day mankind, scowled at their
petty fears and self-centered successes, at their lack of
values—the awful loss of family. Emily knew that was
what she hoped to find in this new life—a return to the

basics. Love, family, home. It was going to be wonderful.

She sat there, feeling the soothing movement of the train, trying to imagine herself as a pioneer a century ago, riding the exact same train on her way to...a new life. Yes, a new start somewhere, a new job. Of course, back then she would have had few choices. A governess, maybe, or a schoolteacher. A bank teller? Did women work in banks in the 1890s?

A century ago, she would have been seeing the exact same scenery, and feeling the same bumps where the rails met. The same mountains and snow and sky and trees. Even some of the same houses would have been there. She closed her eyes and tried to imagine it—the stays of her corset digging into her sides, the smell of wood smoke and men's cigars, the pinch of her high-button boots, the hat pins sticking into her scalp, the taste of the heavy breakfast she would have eaten early that morning in Denver.

In the seat across the aisle would be a man with tight black trousers, a brocade vest, white shirt, skinny tie, maybe even a worn gun belt around his waist. And a handlebar mustache. Yes, definitely a mustache. And a hat, a cowboy hat. A Wyatt Earp sort of guy.

Emily considered giving a disdainful sniff when the man tipped his hat to her, but she figured that was too much. She'd just leave herself sitting there, primly, a hundred years ago and come back to the present. She opened her eyes and sighed. What an imagination she had.

Outside the window the mighty river slid by, dark and wide, meandering through the broad valley whose winter brown fields were rapidly turning white as the storm moved in. It was a dry land, tall trees lining the banks of the river, the rest of the terrain marked by clumps of silver sage. The mountains rose in the distance, from the far reaches of the valley, but curtains of blowing snow were beginning to obscure them from Emily's view. She shivered a little and tucked her feet farther beneath her. It was a raw land, so very different from the softly contoured East. Here the mountains were harsh and bare, cut by dry-land gullies and mesas, sliced by cliffs with layered chunks thrown up by age-old earthquakes still lying naked to the elements.

Oh, yes. Emily could see in her mind's eye rugged cowboys riding across this unforgiving land; it was a perfect movie set. On the bank of the river she spotted a lone ranch house, a trickle of smoke rising from its tin chimney. On the range cattle stood, their heads lowered against the storm. Her heart swelled and she asked herself: could she have endured this life? Could she have left everything behind her if it weren't the 1990s but a hundred years ago? It was a disturbing thought—not knowing if she had the fortitude, the guts.

A strong gust rattled the window and shook Emily from her reverie. It was really beginning to snow hard now, the river totally obscured from view. The train lurched a little in the wind and had to slow down a bit. Emily suddenly remembered reading about the huge plows they used to attach to the old steam engines to clear the tracks of ten- and twenty-foot drifts. *That* must have been a sight.

Deciding to go back to her book now that the storm was blocking the view, Emily wondered if they'd be late getting into Salt Lake City that night. Not that it mattered, she figured, because Judy wasn't expecting her on any particular day.

In her letter, Emily had written:

Well, here I come. No more Bill and his neo-modern thoughts on raising a family. Thank God. How could I have almost married him? Anyway, I'm taking the train to Seattle. May as well see the sights. I might even stop over in a few cities en route. If I hold up any plans you've made you can yell at me when I get there. Can hardly wait to see you....

So it didn't really matter when she got there since Judy already knew her iffy itinerary.

This was heaven. She was free, going to an uncertain but wonderful future.

The train gently rocked from side to side, slowing around wide bends in the river. To the left, she could see the mountains again—though barely—practically right alongside the tracks now.

Suddenly, there was a jerk, a sharp lurch of the train. Emily's right shoulder slammed into the window. Her mind raced. What was going on? But then the ride seemed to settle for a few seconds. She let out a breath. She wasn't flying in a plane, after all.

It happened abruptly. There was another bone-cracking lurch followed by a terrible squealing and grinding of metal on metal. A split second later the car she was in seemed to take flight. There was an ear-shattering sound, indefinable and ghastly. Passengers began to scream as the car started to tumble. Emily

saw a man fly by and she clung even more desperately
to the armrest. Her arms felt as if they were being
ripped from their sockets and she knew she was falling. There was a terrible thundering whoosh and then
sudden, blinding white light. Suddenly, it was black.

CHAPTER TWO

WILL DUTCHER SWUNG the last fifty-pound sack of flour from the Western Mercantile Company onto the buckboard and covered it hurriedly with the canvas tarpaulin, tucking the sides around the sacks carefully.

It was sure snowing, he thought, pulling his hat down more firmly over his ears. He hoped there'd be no trouble getting back to the ranch, but he reckoned he'd get there all right unless a really bad wind came up and drifted the road over. He looked up from under the brim of his hat, squinting into the whiteness. Sure was coming down. The wind was blowing the snow sideways in stinging, wet sheets. Well, if he was late, Antonio could handle things. Of course, there *was* that new housekeeper lady Will was expecting. She could be a problem. Probably wearing thin-soled boots, too many petticoats and one of those little cape things that barely covered her shoulders. And, of course, a big feathered hat that would be the first casualty of the storm. Hell, what could you expect from a city lady? From Chicago, no less.

Pulling aside his long duster coat, he went into his trouser pocket for his watch. Bent over in order to shield it from the blinding snow, he checked it—10:41 p.m. He was just in time. The Number 3 westbound

from Denver City was due in at 10:45. Of course, it
might be delayed because of the storm. Damnation,
then he'd have to wait for the housekeeper. And, if the
flour and sugar got wet, Antonio would have his head.
He might just have to spring for two bits and drive the
whole rig, horses and all, into Collin's Livery Barn if
he had a long wait.

Will wasn't at all sure about this housekeeper. His
older brother, Claiborn, had arranged everything back
in Chicago. Last fall, at their younger brother's fu-
neral, Clay had pushed him: "You took in Jesse's
kids, and you and that crazy old cook of yours can't
raise them. You need a lady. An educated, genteel lady
who can take care of those children."

"Jesse and Clara were ranchers. I don't think they'd
like their young ones raised to be blue bloods, Clay.
We aren't city folk here in Colorado, you know," Will
had replied.

"You need someone," Clay had said. "I'll take care
of it."

And he had. The lady—blamed if Clay had bothered to send her name—was arriving any minute now,
all the way from Chicago where Clay Dutcher lived in
his fancy stone house. He'd written that he'd taken
care of the lady's salary for a year since Will was the
one actually saddled with the three orphaned children. All Will had to do was feed her, give her a room,
then sit back and let her have a free hand.

Well, he'd try it, Will thought, flipping back the
long tail of his duster as he swung lithely up onto the
buckboard seat and unwound the reins from the
brake. He'd give her a try. If she got underfoot, he'd
ship her back to Clay like a sack of flour.

He clucked to the two big bays who pulled the buckboard, slapped the reins on their steaming snow-wet rumps and headed down the main street of Rifle toward the Colorado River and the Denver-Rio Grande train station, which stood near its banks.

At first, he didn't know what made the near horse shy, then he saw Johnny McCrudden racing like a mad dog up the middle of the street. The kid was practically indistinguishable from the snowy, muddy thoroughfare because his wool coat was so plastered with snow. His wool hat was pulled down over his ears, and his mouth was open in a big O. His skinny legs churned like eggbeaters in the morass under his feet.

"Ho up there, Johnny!" Will called out. "You scared my horses."

The boy stopped, panting with exertion. "Oh, Mr. Dutcher," he gasped, "I gotta get to the schoolhouse and tell Mrs. Lindley to ring the bell!"

"What's up, Johnny?" Will asked, frowning.

The boy's chest rose and fell like a bellows under the coat; his eyes were wide as saucers. "A wreck, Mr. Dutcher! The Number 3 from Denver City! There was a big snow slide! Half a mile out of town! I gotta run, Mr. Dutcher!"

Lord Almighty. The housekeeper woman. What a way to start a new position. He clucked his pair into a quick trot, not daring to go any faster on the slippery road. What had happened? Behind him he heard the muffled peals of the schoolhouse bell—the call to the townsfolk to help. Word would get around fast, and everyone would be there. Probably Doc Tichenor was already boiling up his instruments. Damn, he'd never get home today!

His buckboard slid to a stop in front of the train depot, where a crowd was already gathering.

The stationmaster, Jackson Rusk, was shouting something. Will strained to hear through the muffling snow.

"About half a mile east of here," Jack was saying. "Yup, it's a bad one. Hit a drift or something in this storm. All the cars are off the tracks. Men, any conveyance you have would be mighty appreciated, to carry the injured on. Ladies, open your parlors to the wounded. Boil water and get out those bandages. We're sure to need 'em."

"Does Doc know yet?" shouted someone.

"Yessir, he knows. I sent Johnny McCrudden hot-footin' it to tell Mrs. Lindley to ring the bell and Doc to get ready."

Sitting there on his buckboard, Will listened. He took off his hat, slapped the snow from it absent-mindedly, and set it back firmly on his dark head. They'd need his buckboard, he thought, even loaded as it was. What a hell of a day to have a wreck. But, then, if the weather was fine, the train would be pulling into Rifle right on time, its steam whistle tearing at the air. And his new housekeeper would step off onto the platform with her big hat and her thin-soled city boots, climb into his wagon to go home with him and disrupt his easy, comfortable life.

"Anybody want to go with me?" Will called out. "I've got room."

"I will!" Johnny McCrudden yelled out as he dashed back down the street.

"You're too young, Johnny," Will said. "You stay here."

"I'm twelve! I can help! Lemme go, Mr. Dutcher!"

"Aw, Will, let him go," Jack Rusk said. "We'll need every pair of hands. I'm telegraphing Denver City and Glenwood Springs right now, but I can't see them getting any help through to us till the storm's over. Hey, folks! Don't shove. There's plenty of work for all. Half a mile east of here at Maxfields's ranch! Let's move fast. Folks'll be needing help!"

Johnny was up on the seat beside Will before Jack stopped talking. "Gee, thanks, Mr. Dutcher," he panted.

"It may not be nice, Johnny. There're going to be people hurt, maybe dead. Can you handle it, son?"

"Yes, sir, Mr. Dutcher, my word on it."

The two bays must have felt the tension in the air, because they moved quickly, surefooted, through the veil of white that fell steadily, obscuring the other side of the river already. It was only a few minutes before Will heard the hiss of a steam engine, not the ordinary, controlled hiss, but a loud screaming escape of steam, the dying wail of the engine. Even through the storm, the noise was unbearable: clanging, crying, the frantic bellowing of cattle, men's voices raised in panic. Then the snatches became a steady cacophony of shrieks and cries, moans and hisses and the screech of metal grating on metal.

This was a bad one, all right.

"Mr. Dutcher . . ." he heard Johnny say.

"You've been warned, John McCrudden. But go back if you want. There's no need for a boy your age to see this," Will said, giving him a stern look.

"No, I'll stay." But Johnny's voice was shaky.

The train loomed out of the snow like a wraith. It was not there one moment and then it was. To Will it looked like hell. The snow muffled and dimmed and hampered every movement. Sound carried on the wind eerily, too loud one moment, too faint the next. He could smell oil and fire, hot metal and the copper odor of blood. Ugly scents. The train engine lay on its side, still spitting flames and clouds of steam. Down here by the river, wind whipped across the scene, taking with it the steam and the cries.

The sheriff had already arrived. A few horses and wagons were there and more were arriving every second. Train passengers wandered aimlessly, clothes torn, blood on their faces. Townsfolk moved purposefully, quickly collecting those who could walk. Cattle loose from the broken boxcars blundered about, some with dangling legs or bloody gashes.

There were already bodies laid out in rows, rapidly being covered with snow. There would be more, Will knew. And then he thought again about the housekeeper. Was she one of the lucky ones? Or was her trip out West her last trip anywhere? *Lord,* Will thought, *I don't have time to feel guilty, not right now.*

Will leaped down from the buckboard and tied the horses to a tree. His duster flapped in the brutal wind, and he pulled the brim of his snow-whitened hat low. "Come on, Johnny," he said grimly, "we got work to do."

The cars were tilted at odd angles, as if an angry child had kicked at his train set. Inside the first car, close to the engine, it was horror: twisted seats, broken glass, scattered bags. A man lay beneath the wood stove used to warm the car. He was scorched and unmoving, his eyes still open, staring hideously. Will crouched down and, with a steady hand, closed the poor soul's eyelids. He took a breath, glanced at Johnny's pinched face, then began to pull the man out, bracing himself against a broken window. He and Johnny carried the body outside, struggling through the deepening drifts.

"You okay, Johnny?" he asked.

The boy was ghostly pale, but his mouth was firm now. "Yes, sir, Mr. Dutcher."

A woman ran by, her head bare, hair streaming wildly, a baby in her arms. She was sobbing hysterically. Will stopped her, and she looked at him as if he were the devil himself.

"Ma'am," he said quietly, "if you go over there, someone will take you into town."

"I'm going to Salt Lake City," she sobbed. "Salt Lake City. I have to get there. My husband..."

"Well now, ma'am, there'll be no trains through to Salt Lake until they clear the tracks. But there's a telegraph office in town, and you can notify your husband. Johnny, take this lady to the buggy over there. That's right," Will said carefully.

The sheriff needed a team of horses to free some poor souls trapped by an overturned car. Moans came from the wreckage, moans that would rise and fall, stop abruptly or go on and on, until Will wished he could send Johnny on back to town.

He unhitched his team from the buckboard and took it to the car that needed to be moved.

"Here, Dutcher," the sheriff directed, "hitch yours to this side. We'll get a couple of others. You there! Over here, bring those horses here!"

The horses strained, slipping in the churned-up snow, their wet backs steaming. The car moved. Screams came from inside—screams, and the grating of torn metal.

Will swore. The car was slipping, not coming upright. The horses couldn't do it....

More horses were hitched to the car. Men shouted, cursed, yelled at the white-eyed horses. The cold snow whipped into Will's eyes even under his hat brim. His hands were frozen, his union suit soaked with sweat, but he never noticed.

This time the car moved a little, creaking, protesting. Screams filled the air. The snow was trampled and splotched with red for yards all around them. It was hell.

The car teetered on its smashed wheels then settled heavily into the snow right side up. Men rushed inside. Wearily Will unhitched his team and patted their wet flanks. He wished he had blankets for them—and oats. Tonight they'd get plenty. He'd see to that.

"Good boy," he said to one horse, then to the other, rubbing each animal's nose. "Good boy."

The place was a madhouse. Men milled about, carrying hurt passengers. A steady stream of wagons, buggies and buckboards moved slowly, doggedly, through the unrelenting storm, loaded up with wounded. The wind howled, and Will couldn't tell if he was hearing people or just the fury of the storm. After another hour he realized he was exhausted, half-frozen, soaked to the skin with sweat. If he sat down he'd freeze. He had to keep moving.

How did the wounded passengers have the energy to keep screaming? Will wondered. He could barely talk.

And yet the horrible cries kept on and on. None of the rescuers spoke much anymore. They simply labored, their faces grim and cracked with the biting cold.

"Mr. Dutcher!" came Johnny's voice. "Over here, Mr. Dutcher!"

He slogged his way to another tilted car down the line. Johnny hung on to a slanted doorway and waved to him. "Hurry! Mr. Dutcher!" Going over to the car, he pulled himself up the twisted iron stairs to the inside, threaded through broken seats, glass and frozen clots of gore to find the boy. Beneath him the car moved and settled. Will stopped short, holding his breath, but there was no more shifting. He went on, hanging on to the intact seats to stay upright on the tilted floor.

"Johnny?" he called out.

The boy's head popped up from behind a seat. "Here, Mr. Dutcher."

Will pulled himself along until he got to Johnny. The boy was wedged into a corner, crouched over a body. "Look," the boy said, his face incredulous.

Will bent forward. He caught a glimpse of white skin, matted hair, an arm, a woman's hip... "Johnny," he said quickly. "Behind me. Now."

The boy scurried out of the way, and Will took his place over the body. It was a woman, a young woman. Unconscious, perhaps dead. And she was naked. Smooth and white and unconscious, lying there utterly nude, her body gleaming in the dimness.

Shock hit Will like a sledgehammer; his heart leaped into his throat and collided with something, then settled back to beat too heavily.

He cleared his throat, tried to say something. "Well, I'll be damned," he finally got out, staring in disbelief at the full swell of a breast, the womanly curve of a smooth belly. His body felt suddenly drenched and his skin prickled with a flash of heat.

Will tried to clear his head. All the people in the train wreck had ripped clothing, sleeves torn off, pant legs flapping, skirts torn. But no one had been ... no one had been so ... *naked.*

Snow blew in a broken window and settled on her body; he watched, fascinated, as the flakes melted. Then he came to his senses, began struggling in the cramped place to get out of his duster.

"Is she ..." came Johnny's voice, "is she alive?"

"Don't know yet," Will replied, awkwardly trying to bundle the woman into the folds of his long coat. His hands brushed a thigh, her hip, and when he tucked the stiff material around her breasts he couldn't help but feel the heavy swells against his fingers.

Will kept his wits about him, however, aware of the boy's face at his shoulder. *Guess John McCrudden got an eyeful,* he thought as he pulled her into a position where he could pick her up and stagger out of the car. He was tired and she seemed pretty damned heavy, and the tails of his duster kept tripping him up. She moaned once, and he knew then that she was still alive.

"Come on, Johnny," Will said. "We're going to take this lady into town. Everyone's about gone now, anyway."

"Sure, Mr. Dutcher."

"Run on over there and let the sheriff know, boy. Tell him the rear cars are empty now."

"The lady?" Johnny asked.

"I'm gonna take her on to Doc's."

"Sure will be good to warm my hands on the stove," Johnny said, then ran off in the direction of the sheriff.

It was *cold* out. The snow was letting up a bit, but the wind was bad, and the temperature was dropping. Will laid the woman on top of the flour sacks in his buckboard and covered her with the canvas. Was he wasting his time? Maybe the poor thing would die anyway, cold as it was. Maybe she had serious injuries, too. He couldn't tell.

He felt her forehead. It was cool and smooth, like sculpted marble. Her lips were tinged with blue. Her hair was wet and matted, but it would be a dark blond, he guessed. It barely fell to her shoulders, though, as if her head had been shaved in the past, maybe for a bad fever. He saw the pulse throb in her throat, and it seemed steady. He put a finger on it and felt the tiny leap that signaled life.

Who was she? Had she been alone on the train? My Lord, could she be the new housekeeper? It *was* possible. And her clothes—gone. No tatters remained, not even the remnants of a corset. How could such a thing happen? Damned odd, but he supposed there was some explanation. Maybe one of the male passengers had gone crazy, stripped her and left her to die.

Johnny came running back. "Sheriff says go on home, there's nothing left much to do now. Says everyone else left in the cars is dead, Mr. Dutcher."

Will shook his head in sympathy. He was beginning to shiver without his coat, though, the wind biting at him like a live creature. "Let's go, Johnny. Sit up on back, will you, see to the lady. Make sure she stays covered up, now, or she'll freeze for sure.''

The tired horses plodded back to town. He pulled them up in front of Doc Tichenor's, next to a dozen other rigs waiting there.

Shuddering with the cold, Will lifted the woman into his arms and started up the walk. He was moving slowly, numbed by the cold, his mind sluggish. He stopped for a moment and turned to the boy. ''Johnny, there's a quarter in it for you if you take my team to Collin's barn. Tell him to rub them down good and give them a double measure of oats.''

''Sure, Mr. Dutcher.''

''You up to it, boy?'' he thought to ask.

''Yes, sir.''

''Okay. Then you stay there where it's warm and wait for me. I'll drop you home later.''

Doc Tichenor was overwhelmed. His surgery, his whole house, was littered with injured passengers. He'd already tended the more serious cases, and his white shirt was stained with blood. The ambulatory ones he saw to perfunctorily and sent them off with one of the ladies of the town, who took them to the hotel, the school or to their own homes.

It was noisy in Doc's house. The women and children still wailed, the men groaned, the doctor gave terse orders. But it was warm. Thankfully, Will set the woman down on a settee in the parlor, where he was directed, and stood there for a time as if he'd been poleaxed, his hat and mustache dripping melted snow.

''What's wrong with this one?'' the doctor's housekeeper asked.

"I don't exactly know, Mrs. Fisher," he said, remembering only then to remove his hat. "She's out cold."

"The doctor's very busy. It'll be a little bit, Will. Get yourself some coffee in the kitchen. You look like something the cat drug in yourself," she said curtly. "Why, you're soaked to the skin. What's in your head, man, to come out in this weather with no coat? Honestly."

Will barely heard her. *Coffee.* He glanced at the mystery woman. She slept on, peacefully, it seemed, blue-veined eyelids closed, dark lashes lying like fans on alabaster skin. One slim pale arm had fallen loose from his duster and trailed on the floor. She'd be all right for a minute, and he could sure use a hot cup of coffee.

It was black and strong, with grounds at the bottom of the cup. He spooned in two sugars and sipped gratefully, feeling some life flow back into his limbs. He took off his heavy wool shirt and hung it on the back of a chair facing the wood stove to dry. He wished he could do the same with his long underwear, too, but he guessed it would dry on him in time.

What a day this had turned out to be, he thought, shoving a few more pieces of wood into the stove to keep it going. Pots of water simmered on the stove top, ready for Doc's needs. Best keep the stove roaring hot, Will knew.

He carried his second cup of coffee back to the parlor with him and checked on the lady.

She'd moved, his duster lying low across her chest, darn near exposing her bosom. Quickly he pulled it up and tucked it around her. Her eyelids fluttered and she moaned, moving restlessly.

"Easy there," he said, then realized that's how he talked to his horses. But how did you talk to a woman?

He ended up sitting on the settee, holding her because she kept tossing his duster off, and he was embarrassed for her, without even a petticoat to her name. He sat there for an hour, getting warm and drowsy himself, the heaviness of her body sagging against him, the sweet, damp scent of her hair in his nostrils.

Her features, he decided after studying them for a very long time, were not really classic. Her mouth was too big, and maybe her jaw was a bit strong, a little heavy. He didn't know what color her eyes were. Brown, deep dark brown? Or bright cornflower blue? He'd like to know. Why didn't she just wake up and open her eyes? But she kept tossing and making small, throaty noises, like a person in the throes of a nightmare.

The warmth of the parlor brought some color back to her cheeks. Pink. Petal pink. She shivered for a time, trembling against him so that he had to hold her still, but then her body relaxed and her lips became pink, too. Images flashed through Will's mind when she moved against him: white skin, round buttocks, curving hips, belly, thighs. No! A gentleman had no business thinking such things! It was only the accident, the train wreck. If she woke up and knew he'd seen her like that...

It grew darker outside Doc's windows, and the storm seemed to be weakening. Will actually dozed, and his head bowed and touched her hair. He jerked upright, the heady scent of her perfume stirring his senses.

"Well, what have we got here?" It was Doc Tichenor, hands on hips, staring down at him over his spectacles.

"Don't know. Johnny and I found her like this," Will said, disentangling himself swiftly and standing up to his six-foot height.

The doctor briskly pulled back the duster from the woman, stopped short, evidently expecting a chemise, a corset, something. He shrugged then and went on about his doctoring, holding his stethoscope beneath a breast.

Will looked around the empty room quickly, embarrassed. But the doctor didn't seem to notice his discomfort as he felt her body for wounds and listened to her heart. All Will knew was that a hot, prickly sensation was racing across his skin from head to toe.

He tore his gaze away from those round white breasts and mumbled, "I, ah, think I'll get some more coffee." Hands thrust in his pockets, he moved away.

"Get Mrs. Fisher for me," Doc called over his shoulder.

Will stopped short. "Is the lady... I mean," he began, "is there anything...?"

"Heart's strong as an ox," Doc said. "What she needs is some duds. Get Mrs. Fisher."

While Mrs. Fisher searched for clothes, Doc kept examining the lady. Finally he pushed his spectacles upon his nose, stroked his goatee and declared, "She's had a bump on the noggin. Medical term's a concussion. She needs watching for a few days. Might forget things, temporary amnesia. Dizziness, nausea. If she goes to sleep and won't wake up, let me know, Will.''

"Me?"

"Isn't she your new housekeeper?" Doc asked. "The one you were expecting?"

"Well, I don't know," Will said, frowning.

"All the other women are accounted for, Will. This here lady's the only one with no identification, if you know what I mean. She must be. Besides, where am I gonna put her? Every house in town's full and there's many hurt a lot worse. Don't fret, she'll wake up and be good as new," Doc said. "I'll even throw in the clothes for free."

Thoughtfully rubbing his mustache, Will looked down at the woman. "If she isn't the housekeeper," he said, "can I bring her back?"

"I expect she'll tell you what to do," Mrs. Fisher said, "once she wakes up. Now, you two get out of here while I dress her. It's a scandal!''

IT WAS A LONG TREK back through the snow and the darkness. But Will would have had to bed down in Collin's Livery Barn, since there wasn't room anywhere in town, and his horses were rested and fed. So was he, for that matter. So, he guessed, as he sat with a bundled-up Johnny McCrudden, he was better off headed home. Overhead a few stars were beginning to shine. The storm was almost over. The lanterns hanging from the buckboard swung merrily, breaking the utter darkness, and his team knew the road as well as he did.

The woman was dressed and wrapped in three wool blankets and a buffalo robe. He and Johnny each had a heavy quilt wrapped around them and a good meal under their belts. And he'd be home in an hour.

"What's her name?" Johnny asked out of the darkness.

"Don't know."

"But she's your new housekeeper," the boy said. "Ain't she?"

"So it seems. But I don't know her name. Guess I'll have to wait until she comes around and ask her."

"Lucky she isn't dead, huh, Mr. Dutcher?"

"More like a miracle, I'd say."

Every so often he'd hear her moan in the rear of the wagon. Then Johnny would crawl back and check on her. He wondered how long she'd be out like that—hours, days? He should've asked Doc more questions. What if she woke up empty-headed and addled? What if she couldn't remember who she was? All Will needed on top of three young children was an invalid, or a simpleminded female. He should've said no, he wouldn't take her, not until he knew for sure just who in tarnation she was.

He dropped Johnny off at home then continued the last remaining miles to his own ranch, the Dutcher spread, as everyone called it. No fancy names like those rich Englishmen used. Just a plain *D* for a brand. Everyone for a hundred miles around knew the big spreads. And when Jesse and Clara had died, Will got their adjoining land, too: a thousand acres, mostly fenced in now, and good water. Their house came in handy, too, for extra cowhands when Will needed them.

Will usually went directly to the barn, but this night he stopped at the kitchen door. He yelled to Antonio, figuring the old man was asleep, and went around to the back of the buckboard.

Lord, she weighed more than two sacks of flour! Nearer three. But she wasn't fat, he'd attest to that. Maybe he was just plain tuckered out. The blankets dragged on the ground, and he kicked at the back door with his boot. "Antonio!"

A light came on in the kitchen, the door opened. Will turned the woman and sidled in past the half-asleep, astonished Antonio.

"*¿Qué va?*"

"This is the new housekeeper, Antonio."

"She is sleeping?"

"There was a train wreck. She's unconscious. Lord, let me put her down." He walked through the kitchen to the parlor and laid her on the sofa. Antonio hovered.

"I'm tuckered out, Antonio. It's been a long day. I had to help with the wreck," Will said.

"The storm, it was a bad one, boss. I thought you stay in town."

"I would've, but the town's full. There must be a hundred passengers hurt bad. The hotel's full, every house is full. So I had to come home or sleep in Collin's Livery Barn." Will took his hat off and threw it onto a chair. He stood, hair plastered to his head, feet apart, hands on hips, and stared down at the woman.

"She young," Antonio said. "I thought we get old dried-up one."

"Might've been better," Will muttered.

"Maybe she is no going to like it here. Maybe she want to go home, boss," Antonio said hopefully.

"Maybe," he said. "The young ones all right?"

"They sleeping."

"Well, Antonio, I better put her in the spare room."

"I made the bed, like you say."

"Good." Will took a deep breath and picked her up, one arm under her knees, another under her shoulders. Her head lolled back. "Getting to be a habit," he grumbled, striding up the stairs. He carried her down the narrow hall with Antonio holding the kerosene lamp ahead of him and opening the bedroom door. He had to tilt her up to get her through the door and rapped his knuckles on the frame in the process. He swore under his breath.

He was laying her on the bed when Mary appeared from the attic rooms, a small white wraith in her flannel nightgown and blond braids. "Uncle Will," she said in that too-mature way she had, "what's going on? Who is that?"

Will sighed. "It's the new housekeeper, I think. She got hurt in a train wreck."

"A train wreck?"

"A train wreck?" echoed another voice. And then another, even shriller. "A train wreck, Uncle Will?"

Tarnation, they were all up. Both boys and Mary. He'd have to explain. "The Number 3 from Denver City went off the track just east of town. That's where I was all day, helping the people who got hurt. And this lady, well, she's the one they figured has to be the new housekeeper Uncle Clay sent," he explained.

"What's the matter with her, Uncle Will?" asked Burke, the youngest, his eyes wide, his blanket held tightly under his arm.

"She got hit on the head. Doc says she'll come around and be fine soon. Good as new."

"Oh," Burke said.

"Oh," Jesse said.

Will ran a big hand through his dark hair. God, but he was tired. Sweaty, dirty and tired.

He turned from the curious children to the woman lying on the white counterpane. She was wrapped like a mummy in the heavy blankets, her hair tangled, her face pale. He should make her comfortable, he supposed. He stood there looking down at her, feeling helpless and foolish.

Gingerly he pulled the blankets away. Mrs. Fisher had dressed her in a baggy black dress, nothing fancy, black stockings with plain black shoes. Underneath . . . he dared not imagine it. Doc's housekeeper had also bundled up a nightgown, a wrapper and a clean petticoat and thrust it at him as he left Doc Tichenor's. He should put the nightgown on her, he supposed. He just wasn't sure how to go about it.

"Damn," he muttered. He was suddenly aware of the children moving restlessly, disapproving of his language. It was Mary who'd taught them that. "Sorry," he said shortly, but that didn't solve his problem.

Will Dutcher was thirty-four years old. He'd never been married, and he didn't have a notion about women's clothes. He'd never had more than a quick run-in with women, and those were the kind you didn't have to undress. He could rope a cow, break a horse, command men, run a big spread, even cook a decent meal over a campfire. He could kill a man if he had to—and he'd done it. But he'd be goddamned if he knew how to undress a woman.

He'd chosen to stay single, even though there was many a woman over the years who'd made it clear they'd like to have him. But he knew he wouldn't be such a bargain; a man used to his own ways, selfish and sometimes distant. Clay had called him forbidding, and his sister-in-law, Clara, had told him he was considered quite a catch, although one with a difficult temperament. He was just used to his own way—and that was the main reason he'd been real apprehensive about the housekeeper Clay had sent him.

Maybe Antonio could help him with the nightgown. All those goldang buttons and hooks and such. He was going to call the old man, but the idea of another man's eyes on this woman, on her bare skin, made a knot tighten unaccountably in his gut. Another man seeing her smooth, curving hips and legs and breasts—as he had seen her—no, it wouldn't do.

He watched her as she moved. Her features shifted into a grimace then relaxed, her lips trembled but no sound came out. Her fist closed then opened. A woman. How had he let Clay talk him into this?

Hell, he figured he'd have to do it himself or stand there all night gaping at her like a fool. That nightgown, where was it?

He turned to see the three young ones in the doorway of the spare room, staring wide-eyed.

"Get on upstairs to bed or I'll be tanning a few hides," he said harshly. After hearing their doors close upstairs, Will turned back to the golden-haired woman.

Clay hadn't mentioned anything in his letter about how dang pretty the housekeeper was. Only that she was said to be efficient and had good references. Will didn't know whether to be angry or pleased.

He leaned over her, searching for the buttons he knew had to be somewhere around the neckline, then found himself staring into her eyes. They were open. Blue eyes, he had time to note before they clouded over and closed again. His hands went awkwardly to work.

CHAPTER THREE

EMILY FELT as if she were swimming in deep, muddy waters, unable to find the surface. Above her she could occasionally see a face, undulating, unreachable. She knew, somewhere inside her, that the face belonged to a man, but it was no one she knew. And then suddenly she felt dragged from the protective dark waters and thrust into coldness, her skin cringing and too bare, as if someone's hands were on her body, manipulating her, touching her in places that made her moan and shrink away. The frightening sensation lasted too long before those hands deposited her back into the warm, shadowy waters where she could drift again, unharmed.

Time lost all meaning and sensation. She heard a voice occasionally. Deep, gravelly, urging her to come with it. But she was so tired, so bone weary, she resisted the timbre that reached her too often.

There was agonizing pain when she floated too near the surface, terrible pain, sharp and acute. Sometimes the voice and a soothing coolness on her brow helped her ease back into the depths again. It hurt too much to reach the surface, so she let herself drift and drift....

Bright sunlight flashed across her face. Emily's eyes opened to a dizzying pain in her temples.

She was alone. Alone in a cozy room, a coarse wool blanket pulled to her chin. She tried to push herself up on her elbows but fell back, blinking the pain away. Her breath came in short weak gasps. She must have dozed again, because when she opened her eyes once more, the sunlight was spilling onto an oak dresser across the room.

This time Emily made it up on her elbows, though her arms trembled. Yes, she was alone in a bedroom somewhere. Victorian lace curtains at the tall window. An oak dresser with a fine lace doily on top, a single glass and a porcelain pitcher decorated with roses. A rocking chair. And the bed she lay on. She shifted her weight. The brass headrest creaked, and the lumps in the mattress pressed against her thighs and elbows. It felt like an old horsehair mattress, one like her great-aunt used to have.

Emily's hand went to her brow as she settled back down and tried to think. She became aware of a scratching at her neck and found a high lace collar on a white flannel nightgown. The stiff lace tickled her wrists, too, as she felt the soft, heavy weave of the cotton nightgown.

Not my nightgown.

Where was she? How did she get here? Who on earth undressed . . .

The train.

"Oh, my God," Emily whispered, her voice a dry croak. *The train.*

Her memory came flooding back with a whoosh. She'd been on the train. There had been a storm. And then the lurching, the man flying past her as the car tumbled. She must have been hurt. Her head, of course. So she was in a hospital....

Not a hospital. This wasn't a hospital....

The bedroom door groaned on its hinges, and Emily turned her head sideways, confusion swirling in her brain. *Not a hospital.*

There was a man standing in the portal. He was tall, his thick, dark waving hair parted in the middle. He had a thick mustache, too, a handlebar mustache against sun-browned skin. Blue, deep sapphire blue eyes in a handsome rugged face, a face she'd ... she'd seen before ...

"You're awake." The gravelly voice. The same voice as in her dreams. "How do you feel?"

He simply stood there, his body filling the doorway, his weathered hand on the ornate brass knob. He looked ... uncomfortable.

Emily wet her lips and stared.

"Maybe I should come back...."

"No," she managed weakly, "no. Please stay. I...I have so many questions. I..."

"I'm sure you do." His eyes held hers for a moment, and then he seemed to decide something. He closed the door behind him with care and moved across the room to the sunny window. He stood there, still ill at ease, his arms folded stiffly across his collarless white shirt, a shoulder against the window frame.

Emily tried to sit up but only made it to her elbows again. "Who...?" she began.

"Will Dutcher," he said in that unmistakable voice. "You're at my ranch in Rifle, ma'am."

"Your...ranch?"

"Doc Tichenor's was all filled up after the train accident."

"Oh." She tried to clear the cobwebs from her brain. "The hospital? Isn't there a . . ."

"No, ma'am. Nearest one's in Glenwood Springs. Some of the folks were taken there, but Doc said you'd be fine after a spell."

"I, ah, see," Emily said. She didn't see at all. "How long have I been here?" she asked, confused, dreading the thought that she'd been in a coma for days or weeks . . . or years.

"The train wreck was yesterday," he said. "I brought you here last night."

"Oh," she said, relieved. "You brought me here. I see."

"Sure did, ma'am. As I said, the town was full up." He shifted, a hand going up unconsciously to toy with his mustache. Emily noticed no ring or band and wondered.

"Listen," he said, "we couldn't find any identification on you, ma'am, and the Doc and I and some others figured you must be the housekeeper I was expecting from Chicago so I—"

"The housekeeper?"

"That's right. For my niece and nephews."

She shook her head, trying to make sense of his words. "My name is Emily Jacoby. I'm from Philadelphia, not Chicago."

"Well, now my brother back in Chicago didn't supply the name, ma'am, but you were the only woman on the train we couldn't figure who she belonged to so we assumed . . ."

"I'm Emily Jacoby," she repeated. "I'm not a housekeeper, Mr....Mr. Dutcher. Why don't you call your brother and verify things?"

He looked at her oddly. "There's no telephone here."

"No...phone?"

"Not this far out, ma'am."

Emily put a hand to her forehead. It was pounding furiously. She knew the West was still primitive in some areas, but this was really pushing it.

"Look," she said, swallowing, her mouth cotton-dry. "I was on my way to Seattle. I was only taking the train to see the sights."

"Alone?"

"Yes, alone." God, her head hurt.

"Ma'am, Seattle's a dang rough town, I hear. I can't believe..."

"Believe what you want," Emily said, feeling drained and confused as she sank into the feather pillow.

He was across the room in two strides, a glass of water in hand from the porcelain rose pitcher. "Here, drink this," Will Dutcher said, then put a hand behind her head and helped prop her up.

Emily sipped on the water then looked up. He had a penetrating gaze, as if he were judging her somehow. She noticed, also, that there were white crinkle lines around those very blue eyes, identifying him as a man who spent a lot of time outdoors. Handsome, she thought once more, but hard looking somehow, aloof.

"More water?" he was asking, his hand still behind her head.

"No, thank you," Emily replied, and he eased her back onto the pillow. "Mr. Dutcher," she said, "what is wrong with me, anyway? My head..."

"Doc said you hit it real hard."

"Did I have a CAT scan?"

"A...what?" He returned the glass to the dresser and turned to face her.

"A...CAT scan."

"Doc checked you out pretty good, ma'am. He..."

"Emily," she whispered, suddenly exhausted. "My name's Emily." She began to drift. Later, she'd ask all her questions later.

"I'll, ah, be letting you rest now, ma'am," Will said, heading to the door. "Maybe you can eat something in a while."

"Yes," she replied wearily, sinking. Then it struck her. Before sweet oblivion claimed her once more, Emily asked, "Who...who put this nightgown...?"

"I—" he cleared his throat "—I did, ma'am." And then he was gone, the door clicking quietly shut. All Emily could recall before darkness overcame her was the dreamlike memory of cool air on her flesh and warm hands. Will Dutcher's hands.

IF AT FIRST EMILY THOUGHT she was alone at a ranch house with Will Dutcher she was very much mistaken. That evening the cook, a man named Antonio, brought her a bowl of broth. Shortly thereafter there came another knock on her door. It was Will Dutcher. Standing in front of him, crowding the doorway, were three children. They all looked terribly nervous, as if she might bite their heads off.

Dutcher cleared his throat. "These are my wards," he said, "my brother's children. This is Mary." He nodded at the little girl on the left. She appeared to be around ten years old, had two long blond braids and was wearing the most beautiful dress, old-fashioned gingham and lace. On her legs were long, heavy black tights and she wore old-fashioned button-up shoes. She gave a short curtsy, bobbed her sunny blond head and smiled awkwardly.

"Hello, Mary," Emily said, "it's nice to meet you."

"Hello, Miss Jacoby."

Then there were the two boys, Jesse, who was eight, and Burke, a year younger. They could have been twins with their bluntly cropped blond heads and large blue eyes the color of the Colorado sky. Each boy wore a starched white shirt and baggy trousers with suspenders. Their hair was damp looking and neatly combed. Emily had the impression they'd rather be anywhere in the world other than standing in her doorway.

"Let's see," she said, "it's Jesse in the middle and Burke on the right. It's nice to meet you."

"Yes, ma'am," they chorused.

It struck her then. The entire family reminded her of the Pennsylvania Dutch, some sort of Amish or Mennonite sect living in the West. It wasn't just their clothes—rather, it was their whole demeanor right down to the curtsy and politely bobbed heads. No wonder they had no telephone. It wouldn't have surprised Emily to have seen the entire family going to the market in a horse-drawn buggy. Heck, Emily had been born and raised thirty miles from the heart of the

Pennsylvania Dutch country; she knew one when she saw one.

Except...except Will Dutcher. He was somehow wrong for the role. He lacked the humility. He was too...too masculine...and arrogant.

"Now say good-night to Miss Jacoby," he was telling them. Then, "Ah, Mary, you might want to stay and see...I mean, Miss Jacoby might want to tend to...ah...herself."

Little Mary stepped inside the room dutifully, and Will ushered the boys out.

Emily did have to find the bathroom. But she was so terribly weak; her legs were threatening to give out on her as if she were a newborn foal. Mary took her hand and led her out the bedroom door then stopped, frowning.

"You'll need your shoes and a blanket or something for your shoulders, Miss Jacoby," she said.

"My...shoes?"

The girl nodded. "Here, I'll get them." She hurried inside the room, opened a closet door, then rushed back carrying a pair of short black boots that laced up.

"Mary," Emily said, leaning against the doorjamb, "those aren't mine."

"They couldn't find yours," the girl explained, and Emily had to shake the fog from her head. Hadn't she been wearing her tall brown boots? How could they have been lost?

"Tending" to herself was the biggest shock yet to come. Emily, Mary's little hand still in hers, left the house and began to cross the frozen snow toward an outhouse. A real live outhouse with a moon for ventilation carved high on the swinging door. A shaggy black-and-white dog accompanied them on their trek. He wagged his stump of a tail so hard his whole body wriggled, and he pushed against Emily's legs, almost knocking her over.

"Stop it, Shep," Mary cried. "Go on. Sorry, miss." And the dog slunk away, his feelings hurt.

Emily staggered across the yard, shivering. She couldn't believe it. She hadn't even *seen* an outhouse in twenty years. How could anyone in this country still be living without indoor plumbing? What kind of a man was Will Dutcher, anyway? Some sort of survivalist?

Half-frozen to death, Emily made it back inside and passed through Antonio's kitchen. He only glanced at her, then went back to stirring something on the old iron stove.

Her hand still in Mary's, Emily got as far as the staircase before she broke out in a cold sweat. Dizzy and sick, she sank down on the bottom step.

"Uncle Will," Mary cried, "Uncle Will!"

And then he was there, a pipe in hand, crouching alongside her at the bottom of the staircase. "Are you ill?" he asked, irritation obvious in his voice.

Emily found his eyes. "I feel weak. My legs. I . . ."

"Here," he said gruffly, handing his pipe to Mary, "put this in the parlor." Then, to Emily, "Put your arms around my neck."

Obediently she did and was lifted into his arms. He turned sideways and began to carry her up the steps. Emily was embarrassed. The last time she'd stepped on the scales she'd been 132 pounds. Not fat, but still rounded enough that she was sure her weight must have been a burden. But Will Dutcher handled her easily, his strongly muscled arms solid beneath her back and buttocks. She kept her hands locked behind his neck, and her breasts were pressed tightly to his chest as he maneuvered the stairs.

It occurred to Emily as Dutcher held her close that she'd been in this same position once before. He'd carried her unconscious to the bedroom. Then he'd taken her clothes off and somehow gotten her into this nightgown. If he'd been a doctor or something, Emily knew, she would never have given the incident a second thought. As it was . . .

At the top of the stairs, she said, "I can manage now." Ignoring her, he continued on down the dim hall toward her room, and once inside, he carefully placed her on the bed. "You didn't have to . . ." she began.

"Did it before," he remarked dryly, "guess I can do it again."

Emily settled beneath the warm blankets and gave him an embarrassed smile. For a moment their eyes locked and held, awkwardly, before she glanced away. "This is terribly nice of you, Mr. Dutcher," she said, "I mean taking me in like this. I'm sure I can be out of your hair soon."

"Out of my hair?"

"On my way to Seattle," Emily explained.

He was standing next to the bed, his hands on his hips. Unconsciously he reached up and toyed with his mustache. "Doc said . . ." he began then hesitated.

"What *did* he say?"

"Well, he said you might be a touch confused for a time."

"Confused?"

"Yes, ma'am..."

"*Emily*. Please call me Emily."

"Well, yes, Emily," he said, making her name sound different with that husky tone. "Doc said you might have some peculiar notions in your head."

"I can assure you," Emily said, "that I'm perfectly sane. I *know* who I am. And I'm not your housekeeper, Mr.... Will."

He looked at her for a time then smiled thinly. "Whatever you say, ma'— Emily." And then he turned and left her there alone, his tall, dark form retreating along the hall.

She managed to turn down the kerosene lamp—a *kerosene* lamp, she thought in amazement—and closed her eyes, trying to let sleep take her away from this crazy world she'd landed in. But her mind wouldn't cooperate. It worked sluggishly but relentlessly. It was as if she had to work everything out in her head carefully, to make sure it was logical—as if she'd forgotten things that used to come automatically to her. *Confused,* Will Dutcher had said. She might be confused. Naturally, it was the concussion. Perfectly normal.

She wondered if she should be frightened to be alone in a strange place with a strange man, but she couldn't muster the energy. If Will Dutcher had wanted to hurt her, he would have done it by now. She knew instinctively that he would never hurt her, but she did wonder where her money and checkbook were, as well as her credit cards. Oh God, what a hassle it was going to be to call the bank if everything was lost. And no phone.

Well, everything must have been lost because they'd found no ID on her. What a mess. Her Gucci luggage, her jewelry, her good leather jacket and boots, all her underwear, and the new Nikon camera. Did Amtrak have insurance? She'd put in a claim as soon as she could.

And the clothes she'd been wearing. Gone. How could that be? They must have found her with her clothes just ripped to shreds and thrown them out, she guessed. Accidents did that. They said plane crashes knocked peoples' shoes off, so she supposed it could happen in a train crash, too.

Gone, all gone. It was as if she'd arrived here at Dutcher's ranch like a newborn babe, naked, without a thing to her name. The thought made her shiver involuntarily. It was as if without the accoutrements of modern society, she simply didn't exist.

She couldn't pursue it any further, though, because her head ached so badly. Why hadn't they given her any aspirin, at least? Or something stronger if they had it. Surely, even in Rifle, Colorado, the drugstores had aspirin.

THE NEXT DAY she felt awful. It was as if her activity of the day before had worn her out completely. Ridiculous to feel so weak and nauseous and hurt so much. She couldn't help but panic a little whenever she wondered if the doctor had missed something. Perhaps she had something terribly wrong with her. A blood clot on the brain. She'd die instantly—she'd read about things like that. Why hadn't they sent her to a hospital in an ambulance or by helicopter? She wanted to ask Will Dutcher but could just imagine the frown he'd give her. Whenever she'd asked him anything, in fact, he'd seemed annoyed, bothered by her intrusion into his life.

After school Mary came to Emily's room and very kindly read to her since there was no radio or TV in the small chamber. The child read very well, indeed, but Emily couldn't keep her mind on the story.

"Wait a minute, Mary honey, please."

"Does your head hurt, Miss Emily?"

"Well, yes, it does."

"I'm sorry."

"Um, Mary, your uncle said the nearest hospital is in Glenwood Springs, is that right?"

"Yes, ma'am."

"Why couldn't they send an ambulance for me? That way I'd be off your hands. I wonder..."

Mary was watching her calmly and patiently, waiting for her to go on.

"I wonder if your uncle could phone from Rifle and ask them to do that."

"A...an am-bu-lance, Miss Emily? I'm not sure what that is," Mary said.

"A—a kind of car to carry sick people. Like me."

"Oh. Well, I don't know. No one's ever used one of those. Doc Tichenor takes care of everybody here."

"Do you think he'd call?" Emily asked, almost desperate.

"I don't know that you can telephone as far as Glenwood Springs. The only telephone is in the Winchester Hotel, and I think it only...well, I don't really know."

Emily sighed. It was so hard. They seemed so out of touch, so different. She couldn't get any real information from anyone. It wasn't that they kept secrets from her: they just didn't seem to know what she was talking about.

Will came by her room after supper every day to inquire politely how she was. He seemed anxious for her to be up and about, but she still felt dreadful. She wondered if he continued to believe her to be his housekeeper from Chicago.

On the fifth day she felt a little better and was able to eat a small amount of Antonio's rather tasteless food. No herbs, no spices, heck, not even garlic. Plain stuff. She'd brushed her hair and washed her face and felt vaguely human. She found herself looking forward to Will Dutcher's soft rap at her door. She'd organized a few questions to ask him—simple, direct ones. Wouldn't want to put him out.

"Good evening, Emily," he said, in that quiet way he had. "You appear to have improved today."

"I'm a little better. Uh, Mr. Dutcher, Will, could you sit down for a minute? I'd like to ask you a few questions."

"All right," he said unenthusiastically, then sat in the rocking chair, waiting politely.

"You're sure none of my things have been found? Nothing. Not my purse or my suitcase or anything?"

"No, ma'am, nothing."

"What was I wearing when they found me? I mean, do you know who actually found me on the train? You see, I was wondering if they had perhaps kept anything at all of mine."

He was looking away, out the window, stroking his mustache. She waited a moment. Maybe she'd insulted him, insinuating that one of his friends had stolen her things. "I'm sorry, I only meant . . . well, I have nothing, no money to pay for my keep, but if you . . ."

"I found you, ma'am," he said then.

"You?"

"Well, Johnny McCrudden did, but then I came over and shooed him away."

"And nothing, none of my things, was there?"

He faced her full on, his dark brows drawn together in a line over his eyes. "You were . . . uh . . . unclothed, ma'am."

She stared blankly. He met her gaze with determination. "I was, you mean, I was . . . naked?"

"Yes, ma'am."

"You mean my clothes were ripped, ruined," she said reasonably.

He shook his head. "There weren't any . . . clothes, I mean."

She sank back onto the pillows, all her questions dispersed like wisps of smoke. She felt deflated. "I've got to get out of here," she said to herself, feeling panic rise in her throat. "I've got to get out of here," she repeated.

"But where would you go?" Will asked. "If you don't mind my saying so, ma'am, you're not feeling well. That knock on the head. Why don't you rest? You'll feel better tomorrow."

"Will I?"

"And when you start feeling better, maybe you could begin doing a few things around the place. Mary can show you. Just to keep your hands busy," he put in.

"I'm not a housekeeper, Will."

"Then, ma'am, what are you?"

"I'm a loan officer. I *was* a loan officer," she corrected herself.

He regarded her blankly.

"I worked in a bank."

"I see." He nodded. Then it struck Emily, recalling the way they all answered her, looked at her, responded to her. They were *humoring* her. As if she were crazy!

She took a deep breath and tried to recall what it was like to be in control of things. She would be frank, direct, logical. But what came out of her mouth surprised her. "Am I being kept a prisoner here, Mr. Dutcher?" There was a frantic edge to her voice she tried to contain.

"Almighty God, I guess not!" he said. "A prisoner! I brought you here until you recovered. I thought you were the housekeeper Clay sent from Chicago, but if you aren't then that's that. You can go anytime you like, ma'am. You just aren't up to it yet."

"When I am, when I feel stronger, will you take me into Rifle? Will you?"

"Rest assured, I never in my life held a lady against her will. I'll drive you myself," he said, and she believed him. In fact he sounded awfully relieved, Emily realized, as if he were going to get a large burden off his back.

"Thank you," she said, not caring what his motives were. "I am sorry if I seem upset, Will. This is all new to me, and I don't quite know what to do."

"No need for thanks."

Emily lay there after he'd gone and tried to think. She felt better now that she'd asked the question that had been lurking in the corners of her mind. There just wasn't anything she could do right now. Not a thing. She might as well lie back and enjoy it, notice all the details of the odd life the Dutchers lived. Wow, what a story she'd have to tell Judy when she got to Seattle! Weird!

She'd relax, and once she got better she'd get Will to drive her into Rifle to use the phone. Maybe there'd be a fax machine she could use to have the bank wire her some money. She'd have to buy herself some clothes, too. And that insurance claim....

And what about the other people on the train? There must have been many others injured, and some dead, but she hadn't thought to ask Will. Poor people. She was lucky, she guessed.

She snuggled down under the covers and closed her eyes. Yes, she'd concentrate on getting better, wipe her mind clean of the hassles that she was going to have to deal with soon. Credit cards, banks, social security card, driver's license. Oh, what the hell....

CHAPTER FOUR

WILL DUTCHER HAD NEVER been so glad to get out of the house and go to work as he was those last days of February. It was that woman, Emily Jacoby, and all her strange ways. It was more than that, though, he had to admit to himself. It was just her presence in his house—a woman in his nice, comfortable home. He'd never lived with a female, not since he'd left home years ago. He'd chosen not to. 'Course, there was little Mary, but she was still a child. Emily Jacoby was a woman.

It made him edgy. A man couldn't relax, couldn't even have a little doze in his chair without her everlasting questions.

"How many cattle do you own, Will?" she'd asked. "How many acres is your ranch?" "How many men work for you?" On and on. "What's the population of Rifle?" "Where's Antonio from?" And personal questions that could make a man squirm. "What did your brother and his wife die of?" "What does your brother Clay do in Chicago?"

Questions! The woman wanted to know every little thing. Even things like how he got his shirts ironed and why didn't he have a boiler for hot water. Hot water, tarnation. Did she think she'd landed in a big-city mansion with indoor plumbing and servants?

It was a clear, bright morning, one of those perfect winter days that made a man remember why he lived in Colorado. Will stomped down the steps of the porch, Shep at his side, drawing in big breaths of cold air, adjusting his hat brim so he wouldn't have to squint in the sunlight. There was some snow left on the ground from that last storm, but it'd melt soon. Down here in the river valley, the Grand River Valley it was still called, even though the old name of the river had been changed to the Colorado some years back, it was a pretty mild climate. Go a few miles up valley, toward Aspen or the High Tower flattops, and there'd be snow as deep as your waist all winter long. Frankly, Will didn't know how the miners made it, but they did. Down here, three thousand feet lower, snow rarely stayed around for long. Mud, though, mud stayed until the land dried out in April or May.

It was perfect cattle land, a bit dry, but with a stream or water rights, a rancher was fine. And now that the land was all fenced off, and men were breeding for good, fat beef and winter feeding, cattle were going to become more and more profitable. Those Eastern cities couldn't get enough beef, and with all that wealth, the West'd just keep sending it to them and pocketing the profits.

Although, lately, there'd been some talk, some unsettling talk about a problem with the nation's economy, but Will wasn't worried yet. The older he got, the more he realized there was always talk like that.

He went across to the barn and breathed in the familiar smell. Time to go to work.

The men were waiting for him, milling around, rolling cigarettes or already smoking, slapping hands for warmth. Eight good men.

"Hey, boss," Curly said, "you want me to ride out or see to the horses needin' shoeing?" Curly was his blacksmith, an invaluable man on the ranch. He was called Curly because, naturally, he was bald as an egg.

"I wanted to check the horses out in winter pasture," said Hokum, "there's one I've got my eye on to break come spring. A pretty little filly."

"That's all the filly you gonna have till spring," said Tommy, guffawing, "'less you get a bath."

There were jobs to assign, horses to catch and saddle, the big hay wagon to load and hitch up. Breath steamed in misty plumes, twin ones from the horses. Shep danced around Will's feet, frantic to be out on the range, doing his job. The men were dressed in layers of long underwear, shirts, vests, coats, gloves, big-brimmed hats. They all appeared to be fat, even those who were skinny as fence posts, because of all the layers they wore.

And the horses had their winter coats of thick, soft hair, matted almost like felt, so that they, too, looked fat, like overfed children's ponies.

Will led three men out to check on some fences, Curly stayed behind to shoe horses, and Buck, the half-Ute Indian boy, drove the hay wagon out to feed the cattle.

Oh, life was all right out here under the blue sky. Will had his land, his cattle, his men, all he'd ever wanted. Life was simple, easygoing. He'd never asked for anything more. He didn't even mind the young ones, because they were good little bodies and knew their places in this world. They were blood.

But now Clay had sent him a housekeeper, and things were different. Well, Emily kept saying she wasn't Clay's housekeeper, but what was the difference? The housekeeper would have come on that train if Emily hadn't, right? Either way, Will was stuck with a nosy female. All he'd been able to picture, when Clay had written, was a dried-up, silent old spinster, as stiff as starch. He could have lived with that, but Emily—well, now, there was another story entirely.

Odd notions, Emily Jacoby had. Odd questions she asked, things Will had never heard of, not even in the Denver papers. She talked funny, too, not that he couldn't understand her, but funny—he couldn't quite put his finger on it. And she had ways about her, strange ways, like the way she moved, not like a lady at all. Not like a man, though, no, not like a man.

He supposed she was one of those forward-thinking women, like that Bloomer female, who wanted women to wear trousers. Or a suffragette type. Maybe a pro-hibitionist who rampaged into bars, breaking them up with axes. Oh, he could see Emily hefting an ax, all right. With spirit, too. Those kind of women lived in the big Eastern cities, he guessed. What in the devil kind of men lived with those women? Lord above, what a chore!

Well, maybe she *would* leave as soon as she was better. She'd said she wanted to go into Rifle and send for her money and leave. She'd even asked if she were a prisoner! The boldness of her, insulting a man like that. She had less sense of how a person behaved than the young ones. God Almighty, who'd raised her back there in Philadelphia? Is that how folks acted nowadays in big cities?

Good riddance to Emily Jacoby, he thought. He'd write to Clay and tell him never, ever to send another goldarn housekeeper.

He rode his big sorrel mare, felt her move under him with uncomplaining patience, and looked around his ranch to see what needed doing.

Fargo got off his horse and undid the wire gate so Will and the others could ride through into a new field. The cows who'd calved last year were there with their offspring, and he wanted to check them out, see how the young ones were wintering after that blizzard.

"Looks good, boss," Fargo said, doing up the gate behind them.

"Yup."

"We lost a couple in the storm, but the rest are fine," another young hand remarked.

"Years back, on open range, you would've lost thirty percent in a winter, maybe more," Will said.

"Yessir, my daddy lost 'em all in the blizzard of '87. That's why I'm here 'stead of runnin' my own spread," Jonah said without a hint of rancor.

They moved on to the next field, where cows expecting that spring were eating the long lines of hay that Buck had forked off the back of the wagon. Heads down, breath fogging, sides bulging with this year's calf drop, the cows ate patiently, endlessly, their backs steaming in the warm midday sun.

Will sat, forearms crossed on the pommel of his saddle, and counted up in his head what he could expect. A few would drop next month, then in April and

May the calves would come, a few every day. Funny how these shorthorns ran into more trouble calving than the old wild longhorns. But, he guessed, you got the bad with the good.

They rode back, Shep panting alongside the horses, chasing a rabbit once. Some deer had jumped a fence and were eating hay along with the cattle, but when they saw Will and his hands they panicked and took off in their stiff-legged leaps.

"Come out here someday with a rifle," Will said, "and get one of those for dinner. Antonio would sure like that."

"I'll do that, boss," Fargo said, nodding.

The sire of his herd, the lord and master of the ranch, Will's prize bull, had his own field. He snorted and pawed the ground when he saw Shep, his arch enemy. The dog darted at the big red bull, just to tease, and the animal lowered his horns, swiping sideways at the place Shep had been a second before, his hump rippling with muscle.

Will whistled, calling Shep off. "Leave him alone, Shep," he admonished.

"He needs his strength," Jonah said, laughing. Then he called out to the bull, "Save your strength, *toro*, you'll need it come spring."

"Come on," Will said, setting his spurs to his mare's sides, "time to head on in."

Shadows grew long early in the winter. It got cold early. The men straggled in from their chores, disappearing into the brightly lit bunkhouse. Will rubbed down his mare and gave her a measure of oats. He could see his house through the open barn doors all lit up, too. A shadow kept flicking across the kitchen window, a person moving around inside. Emily? No, probably Antonio.

But it could be Emily, up and dressed, feeling better. Sticking her nose into every corner of his domain. Antonio would never be able to handle her.

He turned his mare out for the night and shot a last, lingering glance at the cheerful bunkhouse, with the stream of smoke coming out its chimney pipe. In there, the hands would be joking, talking, smoking, laughing, cussing. They'd have a few belts of whiskey, deal some hands of poker and josh one another.

In his house, Will had the strange Emily Jacoby. In retrospect, he figured the hands had the better deal.

THE DAYS AT THE RANCH took on a sameness as Emily recuperated slowly. The house was heated entirely by the potbelly stove in the parlor and the wood cooking stove in the kitchen, so life centered around those rooms. The rest of the house was distinctly chilly. Each morning Antonio fired up the big black stove and fixed breakfast, then Will rode out onto the frozen range with his ranch hands. She watched through her windows, fascinated, and it was as if she were seeing an old movie, correct in every detail. The men never used Jeeps or pickup trucks—only horses—but Emily chalked it up to the rough terrain, or simply their own preference.

At lunch she usually stayed in her room, reading books she'd found in the parlor, sitting by the sunny Victorian window that overlooked the vast land of western Colorado. It was a harsh winter landscape beyond the ranch house. The range was dotted with cattle that grazed on hay collected for the long winter months. Close to the ranch were piñon and cedar trees and just outside her window were bare-branched apple trees, frozen and brittle under the weak February sun.

But it was the distant mountains that held Emily's attention for hours on end each day. As the sun moved across the afternoon sky she watched the colors brighten and then darken on the bone-dry, striated mesas—red and pink and orange colors that stood out in the shalelike layers of rock. Browns and ochers and golds against the clear blue of the Colorado sky.

Emily learned that these were called the flattops. Mary told her the names of the mesas and the mountains beyond. There was Hubbard Mesa and Graham Mesa and Cactus Valley. There was Book Cliffs and Burning Mountain. Was that where the oil shale development sat?

It was beautiful, evocative land. Distant, snow-capped mountains covered in mantles of evergreen and aspen trees and tall, majestic spruces. Dazzling white meadows and sharp, craggy cliffs. An endless, empty land that both beckoned and repelled. Often, Emily wondered just how the pioneers had managed.

Of course, she periodically thought, Will and his family were not so terribly different than pioneers. He'd apparently chosen a simple, basic life despite the riches of the land. She longed to ask him if he was connected to some sort of an Amish sect but kept her counsel—it wasn't her business. And besides, Will wasn't one for too much conversation.

At night, Emily would sit in his cozy parlor beneath a kerosene lamp while he read one of his beautifully bound books. At first, when she'd been asked to join him after supper, Emily had sat quietly, still weak, and listened to him converse with his niece and nephews. The dog, Shep, always lay with his muzzle on Will's boot. He adored Will unreservedly and followed him everywhere. He was a nice dog, Emily thought. He liked her all right, was protective of the kids, but he *loved* Will. He was a cow dog, Will had told her, trained to herd them. He earned his keep, Will added soberly, as if to point out that Emily did not.

But she ignored Will, or rather, she ignored that authoritative tone in his gruff voice. Instead, Emily studied the children and watched them relate to the world around them without the trappings of television and radio. There were word games they played with Will and talk of school and mathematics—the boys hated their math. But Mary was a true reader, very mature in her tastes, and loved to talk to her uncle about the books she was reading: *Uncle Tom's Cabin* and *Jane Eyre.* Every so often Emily put in a word or two on a subject, though she had to stretch her memory all the way back to high school.

This always seemed to surprise Will. He'd look up from the children and study her for a moment, a quizzical expression on his rugged features.

The children turned in early. But their days were long, beginning at six for breakfast. Afterward, they'd walk down the lane to school. Emily asked once how far they had to go to catch the bus.

"The bus?" Will had replied.

"You know, transportation."

"Sometimes they ride with the McCruddens," he'd said with a shrug.

Will Dutcher's buckboard perplexed Emily. Shunning modern conveniences was one thing, but hauling all his supplies in a buckboard was really absurd. The horses alone, she decided, had to be more costly than gas for a truck. It was another question she was dying to ask but feared he'd take her curiosity as an insult to his life-style. With men, Emily had learned in her very competitive job, you never knew. Best to stay quiet, listen and learn.

It snowed again on the last day of February. Snowed hard. Wind whipped around the wood-framed siding of the three-story building and sang in the chimneys. Will had gone out early to help feed the cattle and wasn't expected back till late afternoon.

It was the first day Emily had felt well enough to get dressed. But before attempting to clothe herself, she approached Antonio in the kitchen. She'd washed up every day using the pitcher and washcloth, but she was ready for a bath—a real scrubbing, hair, feet, everything bath.

"Antonio," she said, standing in the doorway to the kitchen, feeling ridiculously shaky, "I know there's a tub in there," she pointed toward a small room off the kitchen, "but how do I fill it?"

Antonio grumbled something in Spanish.

"I can do it, if you'll just tell me how."

He then nodded at two large metal pots that sat in a corner.

"You heat the water," Emily said, "on the stove?"

"*Sí.*"

"Um," Emily said, going to lift the pots to the pump over the sink.

Somehow, with help from old Antonio, Emily managed. It wasn't the best of systems, but it worked. The trouble was, the water only stayed warm for a short time in the big iron tub. And then Emily had to pour water from a fresh bucket over her head to get out the harsh soap. Her hair, she was certain, was going to look like a rat's nest.

She dried off, dripping water out onto the wooden floor and shivering in the uninsulated room. Then, she had to manage the clothes Mrs. Fisher had sent out from town a few days ago. Unbelievably, there was a corset. Mrs. Fisher's? Was she a member of this sect, too? Emily tossed it aside, shaking her head. The bloomers and petticoats she donned. They provided warmth. The skirt, a long, navy blue serge with a flounce at the bottom was much too big, but the blouse was lovely. Antique white with a high collar and a tucked yoke and dozens of tiny pearl buttons down the front. It was her hair that gave her the trouble. She'd meant to have it trimmed above her shoulders and thinned when she got to Seattle, but for now the best she could do was brush it out with Mary's silver hairbrush and twist it at the nape of her neck, fastening it with hairpins.

She was ready. She gathered up her nightgown and damp towels and opened the door to the kitchen only to be met by Will, standing next to the big iron stove still in his long duster, warming his hands, the dog Shep dripping muddy water beside him.

Will looked frozen. Ice dripped off his mustache and from the long curling hair around his ears. His lips were blue, his face pale.

"My God," Emily said, dropping the bundle of laundry onto the table. "Will. You're half-frozen to death!"

"Normal winter," he said, turning back to the stove.

"Well, if this is normal," Emily said, "I'd hate to see a cold spell."

Will turned his head slightly and regarded her with a raised brow. "We survive."

But Emily was ignoring his brusqueness. "Antonio," she was saying, "help me with these pots. I think Mr. Dutcher here can just thaw out in a hot tub, himself."

Will spun around on his heel. "I won't," he said, shocked, and Antonio merely looked from one to the other.

"You want to lose some toes and fingers?" Emily said.

"I..." Will was speechless. "I don't need..."

It was no use. After several more minutes of arguing, Emily ushered him into the bathroom—or, as she thought of it now, the room for baths—and instructed Antonio to take in the pots of water while she heated more. Through the closed door, Emily could hear Will grumbling, but she could also hear his boots being kicked off and a belt buckle hitting the floor. *Stupid,* she thought. He'd worn that duster thing and thin leather gloves out into a blizzard. Didn't he own a down parka? Probably not. And then he'd stayed out on the range for five, six hours. Most likely his ranch hands over in the bunkhouse were in the same shape. She'd have to instruct Antonio to bundle up and check on them, making sure they had hot coffee and soup.

Will was not one for singing in the bath. But he did protest, his grumbling never stopping the whole time. Emily sent Antonio for clean, dry clothes from Will's dresser upstairs and made him hurry down with them, pushing Antonio through the bathroom door. When Will finally emerged he was still miffed, his unyielding masculinity challenged.

A bachelor, Emily thought, of course. Everyone knew that most bachelors were helpless when it came to taking proper care of themselves. Oh, there were the health food nuts and joggers out there, but even the more sensible singles still could use a woman's touch from time to time....

Will threw his dirty clothes on top of hers. "Satisfied?" he growled.

Emily faced him, hands on her hips. "Your color's normal now. Yes, I'm satisfied."

He only mumbled under his breath and headed to the parlor. For the rest of the afternoon he sat near the potbelly stove, pipe and book in hand. Never once did he glance up.

The children arrived home at four. Evidently, the McCruddens had given them a ride due to the storm. They were chilly, naturally, but not frozen like their uncle had been. Emily took their book bags and placed them on the stairs while they stomped their feet and blew into their mittened hands.

It was then that she saw it. A book. It had slid out of Mary's bag and thumped onto the floor. Emily picked it up, meaning to replace it, but then suddenly the title caught her eye: *A History of Astronomy*. The book was thin, beautifully bound but certainly anti-quated, Emily could see, because the embossed gold markings on the front—a rendering of the solar system—was missing a few outer planets.

"Why would your teacher give you this, Mary?" Emily asked, opening the book, flipping pages.

"I like the stars, Miss Emily," she said.

"Well, certainly there's something more modern you could study. I mean—"

But then Will was there, taking the book from her, scowling. "Mary's teacher is a fine woman," he said. "I'm sure Mrs. Lindley knows what she's doing."

"I didn't mean—" Emily began but decided to let it drop. She was almost completely well. In a day or two she'd get Will to take her into Rifle, and then she'd leave these well-meaning but strange people, the Dutchers, behind. Let them live in the past. They were happy enough, it seemed. It might take a little time to get her affairs straightened away—money, credit cards, a thousand phone calls—but perhaps she could stay in the hotel Mary had mentioned, if they'd believe she had money. If not, she'd just stay with the Dutchers until her money arrived. And Will had promised to take her into town as soon as she felt better. Yes, maybe tomorrow. If the storm let up, she'd ask him first thing in the morning.

They ate thick venison stew for dinner and the children went to their attic room early. Emily helped Antonio clear the dining room table, but he liked having his kitchen to himself.

She felt unsettled. Out of place. The children had already retired, and Antonio was chattering away to himself in the kitchen. Will had gone back to his book and pipe, Shep at his feet, and, Emily knew by now, he would probably also retire early.

She was bored. The fogginess in her head had finally cleared, and Emily no longer felt comfortable whiling away the hours. She'd needed to heal, naturally, and the ten days she'd spent at the Dutchers' had really been special. But now her mind sought other vistas, new environments, something akin to her usual, more compelling life. *Face it,* she thought, standing alone in the dining room, *this old-fashioned existence is for the birds.*

Emily wandered into the parlor, her fingers playing with the lacy cuffs on her sleeves. Will glanced up, then went back to his reading. At least he was reading a newspaper, she saw, then settled herself into the chair on the opposite side of the wood stove.

After a minute or two, she said, "Anything interesting in the news? I really have been out of it lately."

He glanced at her again with those penetrating blue eyes, rattled the paper and said only, "Nothing to interest you, I'm sure."

Emily cocked her head but let it go. Soon, very soon, she'd be on her way. Instead of hounding him, she sat and studied the man. He was oblivious to her—as usual—keeping his dark head buried in his paper. He *was* an attractive man; Emily would give him an eight on the one-to-ten scale. But as for his attitude toward her, and probably toward most women, she'd give him a two. No, a one. He was decidedly arrogant, one of those males who believed he was superior in all ways to a woman. He never tried to hide his feelings, either. He let his sexism exude from every long, tapered sinew and rippled muscle, from every blue-eyed glare and tensing of his jaw.

Emily hated labels. But in Will's case she couldn't help it: male macho pig.

She sighed and looked down at her hands, bored again. Still, she wouldn't annoy him. He'd basically treated her very honorably and if he couldn't force himself to be companionable, well, that was just life.

But it wasn't five minutes later when she asked, "The Mideast hasn't erupted again, has it?" She played with the lace and gave him a wide, false smile.

Again the paper rattled. "Nothing about the Mid— What did you say, the Mideast, Emily?"

"Yes, I was just..."

"There's nothing." He turned a page, adjusting the paper.

"Um," Emily said, wanting to reach for the newspaper, but she'd have to wait till he was done, she guessed.

She watched him some more, her head cocked slightly, her brain dulled with the boredom. He *did* have a certain ease to him, a way of sitting in repose in his chair with his long legs stretched out in front of him, crossed at the ankles, as if he owned the space he occupied and wanted no intruders. It made her want to smile unaccountably. Will Dutcher, bachelor. She pitied his housekeeper, whoever and wherever the woman was.

Will turned a page, refolded his paper and glanced at her before going back to the print.

A ten, she thought again. She'd definitely give those bottomless blue eyes beneath the heavy dark brows a ten. He had a generous, full nose and finely chiseled lips that rarely smiled. Hollow cheeks and a square jaw—a rugged, outdoorsman's face lined by the sun's strong rays. Not bad, she thought, not bad.

And there was that boyish way his hair waved over his ears and his shyness around her at times. Emily could only imagine what it must have taken for him to lift her, naked, into his arms or to have put her into the nightgown. Thinking about it, she found a strange, unaccountable heat spreading through her limbs and belly. Her skin felt supersensitive. Will's hands on her skin, his eyes resting on her hips and breasts—no matter how shy she knew him to be, Emily also realized he must have *looked*. He was a man. She was a woman. He'd looked, all right.

She cocked her head again and openly kept studying him, wondering if he was even vaguely aware of her perusal. How *did* handsome Will Dutcher see her, anyway?

After a time Emily turned away and stared out the window. Yes, it was going to be good getting back to civilization. The storm looked as if it were breaking; stars could be seen in between the tattered clouds of night. It would do her good, too, to get away from Will. This close proximity could get on a girl's nerves.

She glanced back at Will. Her heart gave a sudden leap to find him staring at her over the top of his paper, his eyes seeming to probe to her very soul before he cast his glance downward again.

Oh, yes. She really did have to get out of here.

Shortly Will dropped a section of the paper to the floor, finished with it. Emily sat up straight. "Mind if I read some of the paper?" she asked, hungering for the morsel he'd dropped. He couldn't deny her *that*.

"Um," he said, reaching down past Shep to retrieve it. He leaned over and handed it to her, mumbling something like, "Darn odd, a woman caring about politics and such."

But Emily hadn't really heard. Before she'd even straightened out the section, she was reading. Lord, a newspaper, she thought, feeling much better already. Her eyes scanned the headlines—odd headlines, apparently about local Rifle doings. It wasn't a national paper, then. Darn.

She glanced at the top of the paper. *The Rifle Reveille,* it read. *March 2, 1893.*

Emily giggled. A typo. Lousy small-town newspaper. She shook out its folds and searched for an item of interest. But there wasn't any. She read on. And on every heading of every page the same typo: March 2, 1893. Ridiculous. Five minutes later, after finding nothing in the paper whatsoever that resembled reality, Emily suddenly glanced up at her surroundings. A fist of indefinable fear was tightening around her heart.

Silly, she told herself, *don't be so silly.*

She looked harder at the house, the kerosene lamps, the wood-burning stove. The outhouse. The bathtub. No phone. No TV. No cars or electricity or... Mary's book on astronomy.

Her eyes snapped back to Will Dutcher. Hair parted in the middle. That mustache. The style of his clothing. *Her* clothing... The...

"Something the matter?" Will was asking. "Are you ill, Emily?"

"Ill?" she repeated, her throat closing around the word, a bubble of hysterical laughter ready to burst forth. "Ill," she said. "Yes, I think I am going to be sick."

CHAPTER FIVE

IT WAS A JOKE. Some sort of misunderstanding. It had to be. Emily lay in bed, on her side, staring at the moonlit rectangle of the window, hearing the soft night noises of Will Dutcher's house, trying to make sense of things.

March 2, 1893. It simply wasn't possible. There was some logical explanation. This must be a group, a colony of people who chose to live in the manner of a century ago. Survivalists, with their own rules and customs. Sure, there were all sorts of nuts in the world.

On the other hand, Emily mused, perhaps this really was a theme town—the whole town, right down to the local newspaper. Tourists must have gotten a real kick out of it. She'd bet at four o'clock sharp every day there was a staged bank robbery and shoot-out on the streets of Rifle. Of course. But then, why did the outlying ranches—where no tourist ventured—have to keep up the farce?

Oh, well. She'd have her answers soon enough. Thank God, she *was* feeling better now, well enough to go into Rifle, wire for her money and go on her way. Will Dutcher had been generous enough. He'd taken care of her, and she was grateful, but she couldn't stay here anymore. For heaven's sake, she had a life of her own.

If Will Dutcher chose to live according to the old-fashioned traditions of some weird sect, or whatever, that was fine, but how could he expect Emily to put up with it? No TV was refreshing, for a while, but this was getting serious. She didn't even know how the stock market was doing.

What was so very peculiar, though, was that Will didn't even acknowledge that the outside world, the *real* world, existed. Whenever she'd mentioned it, he'd given her that blank look, a combination of pity and bare tolerance. Doc had said Emily might be confused for a time, and maybe she had been—at first—but she wasn't now. Her mind was as clear as a bell, and she knew without question that it couldn't actually be March 2, 1893.

She lay there and tried to imagine Will in modern jeans and a cowboy shirt or a three-piece suit or a set of sweats. Driving a car, sitting at a desk in an office. He must have done something like that once in his life. Surely he hadn't been born and raised the way he lived now.

But she couldn't. In her mind, he remained a man of the past—mustache, hairstyle, clothes—a rancher. She just couldn't picture him any other way. What was it about Will that defied her understanding? He was a man, that's all, just a man.

In the morning the sun was out, the brilliant Colorado sun glaring off the new snow. Emily dressed, visited the outhouse, then found Will at breakfast, Shep asleep under the table.

"Good morning, Emily," Will said gravely. "You're looking better today."

"Uh, yes, thanks, I'm feeling fine. Will, look, I'd like to go into Rifle today, if you could take me. You said, I mean, you told me you would, and I definitely feel well enough now," she said.

He sat at the table, both big hands wrapped around a thick mug of coffee, and regarded her. "Yes, I guess I could do that today."

Emily let out a breath she hadn't known she was holding. "Oh, good. Thank you. I really appreciate it. I'll...well, as soon as I get my money, I'll pay you...."

He made an impatient gesture with one hand. "No need. I only did the neighborly thing."

"But I insist. I've been here for, gee, over a week, living off you."

He frowned. "You keep talking about money. This isn't about money. There was an accident, you were hurt, someone had to take you in. What's money got to do with it?"

Emily opened her mouth, but no answer came to mind. His statement was so sure, so simple, so absolutely right. Meekly she replied, "Nothing, I guess," and poured herself a cup of Antonio's powerful coffee.

"I'll get the men set on their work, and then we can go. That suit you?" he said, pushing his chair back and stretching his legs out.

"Oh, yes, that's fine. Whenever it's convenient."

"It's cold out today. Think you're up to it? Wouldn't want to set you back any," he said, averting his gaze as if mention of her health were a delicate subject.

"I'm okay," she said, "really."

"Well, then, I'll get going."

"I'll be ready whenever you want," she said, smiling, trying very hard to be pleasant.

The three children came into the kitchen shortly, squabbling, hurrying, grabbing hunks of Antonio's bread. Emily noticed that Mary's braids were untidy, full of escaping wisps. It looked like the child had slept in them, for goodness' sakes. She wondered if she should say anything, then decided to. Mary had no mother any longer, poor kid, and maybe she could do with some female advice.

"Mary," she ventured, "have you redone your braids this morning?"

The girl looked down, one hand fiddling with a braid. "I'm not very good at braiding, Miss Emily. I usually get Mrs. Fisher or Mrs. McCrudden to do it Sundays at church. But this week they aren't staying very well."

"Oh, Mary," Emily said, "you get your braids done once a week?"

"Yes, ma'am."

"They should...well, I guess what I mean is, you'd be even prettier than you are if your hair was done every day."

"Mama used to do my hair every day," Mary offered.

"I bet she did."

Emily brushed Mary's hair, braided it, washed the boys' faces and sent them off down the long lane to meet the McCruddens.

She sighed and looked around the kitchen. Antonio was nowhere to be seen this morning, and she wondered who was going to clean up the place. It was getting cold, too, the fire in the living room not started, the one in the kitchen stove dying down.

Emily had seen Will and Antonio put wood in the stove. They lighted a section with a kind of hook. Yes, there it was. And a neat stack of split wood was piled right there next to the stove. She might as well load it up and stay warm. Damn these primitive conditions! Either you were in bed, right in front of a hot stove— or you were chilled through. And people used to live like this! She shivered as she jammed wood into the stove on top of the last few glowing embers.

She sat at the table and leaned her cheek on her palm. Her head ached on and off. She was weak still, with an unfamiliar shaky feeling in her limbs. But she could manage. She'd get into Rifle today no matter what.

Will came back to the house later that morning. By then, Emily was consumed with impatience. No one seemed to have any sense of time around here, she'd thought a dozen times. No one even had a watch, except for Will, and his was an old-fashioned pocket watch. But, she guessed, as she waited, drumming her fingers, that went along with their life-style.

"So," he said, slapping his dusty hat on his thigh, "you still set to go into town?"

She looked at him, startled. "You haven't changed your mind, have you? We're still going?"

"Yes, ma'am, if you want."

"Oh yes, please." *Careful,* she told herself, *don't sound too anxious.*

It took another half hour for him to hitch up the horses, and to find her a coat and hat to wear—a woman couldn't go into town with her head bare. But

Will dug out some things that had belonged to Clara, his dead sister-in-law, which Mary had been keeping in a trunk. There was a hip-length gray wool coat, fitted and flared, with black frogging up the front and around the collar. The hat was small and round, a black felt thing that tied under the chin. She noticed Will looking at her, studying her.

"Is something wrong?" she asked.

"Yes, ma'am, something is. I'm just not sure what," he said. "You don't look like Clara did in that getup."

Lord, Emily thought, she probably had something on backward. How was she to know?

Finally he helped her up on the buckboard seat. Oh, God, she was anxious to be going, to reach civilization again! To see the news, talk to real people who knew what was going on in the world, to get out of these confining, heavy clothes, to get her identity back.

"Just a minute," Will said then, and went into the house again.

Emily sat there in the brilliant sun, her nerves thrumming with impatience. One of the horses shook his head, jingling the harness, and the buckboard rattled a little. Will emerged from the house, carrying something over his arm. He climbed up to the high spot and turned to her.

"I was afraid you'd get cold," he said, "so I got one of my coats." He put it over her shoulders, tugging at it to get it straight, a heavy wool coat, rough tweed, smelling of pipe smoke and horses, Will's scent, and she burrowed down into it.

"Thanks," she said.

"It'll keep you warm," he replied. "Doc'd have my head if I let you catch your death after he pulled you through that accident."

He unwound the reins from the brake, released the handle and slapped the horses' rumps. "Get up," he called, clucking and, at last, they were off. The air was clear and brittle, the sun blinding on fields of glistening snow that spread flat and even up to the foot of the mesa. Emily had to shade her eyes with her hand as they bumped along the snowy track away from the ranch house. Behind fences were hundreds, no, thousands of shaggy red cattle with white faces. The ranch hands were forking hay off wagons in the fields, feeding the cattle. The wagons, of course, were pulled by teams of horses. Some of the hands were on horses, too. Wouldn't it be much more efficient to do this kind of work with a pickup truck? But, Emily knew, if she asked Will, he'd give her one of those looks.

"Um," she finally ventured, "those cows are Herefords, aren't they?" God knew where that tidbit of information had been dredged up from.

"Yup, shorthorns, purebred Herefords. The breed of the future," he said.

"How many do you have?" she asked, gripping the edges of the seat as the wagon lurched out of a rut.

"Don't know for sure. There'll be some winter kill. Last roundup I counted six thousand some."

"And you sell them," she said, "to meat companies."

"That's right. Now that the train got here, it's real easy. Years past we had to drive them up to Wyoming or as far as Pueblo."

"Is your ranch profitable?"

He gave her a sidelong glance. "Don't know as I ever discussed that with a lady before."

Exasperated, Emily asked, "Why not?"

He hesitated, thinking. "Guess no lady ever asked before."

"Sorry," she said shortly.

The wagon swayed, and Emily was thrown against Will's arm. She straightened, pulled the heavy coat around her. "Excuse me," she said.

He only nodded, not looking at her.

"Is there an airport nearby?" Emily asked, unable to hold it in any longer. "Something that connects with Denver, say?"

He did look at her this time, a puzzled glance. "A what?"

"An airport. For airplanes. So I can fly out of here."

"Fly?" He shook his head. "You do come up with some strange notions."

"An *airport,*" she said. "Everyone's heard of airports, for goodness' sakes! Why are you acting like this? Why are you pretending?" She hugged herself, pushing down the frustration, the welling panic. She took a deep breath and turned to him with absolute resolve. "All right," she said. "You can stop the masquerade now. It has to end. I demand some answers. Will, really, this has gone on long enough!"

He said nothing, only pulled up the horses, wrapped the reins around the brake handle and regarded her stolidly, a rugged man with frost on his mustache and dark hair curling from under his well-worn hat. A man with no deception in his gaze, no joking, no levity at all.

"Stop it," she breathed, "stop looking at me like that! I mean it. All right, if you choose to live like people did a hundred years ago, fine! That's your choice. But don't pretend you haven't heard of the real world!" She glanced around—the sky, the white rangeland, the sagebrush—but there was no help in any of that stark winter landscape. Panic was near to suffocating Emily; she felt herself sliding under, cold and hot, her head pounding, bile rising in her throat. She swallowed convulsively.

"Now, Emily, ma'am," he started to say, "you take it easy."

"I won't. I don't want to take it easy! I've been taking it easy long enough. I want to get out of here now. I want to go home!"

"Yes, ma'am, you can do that," Will said reasonably.

"Oh, God." She felt the way a sane person must feel trapped in an insane asylum. "Why are you doing this to me?"

"I'm not doing anything to you," Will said stiffly. "I do believe you're still confused some, like Doc said. He told me . . ."

"Doc! That quack. What does he know? If he even exists! I . . . I feel like—like you kidnapped me. It's like you kept me a prisoner. I bet you have my wallet, my money, my credit cards! You kept them. You have them somewhere, and you lied to me!"

"Now, ma'am." He put a restraining hand on her arm, but she shook it off.

"I can tell the police about you, you know. I can report you. I can file charges! My God, you could go to jail." She moved to the far side of the buckboard seat, away from him. She knew she was making crazy accusations, but she couldn't help it. "Go on, aren't you going to take me into town? Aren't you?"

"Yes, ma'am, I . . ."

"I'm an intelligent woman," she cried. "Please, just give me back my wallet, and I'll leave today. Keep the clothes, keep the money. I'll leave, and you'll never see me again."

"Emily, you best calm down," Will said. "I'll take you to town, if you want. The way you've been acting, I wonder whether you're well enough, but I can see you're set on continuing." He frowned. "Maybe you should see Doc. Maybe a dose of laudanum would help settle you."

She couldn't get through to him. There was no way. He just sat there, humoring her, not reacting in any way to her ravings, her threats. It was as if he didn't hear a word she said.

"Please," she finally said, beaten, "let's go. Take me into Rifle."

He unwound the reins and clucked to the horses. The buckboard bounced and rattled over the snow, the horses' hooves crunching.

Stupid. She'd been stupid. You couldn't get to a man like Will Dutcher with hysterics. She'd have to be calm and reasonable; otherwise, he'd think she was still dotty from her concussion. Control was the key, logic and a cool head. She'd take some deep, cleansing breaths and start over.

"Okay, I'm sorry," she said. "I'm fine now, just fine. Take me into Rifle, please. Let's see what comes next."

"Yes, ma'am, that's where we're going."

She sat there, hardly feeling the rough ride. Could Will be right? she wondered. Could she still be feeling the effects of a concussion? Was she seeing things wrong? Was her reality skewed because her brain was shaken up? Her heart skipped a beat. Lord, maybe she was caught in the middle of a nightmare, lying in her own bed at home. Maybe she was dreaming. Oh God, what if... what if... She sat there, swaying and bouncing, clutching the seat so hard with her fingers that they hurt.

Rifle was a bustling town. The streets were clogged with buggies and buckboards like Will's. Men and woman walked on the wooden sidewalks under porch roofs. The men were dressed like Will, in dusters or wool or corduroy jackets, baggy pants tucked into tall, muddy boots, wide-brimmed hats on their heads. Women in long dresses, bonnets and wool coats like the one Emily had on stood in front of the Western Mercantile Company talking. There was the Western Union telegraph office, the First National Bank of Rifle, Collin's Livery Barn and Doc Tichenor's office.

The sun had begun to melt the snow, and the main street was a quagmire. Horses were tied to hitching posts, there were men going through swinging saloon doors and a hotel—the Winchester Hotel, a two-story wooden building with a portico all around the second floor.

Emily took it all in, not blinking, breathing shallowly, her heart pounding in a heavy rhythm. From somewhere came the sound of a train whistle, an old-fashioned steam whistle.

It was a movie set, of course. Perfect down to the last detail. The people were actors, extras, and a scene was about to be shot. Or—yes—it had to be a theme town like Williamsburg, Virginia, or Sturbridge Village, Massachusetts—towns set up for tourists to see how people really lived in the past. That was it, a theme town.

A man tipped his hat to Will, got a casual wave in return. Emily glanced at Will; his face was unemotional. This town, this insane, impossible town was normal to him. Oh, God...why hadn't he just told her?

Rifle was only a few blocks long, with cross streets lined with houses, stores and saloons. A newspaper office was on the corner, *The Rifle Reveille*. And then it occurred to Emily that there were no electric lights anywhere. Gas lamps, yes, ornate gas lamps down the main street, fancy gilt signs, lace curtains, etched glass windows and marvelous gingerbread Victorian detail on the fancier buildings, but no neon, no electric lights, no electric lines or telephone poles, no cars or buses or taxis or telephone booths....

No tourists snapping pictures of the theme town, no cameras or station wagons or tour guides or ticket booths or parking lots. And the street was so muddy, no tourist in his right mind would cross it. If they wanted to attract tourists, for God's sake, they'd better provide *some* amenities. Of course, Emily realized, she hadn't seen any tourists, had she?

Her eyes saw it all, but through some illogical internal alchemy, she didn't lose her mind. *Wait,* she told herself, *wait and watch. Don't judge yet, don't make irrevocable decisions. Just wait and see.*

"Now, Emily," Will said, stopping the horses, "where do you want to go first?"

She took a deep breath. "A telephone, please. Where is a telephone?"

"The Winchester, but it's only local. We don't have a real system here, yet, like I hear they do in some big cities. If you want to wire for money, then you'll need the telegraph office."

"The telegraph office," she repeated.

"Right over there."

Her legs were weak, her knees like jelly as she walked into the telegraph office. Behind a wooden counter was a burly, bald-headed man in a white shirt and visor, black bands holding up his shirtsleeves above the elbows.

"Help you, ma'am?" he asked.

"I'd like to, that is, can I telegraph a bank in Philadelphia?" Emily asked.

The clerk pushed a Western Union blank across the counter to her. "I'll need the full address of the bank, ma'am. Also your name and address. Now, I've gotta warn you, this might take some time, maybe a day or two. The message has to be relayed to Denver, St. Louis, Chicago, then Philadelphia. So, I'm just letting you know up-front."

Emily looked at the blank paper, her mind whirling. What should she say? How should she start? She couldn't remember her account number, so she'd have to ask the bank to look it up and send it to...

The knowledge hit her with absolute, cold surety. The bank she'd worked for in Philadelphia didn't exist in the world of Will Dutcher in Rifle, Colorado. The man waiting for her to fill out the telegram form wouldn't be able to send a message to her bank—it was too far away from here, so far that even Emily had to question its existence.

"Uh, I . . . I changed my mind," Emily said breathlessly. "I'll do it some other time."

"Fine. Suit yourself," the clerk said.

"Thank you, thank you very much."

She tottered outside, feeling sick. Tears blurred her eyes.

"Emily, ma'am? Are you all right?" came Will's voice. "Did you send your telegram?"

She shook her head.

He was beside her then, tall and unerringly masculine, protective as he took hold of her arm, supporting her, and she felt so dizzy and shaky, everything distant and whirling around her.

"Sit down here, right on this step. That's it. Put your head down," Will was saying. "Lord Almighty, I was afraid of this. *Women.*"

"I'm all right," Emily gasped, feeling the dizziness recede.

"You sure? Maybe I should call Doc Tichenor . . ."

"I'm all right." She sat there, holding her head, not only feeling embarrassed but deeply, achingly frightened in some indefinable way.

"I was coming back because I realized you'd have to pay for the telegram," Will said.

"I didn't send it," Emily said faintly. "I don't know the address, I don't know my account number. I . . . ah . . . don't even know if there's any money in my account." She looked up at him, feeling utterly drained. "I made a mistake, a terrible mistake. I'm sorry. Oh, God, I'm sorry. I don't know how I could have..."

"Now, don't fret. It could happen to anyone who got hit on the head the way you did."

"I don't know. I don't know anything anymore. What am I going to do? I have no money, nowhere to go." She sat there on the step, trembling, feeling lost, drowned in confusion. Will Dutcher stood over her, and she was aware of his impatience, his discomfort in dealing with her. She looked up at him, not caring, just needing to belong somewhere, grasping at the security he offered.

"Emily, ma'am, you can't sit here like this. If you're feelin' poorly I'll take you to Doc's. If not, we'd best be on our way," he said.

"Yes, yes, I'm coming, I'm all right," she murmured.

He put his arm around her to help her up. "There," he said, "that's better. Now, you're not going to go all faint on me again, are you?"

"No," she replied, straightening.

"I bet you need some food. Darn women never eat. Some food, that'll cure your ills. We'll have lunch at the Winchester. That suit you?" he asked.

"Yes," she agreed humbly.

She had to go on; she couldn't just stop in the middle of life and quit. She knew that. *Don't panic,* Emily told herself. *You're okay. Just put one foot in front of the other. It will all work out somehow.* She had to believe that. She straightened her shoulders and wiped at her eyes.

A woman said good-day to Will; he tipped his hat politely. Emily could see the woman give her an assessing look, but Will didn't stop to introduce her. They passed Zimmerman's Drug Store, and Emily caught a glimpse of a stack of newspapers inside. "Wait," she said to Will. "I'd like to go in here for a minute."

"Suit yourself," he said.

The newspapers were from Denver. The copies of the *Rocky Mountain News,* a few days old, read "March 1, 1893." But this time Emily wasn't so easily shocked. It was as if her system were overloaded and had gone numb. She accepted things now, almost with a pure animal acceptance.

Will waited outside. He took a look at her when she came out. "Did you need to buy something?" he asked.

She shook her head. "No, just looking," she replied.

The bank was a brick building with two tall, deeply recessed windows. First National Bank of Rifle was written in gilt paint in an arc on each window.

"Could I go in here?" she asked.

He merely shrugged.

The date at the teller's window read March Third. Emily stepped up to the teller, a young man with spectacles and black bands holding his shirtsleeves up. "What's the real date today?" she asked.

"March the third, ma'am," he answered, indicating the sign.

"What *year?*" Emily asked.

The teller looked at her oddly. "Why, eighteen and ninety-three, ma'am."

Before she could say anything else, Will was there, taking her arm and pulling her away.

Lunch was beef steak or mutton and potatoes. No salads or quiches or croissants. Will had a beer with lunch, and Emily had a glass of wine.

The other people in the Winchester Hotel dining room were all men, mostly businessmen, Emily thought, and they were all eating meat—big plates with large slabs of meat. Emily felt slightly nauseous, picked at her potatoes and sipped at the wine.

"Eat something," Will said. "Put some color back in your cheeks."

"Why aren't there any women in here?" Emily asked.

"Why, they're home, I guess. No reason for them to be. There's more women for Sunday dinner. Families, you know."

Men puffed on fat cigars until the air was blue with the smoke. There were no signs prohibiting smoking—only ones that warned patrons to use the spittoons. Emily could see the bar through a doorway—ornate wood, fancy mirror, a floor of small tiles in a design. A few men stood at the bar drinking and talking.

A movie set. But where were the tourists, the gaping onlookers?

Will left two shining quarters on the table then threw down a dime, as well. He helped her on with her coat and they left. Emily was aware of every man in the room watching her, following her progress. Unconsciously she straightened her shoulders and smoothed back a strand of escaping hair.

"Don't mind them," Will said. "They're curious. It's a small town, and they all know I was expecting a housekeeper from Chicago."

"But I'm not your housekeeper from Chicago," Emily protested.

He shrugged. "They don't know that."

Outside, Will paused and toyed with his mustache. "Well, is there anything more you need to do in town?"

Emily looked around at the town—the people, the blue sky and muddy street, the horses, the wide river in the near distance, the narrow wooden bridge that crossed it, the train depot at the foot of the street. She looked and swallowed and turned to Will. "No, I guess not. I...I guess I'll go home with you. I have nowhere else to go. Is that all right?"

"Well, ma'am, I wouldn't turn you out," he said.

"Look, I'll take the place of your housekeeper, how's that?" Emily said quickly. "I'll earn my keep, I swear I will. And then, when I have some money saved, well, I'll...I'll...oh, damn, I'll go *somewhere.*"

"No need to swear, Emily, and I'd take it kindly if you wouldn't use cuss words in front of the children. Mary's a real stickler on that," he said gravely.

"I'm sorry. I'll remember," she said.

"Let's be getting on home now. I still have chores to do," he said, taking her arm.

But she stopped short in front of the Satille and Gallow Saloon. Tinkling piano music came from inside and men's voices, raucous laughter. "Who's president of the U.S.?" she asked abruptly.

"Grover Cleveland, of course," Will replied. "Come along, now."

Emily clamped her mouth shut. She wanted to scream, to rip open the tight, uncomfortable coat she was wearing, to tell Will that she didn't belong in this crazy town living in the past, but she knew he wouldn't believe her. "Grover Cleveland will prove to be a lousy president," she blurted out.

Will regarded her with barely concealed disdain. "And that, ma'am, is why women will never have the vote."

"Don't count on it," Emily said under her breath, feeling as if she'd gone utterly mad.

The ride back to the ranch was long, cold and exhausting. Emily's small store of energy was long gone, used up in mental gyrations. She shivered incessantly, dozed a few times, waking to find herself slumped against Will, his arm around her to keep her on the hard-sprung seat. "Sorry," she said each time, and pushed herself upright, horribly embarrassed, but then weariness would overcome her again. Shep's barking roused her as they drove into the yard. She sat up just as Will was bringing the team to the front door. He jumped down and came around to her side. Emily stood too fast, and the blood drained from her head. Will's hands held her, thank heavens, because she felt so shaky she wasn't sure she could have managed to clamber down from that high seat by herself. Then she was standing, wavering a little, and Will's hands were still spanning her waist. He gazed down at her from under his hat brim. "You all right?" he asked gruffly.

She looked up into his dark blue eyes, seeing the frown that drew his brows together and the thick mustache. She felt her heart give a sick lurch. Eighteen ninety-three. No, it wasn't...wasn't...

The next thing Emily knew she was on the sofa in the parlor, someone's hands, Will's, were at her throat unbuttoning her shirtwaist, and Antonio was fanning her.

CHAPTER SIX

"MARY," EMILY ASKED one night after dinner, "do you or any of your friends ever ski?"

"Ski?" Mary looked up at her as Emily tucked her into bed.

"Yes, you know, up in Aspen or... Vail?" Emily knew Vail had been founded in the 1960s. "It's a sport, with skis on your feet so you slide down the snow."

"Oh," Mary said, "Norwegian snowshoes, you mean."

"Norwegian snowshoes," Emily muttered.

"I've heard of that, but I don't know anyone around here who does it. They do it in Aspen to get down from the mines, but what was that other place...?"

"Vail."

"I don't know where that is, Miss Emily."

"What about Aspen? Did you ever go there?"

Mary shook her head. "It's too far. But I know there're lots of rich folk there. Big houses."

"How did they get so rich, hon?" Emily asked, tucking Mary in snugly.

"Why, from the silver mines, Miss Emily."

It didn't matter how many questions Emily plied the Dutchers with, the results were the same. They lived in 1893. But Emily didn't. She couldn't. She *wouldn't*.

She thought often about how she'd come to be in this place. Why *her?* But no answers came to mind, and it made her head ache to ponder the unanswerable. She'd figure it out, though. Someday she'd find out what happened and get back to her real life.

At night when the children were finally asleep, Emily sat in the parlor with Will while he mended a harness or went over his ledgers.

Oh, how she'd like to snatch those ledgers out of his hands and tell him how antiquated his bookkeeping system was. After all, she was a graduate of the University of Pennsylvania's business school—Wharton. She had an M.B.A., for heaven's sake, and had worked in the banking business for years now.

Emily glanced up from sewing buttons on the boys' shirts and wanted to scream, *I'm vice president of a loan division! I'm a highly educated, powerful...*

She went back to fiddling with the needle and thread, a lump in her throat—he'd think she was utterly mad. No, she'd have to hold her tongue, and then somehow, someway, she'd escape.

Escape. The word was on Emily's mind incessantly. Maybe if she could get to Denver. Maybe in Denver everything was normal. Sure. The trouble was she had no money, no phone, no car—nothing. And yet she was not a prisoner. Will certainly treated her courteously enough. Oh, he was an arrogant loner of a man, all right, unused to women and children in his male domain... yet he was hardworking and generous. He'd taken in his nephews and niece and was putting up with her despite the fact that she had yet to do any real work for him.

Emily let out a sigh then saw him glance at her over his ledger book. She hated the way he looked at her, as if she were a nuisance.

She'd just have to go with the flow, Emily guessed, meeting his gaze boldly. She'd have to live in Rifle, in Will's home, until she could figure out where she really was or—did she even dare think it?—*when* she was.

"Any problem with your bookkeeping, Will?" she asked. "I'm really quite good with numbers. If you..."

"Everything's fine, ma'am...Emily," he said, turning back to his pages.

"Well, then," Emily said, putting aside the sewing, "I guess I'll turn in. You don't mind, do you?"

"Um?"

"If I turn in, Will?"

"No, no," he said, partially rising, not looking up, "go right ahead."

"Thanks." Emily got up, frowning at him.

Panic seemed to overtake her at odd moments, a seething fear that maybe she *had* gone insane. Maybe she really was Will's housekeeper, and the accident had addled her mind. Could a person go mad and dream up things such as airplanes and computers and nuclear bombs? Maybe. Perhaps. Trying to overcome the panic, she'd tell herself over and over, *It's fine. I'm going to be okay. I just need to figure things out.*

One thing Emily had finally figured out—or at least thought she had—was why Will had found her na-

ked. She had somehow traveled through a time warp!
Flesh and blood had slipped through a hole but, just
like in the movies, inanimate objects, clothing, jewelry, purses, were left behind.

Jeez, she thought, wait till she got home and told
them that! Of course, she still wasn't absolutely convinced it was 1893. Maybe if she could get to Denver...

It was two days after Emily had offered to help with
his bookkeeping that boredom finally drove her to
bundle up and seek Will out in the barn.

"You in here?" she called, closing the heavy doors
behind her against the cold. "Will? Are you...?"

"Over here."

Hay crunched under her feet and got caught in her
long hem as she made her way toward a far stall where
Will was tending to a frisky mare. The big horse shied
and threw her head up as Will carefully rubbed some
sort of ointment into a cut on the beast's neck. A tortoiseshell cat balanced gracefully on the partition,
watching and keeping a sharp eye on Shep.

"Be careful," Emily breathed when the horse tried
to rear.

Will only gave her a disparaging glance.

A man's world, Emily thought as she watched Will
Dutcher work on the nervous mare. She was hope-
lessly trapped in a world where men were dominant
and women subservient. Will's hands glided over the
mare's smooth flanks, settling her, and Emily kept
staring and wondering. A man's domain. A woman
wasn't worth much more than that horse. A woman
did certain work and bore a man's children. A brood
mare.

She kept watching Will's hands, staring at them in mute fascination. He was gentle with the mare, his big, work-worn hands moving fluidly on the animal, back and forth over curves and leanness, acutely sensitive, the way his hands might move on a woman...calming, soothing, knowing....

"Did you want something, Emily?" His voice broke her reverie sharply. "Are you all right? Not ill, I hope?"

Emily started, but soon found her voice. "I'm fine. Perfectly fine. And that's the problem."

Will washed his hands in a bucket and dried them on an old towel. When he rolled down his sleeves, she couldn't help staring at those powerful forearms, sprinkled with dark hair, the long, corded muscles... "There's a problem?" he was asking, his voice harsh as always.

"I'm...I'm ready to go to work, Will," she said, looking up into his eyes earnestly.

"Well, now," he said, and studied her. Studied her so long, so silently, that Emily wanted to crawl off into a dark corner like some sick calf. "Well," he repeated, and gave her one last look, shouldering past her toward a bucket of oats.

"Well *what?*" Emily said, swallowing, following him.

"I don't want you having a relapse on me, Emily," he began.

"I am *not* some sick...sick horse, Will. I'm a human being. I'm a *woman*. I know when I...oh, never mind." She folded her arms stiffly across the heavy wool coat she'd worn and looked at him, waiting, patches of red staining her cheeks. He went on about his business, bending, lifting, sometimes stopping to talk quietly to one of the horses. And all the while she watched him and felt diminished, small.

How *did* Will Dutcher see her? Had he ever thought of her as a woman? He'd seen her naked.... Emily's far-off gaze darted back suddenly to Will. He was standing near the tack room, doing something with a bridle. His feet were slightly apart and the muscles in his broad shoulders moved fluidly as he worked. He had a strong neck, thick and long, and as he bent his head, she could see his thin lips moving a little while he talked to himself. "Damn thing. I'll have to get to town to..."

Yes, he was an uncommonly handsome man—attractive in any time or place. His brand of manliness would cut it just fine a hundred years from now—two hundred years, if necessary. There were always going to be women who'd go for the likes of Will Dutcher.

"Something else I can do for you, Emily?" he asked, glancing once in her direction.

"No," she said, clearing her throat, "ah, no. We'll talk more about it later."

"Um." He went back to the bridle and never looked up when Emily left.

"THAT WILL DO JUST FINE," Emily said to the shopkeeper in the Western Mercantile. "Just fine."

"This is on Mr. Dutcher's account," the woman said, not asking, but telling Emily.

"Yes, I'm his housekeeper."

"I'm aware of that, miss. Everyone knows who you are," Mrs. Tate said coldly, her pale eyes meeting Emily's in a kind of challenge.

It took Emily aback for a moment. She could feel the vibes; this woman did not like her one bit. But she'd never even seen her before.

"I'll just write this up and wrap the dress for you," Mrs. Tate said grudgingly.

"Thank you so much," Emily said, trying to be gracious. *Nasty woman,* she thought. *What's got her goat?* But she was so happy with her new dress, she decided not to let it get her down. Lord, but she was tired of her two outfits: the baggy black dress and the awkward blue skirt. She'd asked Will if she could buy something new, and he'd told her, "Sure, fine," without even looking up from his newspaper.

The dress was beautiful—every stitch done by hand, of course. A deep Dresden blue in a fine wool with a bustle and a yoke of pleats and fringe around the hem. A real work of art. It cost $9.95, an exorbitant price, but it was from New York, Mrs. Tate said. Emily couldn't wait to put it on for supper that night.

It was a ploy as old as time, Emily knew as she came down the stairs to dinner, her new skirt swirling around her ankles. A ploy to get Will to notice her. It wasn't romance she was seeking—not at all, not in this mad charade she was caught in—rather, it was a way of getting him to see her as a woman. No man, in any day or age, could be allowed to be as oblivious and aloof as Will Dutcher, gentleman rancher. If it took parading her femininity in front of him, well, why not?

"Good evening, Will," Emily said, poking her head into the parlor, "I think dinner's ready. The children are already at the table." She turned, her skirt rustling, and headed into the kitchen to help Antonio serve.

If Will hadn't immediately noticed Emily's new dress, Antonio did. *"Dios"* the old man said, his brown eyes as big as a calf's.

"You like it?" Emily swung around for him, doing a full circle.

"Dios," was all she got.

The boys were oblivious. And Will. Well, Emily couldn't decide if he was his usual, preoccupied self at dinner or if he purposely avoided looking at her. "More potatoes?" she asked, leaning toward him. "Another piece of meat, Will?"

"Yes, thanks." He went back to his roast.

"You know," Emily said over Antonio's pie, "it wouldn't hurt for this whole family to cut down on red meat. It's really bad for your cholesterol levels."

Will looked up and raised a dark brow.

"The fat level in your blood. It can clog...oh well, never mind."

"What's wrong with the meat?" piped up Jesse.

Emily smiled. "Nothing. It's good for you. But more fruits and vegetables are better."

"I hate vegetables," Burke said.

"I like them," Mary said, "they're good for you." She gave Emily a smile.

After dinner the boys played in the attic while Emily and Mary worked fashioning a doll's wedding gown that was proving to be a challenge. Will sat in his usual chair in the pool of light from the kerosene lamp, with Shep dreaming and twitching at his feet and the wood crackling cheerfully in the stove next to him. He was reading *The Rifle Reveille.*

Emily glanced up from the sewing. "Anything exciting happening in town?"

"The usual. Cattleman's Association meeting next Wednesday. Ladies' Literary Society on Monday." He rattled the paper. "If you'd like Antonio or one of the hands to drive you into Rifle for the meeting, you know you'd be welcome."

Emily frowned. "I wouldn't be so sure," she said, mostly to herself. In truth, whenever Emily had ridden into town on errands, she'd gotten a cool reception from the local women. If the men didn't sense anything strange about her, the women did. Perhaps it was female intuition. Perhaps it was jealousy—after all, Emily was living under the roof of the most sought-after bachelor in the county. She had a feeling all the women in town had heard how she'd been found in the train wreck. Mrs. Fisher had dressed her and given Will clothes for her. And, according to Mary, Mrs. Fisher was the worst gossip in town. A tidbit like that would be too good to pass up. Now, she was sure that everyone, men and women alike, knew Emily had been stark, staring naked when Will had found her. Obviously they disapproved. Damn Victorian morals, Emily thought, as if it had been her fault.

"What did you say?" he asked.

"Oh, just that I think I'll pass on the literary society."

"Suit yourself." The paper rattled.

The boys turned in at nine. Mary at nine-thirty. Antonio had long since gone over to the bunkhouse—it was poker night. But Will was still up, dozing on and off, drowsy from the big meal and the warmth of the stove. Emily came down the stairs after tucking Mary in and silently entered the parlor. For a time she stood in the center of the Oriental rug, poised between going to bed herself or waking Will. She told herself she really needed to talk to him about her chores—just what he expected now that she was fully recovered. But there was also that something else inside her, that part of Emily that craved his attention, that kept nagging her, telling her in a seductive inner voice that he should acknowledge her, treat her as a human being, a woman. What was wrong with Will Dutcher? Other men, plenty of them in town, stared at Emily and tipped their hats. Other men saw her as available and female. What in the devil was wrong with Will?

She stared at him, taking in his long, slightly bowed legs and narrow hips as he dozed. He was wearing his underwear—his union suit—beneath a white collarless shirt open at the neck. Beneath the union suit crisp black hairs curled on his chest. His lips were parted very slightly, and he breathed with a faint, husky rumble, like a well-kept engine.

God, he *was* handsome, Emily saw. A pool of golden light from the lamp was falling on his curling dark hair and touching his jaw and cheek, gilding one side of his long, straight nose and lying gently on thick eyelashes that hid those discerning blue eyes. In Emily's day she would have laughed with a friend and said he had a face and body that wouldn't quit. But now, well now, standing in front of him, unmoving, unable to move, Emily wasn't at all sure how she felt. She'd told herself she'd gotten the dress—his gift to her—so he'd see her as a person, perhaps sit and talk to her.

But that had been a lie, she suddenly knew; the dress was a symbol of her loneliness, the growing hunger inside her, the...

"Um." Will stirred, stretched and opened his eyes. "I must have drifted off," he said, straightening.

"Ah, yes, you did." Quickly Emily began moving around the room, picking up Burke's wooden soldiers, Mary's hairbrush. "You must have been tired," she said, turning toward him. And suddenly she got that long-awaited response. She saw it in his gaze that was locked, held against his will, on the swell of her bodice, the slimness of her waist and flare of her hips.

After an agonizingly long moment, Will finally tore his gaze away and began picking up his newspaper, piece by piece. His jaw was locked tightly, the muscle working.

Suddenly she felt awful. Felt as if she'd betrayed herself, betrayed her whole gender. This must be the way a whore feels the first time, Emily thought, with a sick, sinking sensation. What had gotten into her? Was she really trying to *seduce* Will Dutcher? She felt like covering herself—covering herself and running. The hairbrush slipped out of her trembling fingers, wooden soldiers scattered on the rug.

Will was on his feet. "Here, let me. You're not..."

Tears sprang into Emily's eyes. "I'm fine," she cried, "I'm perfectly fine, Will! Can't you get that through your thick head? I'm *fine!* I just want to be treated like... like a human being. I want someone to *talk* to, Will. I want you to tell me how I can help you. Anything. Just let me do something around here. And... and for God's sake, stop pretending I don't exist!"

But Will only regarded her without expression. He finally said, "No need to get yourself riled up, ma'am. I'm not about to debate your existence."

THE DAYS PASSED. Spring blew into the valley, and fragile green touched the leaves of the apple trees beneath Emily's window. The road turned to mud. And Emily got to finally take over the household management.

It was hard work. Long and hard. The harsh lye soap stung her hands, and the cold water drove her crazy. And the iron was incredibly heavy. God, she'd invent wash-and-wear herself if this went on much longer. The work was beginning to seem endless— endless and without reward.

Until the day Will appeared behind her and emptied the heavy washtub out back.

Emily wiped her brow in the late April sun and tucked wisps of her hair behind an ear. "Thanks," she said, watching him handle the tub with ease.

"It's nothing," he said, straightening, hanging the tub on a peg outside.

Emily smiled. "Well," she said, "that's done."

He stood there, studying her unabashedly, as if he were judging her worth. Finally he said, "I've been meaning to tell you, Emily, what a fine job you're doing."

"Oh, well." Surprised, Emily waved a hand in the air. "It's no big deal. Have to earn my keep."

"Um." He still stared, hands on hips.

"I'm . . . I'm glad you noticed, though," she said at last, and oddly enough, this time, it was her eyes that turned away first. For the entire rest of the day she went about her business feeling like a newlywed who'd just cooked her first decent meal.

And that was the trouble, Emily finally realized—she was accepting her bizarre existence.

She didn't belong here. And no matter how easily she was falling into the routine of life in Rifle, and Will's life, she still longed for her own time, her own place in this crazy, mixed-up world.

Time travel couldn't exist, Emily had often thought. And yet it did. And she wanted out of this time. She needed the intellectual stimulation of the 1990s. Her health club. Museums. Travel. Eighteen-hour bras, for heaven's sake. A woman to talk to. Women in Rifle, as Emily had already learned, found her intimidating. They didn't like her.

"I'm an aberration," Emily mumbled over the ironing board, "I don't belong here."

She could even be dangerous, she frequently thought. What if she were to somehow change the course of history? What was that old adage? If a man were to travel back in time and shoot his grandfather, would he cease to exist? And what if Emily were to alter history? Maybe there wouldn't be a future, certainly not the one she'd come from.

Strangely, Emily was managing to live daily life without going completely crazy. She was growing fond of the two impish boys and dearly enjoyed Mary's company. Even Antonio was warming to her in the kitchen. But Will—Will still stood his distance, and she hadn't a clue how he really saw her.

It didn't matter, Emily convinced herself, because somehow, someway, she was going to find the path back to her own time. To heck with Will Dutcher, she'd think, even as her gaze betrayed her when she'd watch for him coming in off the range, tall and distinctly handsome in the saddle. She *had* to get back to her own time. If only she had some money, could somehow reach Denver. She had to get away from Rifle, from Will—especially from Will, because, despite her best intentions, Will Dutcher was getting under her skin.

Emily's thoughts were along the same line as she sat dining with Will and the local bank president, Bob Bergener, who'd come out to the ranch for a business dinner. *I have to get away...*

"Excellent dinner, Miss Jacoby," Bob Bergener was saying, pushing himself away from the table, his forty-five-year-old stomach protruding under his gold brocade vest.

"Thank you," Emily said, "but it was mostly Antonio's doing."

"Well," Will said, "how about a cigar and brandy, Bob?" He, too, pushed himself from the table and rose, tall and trim, the exact opposite of the balding banker.

The two men retired to the parlor, but Emily, much to her annoyance, was relegated to the dining room and her sewing. For some time she sat in the adjoining room pricking her finger with the needle and listening to the men's conversation. God, how she'd like to join the talk—banking. She'd bet she knew a whole lot more about it than old Bob Bergener, too.

"So," she could hear the banker saying, "how's the new livestock acreage working out for you, Will?"

"Fine," Will replied, and Emily could smell the cigar smoke as it wafted in blue streams through the house.

"Good, good." Bergener cleared his throat. "I sure wish the banking climate was going as well."

"What's that, Bob?"

"Oh, the climate's a bit nervous lately. Clear across the country. A lot of us bankers are having to pull in some reserves, Will. You understand."

"No," Will said slowly, "not really."

Again, Bergener cleared his throat. "It's like this, Will," he said, his tone guarded, "that money you borrowed last autumn to expand the herd...well, I'm afraid I'm going to have to up your payments. You understand. We bankers have to start tightening the old belts, as they say."

"Increase my payments?" Will asked, his voice hardening. "And just how much of an increase, Bob?"

There was a moment's silence. Then, "Double."

"You're *doubling* them?"

"Now listen, Will, I sure wouldn't be doing this if there were any other way."

"Am I the *only* rancher in this goldang fix?"

"Oh, not at all, Will. Certainly not. There's the McCruddens and the Smiths and..." But Emily was no longer listening. Eighteen ninety-three, she was thinking. There was something about that time period... and then she had it. Part of it, anyway. Something about a panic occurring in the U.S. A panic, yes. Banks collapsing. Right. It had to do with the gold reserve in the U.S. Treasury. Sure. But when had the panic happened? And exactly why?

Before Emily thought about her actions, she was standing in the parlor door, her sewing still in her hands. "Your gold reserves are down, aren't they?" she asked Bob Bergener.

He looked up, surprised. "Excuse me?" he said.

Emily's brow was furrowed. "I asked if you were overextended at your bank, Mr. Bergener."

"Emily," Will was saying, astonished.

But she ignored him. "I was only curious about whether you have enough gold in reserve, Mr. Bergener, to cover your deposits. I was wondering if your balance sheets are—"

"Emily," Will said, striding over to her, taking her arm roughly.

"Well, I never," Bergener was saying, rising also, stubbing out his cigar. He reached for his coat. "I'll talk to you in town, Will," he said then, and shot Emily a disgusted glance before he escaped out the door to his buggy.

"Damn, Emily," Will said, grabbing her arm and half dragging her over to a chair, pressing her down into it. "How could you embarrass me like that? What kind of woman are you?"

Emily looked up at his angry scowl. She shrugged. "I'll tell you what kind of a woman I am. I'm an *educated* woman. I happen to have a degree from one of the top business schools in this country, Will Dutcher." She kept staring at his disbelieving face, refusing to give in. "And what's more," she said, hot now herself, "I'll bet I know a whole lot more about banking than Bob Bergener does!"

For a long moment, Will continued to regard her gravely. Then, in a very quiet voice, he said, "If that's true, Emily, why did you hire out as a housekeeper?'' His sapphire blue eyes bored into hers.

Emily swallowed and looked down into her lap. Now she'd gone and done it. "I, ah," she said, fumbling for words, "I, ah, had this...ah...relationship and it...ah...it didn't work out. I left the...East, Will, and..." Abruptly she fell silent. She could only imagine what he was thinking.

Will's hand went to his mustache automatically while he stared at her, and a chill crawled up Emily's spine. "I knew you were running from something," he finally said, "I suppose I should have guessed it was...a man."

The evening wore on miserably. Emily felt torn apart inside, convinced on the one hand she'd stood up for herself just fine in front of those two men. But on the other hand, she knew she *had* embarrassed Will. If this really was 1893, she'd had no business interfering in their conversation. And then, of course, she'd come up with that lame story about a sour relationship. *Damn.*

But she wouldn't turn tail and run. She'd sit there on the settee, her back straight, her chin up, her stomach churning. Why had she gone and told Will that? Had she wanted his pity?

Damn, Emily thought, stabbing the needle in and out of his white cotton shirt. *Damn.* She could have concocted dozens of stories—why a bum relationship? *Stupid.*

She looked up and found his eyes on her, questioning, accusing, and her heart began a slow, heavy rhythm in her chest. Outside, a late spring storm was racing across the valley and the shutters rattled. But inside, in Will's parlor, the lamp laid down warm circles of gold on the carpet, and Emily felt sweat break out on her brow and upper lip.

Will kept staring, a thousand unspoken questions on his rugged features, questions Emily could only guess at. She held his gaze and commanded her heartbeat to slow. And then in his eyes she thought she could read something new, something beyond accusation. It almost seemed as if he were envisioning her in that other man's arms, and wondering, himself, what she would feel like pressed to...

Suddenly Emily stood, her heart in her throat. The buttons scattered on the floor and his shirt drifted from her fingers. She didn't notice.

And then he was there. But he wasn't reaching down to collect the buttons. Instead, his hands were on her arms, gentle yet imprisoning. And his eyes. Those deep blue eyes were searching hers. Emily held her breath, her whole body brittle, ready to shatter like glass.

The moment stretched out, unbearable. Finally, in a husky whisper, she heard him say, "You *are* different, Emily. There's something..." But he faltered suddenly, and Emily wanted to scream, to cry, to lean up against that steel-hard chest and sob out her fears. He'd let her do it, too, Emily knew. He'd hold her and comfort her and save her—save her just as he had in that train wreck.

"Emily," he started to say, but she was pulling back, twisting away from him. Then somehow she was free, hurrying from the parlor, from the man, rushing from herself and her aching fears. Later, much later, when the storm outside had fled the land and a curtain of stars fell over the mesas, Emily heard his footfalls as he climbed the stairs, paused for a moment, then opened his bedroom door and closed it quietly. She pressed her eyes shut tightly and prayed she'd awaken from this terrible nightmare.

CHAPTER SEVEN

EMILY BECAME OBSESSED with this new idea of hers. If she got out of Rifle, if she could get away from the town to a real city, she'd find that everything was normal. She settled on Denver, or Denver City, as they called it in 1893. The train went from Rifle to Denver, an easy trip. She even knew the schedule by heart.

The obsession controlled her life, even as she dressed in bloomers and chemise, corset and petticoats and uncomfortable, tight jackets, even as she cleaned Will's house, did laundry, took lunches to the men at work in the fields when Antonio was too busy, even as she heated bathwater, and scrubbed and mended and helped the children with their homework. She never stopped planning, weighing possibilities.

She had to get away. She had to prove there were planes and cars and computers and that she wasn't completely nuts.

And she had to escape Will Dutcher. There were times when he was around that she actually did forget her obsession, moments when he looked at her, their eyes met, moments when his hand brushed hers accidently or he helped her with a heavy chore. Stolen moments.

She had come to appreciate his strengths, the curious gentleness Will could show the children or a sick horse—though seldom did he display that gentleness toward her—the power that made him so self-sufficient and so very attractive. His homespun, old-fashioned virtues such as loyalty, independence, pride, a fierce sense of responsibility for family. He even drove the children to church on Sundays. There wasn't a man she could think of who matched up to Will Dutcher. Certainly not Bill.

She was in a precarious situation, a spinster lady under the roof of an eligible bachelor. And the stories Mrs. Fisher had apparently circulated about her scandalous condition when she'd arrived at Doc Tichenor's surgery—well, Emily could just imagine. It made things so much worse. Will, and the whole town, no doubt, had expected a homely, dried-up hag. Emily was wrong for the part, and every woman in Rifle made no bones about bringing it to her attention. They all had daughters or nieces out to nab Will Dutcher, and they resented Emily. She didn't belong, and the women knew it.

Will would be better off without her. Some strong, uncomplaining female would get him eventually, someone who'd make a good rancher's wife, someone who fit in.

As the weeks went by, and nothing occurred to whisk Emily back into the world she'd left, she came to one conclusion: she had no choice but to run away to Denver. She'd just have to take the money from Will and leave.

Oh, she'd asked about the salary, all right, but it hadn't gotten her very far.

"Well, now," Will had said, "my brother Clay paid the Chicago employment agency for the whole year. Other than that it's room and board."

"He didn't pay *me*," she'd pointed out. "I'd like a little pocket money. I don't have a cent, Will. It's embarrassing."

"You have everything you need, don't you?" he'd said. "You can charge anything you want at the Mercantile store."

"Yes, but..."

"I can't figure what else you have to spend money on," he'd said.

"To save. What if I wanted to save money, so that when I leave..." she'd said.

"You planning on leaving?" he'd asked.

"Sometime I am."

"Tell you what, I'll write Clay and ask him where that money is. I figured the agency would have given you your cut. How's that?"

She'd given up. "Okay, fine."

But she couldn't wait to hear from Clay in Chicago. She had to go—she had to find out if the rest of the world existed in 1893.

It was a Wednesday morning in late April. The land was coming alive, pale green and fertile after the long winter. Will and the hands were busy with the calving. He'd even been out all night a couple times. This particular morning he'd left early, and Emily was alone in the house with Antonio.

It came to her with sudden clarity. She put the pans of bread dough near the stove to rise, carefully laid towels over them, put more wood in the oven to keep it going, took the hot water off the stove to do the dishes. Routine chores. When everything was in order, she untied the long white ruffled apron and hung it carefully on its hook.

Antonio was in his room at the back of the house. The place was quiet, neat, empty. She strode from the kitchen to Will's desk in the parlor and deliberately, thoroughly, searched every drawer.

In a tin box in the top right drawer she found thirty-five dollars, funny-looking big bills like play money. Greenbacks. She closed the tin box and the drawer, clutched the bills in her hand and went upstairs.

She packed the few clothes she had in a small carpetbag, her heart pounding. She wasn't stealing, she wasn't running away. This was something she had to do. If Will Dutcher hated her for doing it, then he hated her; it made no difference. She couldn't stay.

One regret assailed Emily. She'd have liked to say goodbye to the kids. She'd have liked to believe they'd miss her, especially Mary. But there was no other choice. They'd do fine without her. Clay could send a real housekeeper out from Chicago, an old, sensible one, a woman who would fit right into the community—someone Emily could never be.

She went downstairs and rapped on Antonio's door. "I feel sick," she said when he roused himself from his nap. "I need to see Doc Tichenor. Could you please drive me into town, Antonio?"

It seemed to take forever for the old man to hitch up the horses. She prayed Will wouldn't come home for some reason. She sat on the porch, waiting, her fingers clutching the carpetbag, her heart beating a sick, heavy cadence.

Antonio let her off in front of Doc's. "You goin' to be all right, Miss Emily?" he asked, concerned. "The boss murder me if anything happens to you."

She stood on the flower-bordered walk and looked up at Antonio. "You go have a beer or something. I'll send someone for you when I'm done. Thank you, Antonio. But I'll be fine now that I'm at the doctor's."

When the rig was out of sight, Emily walked swiftly down the wooden sidewalk past Zimmerman's Drug Store, the bank, the Western Union office, the saloons and shops and houses, toward the train depot. She was just in time. The 10:18 Denver and Rio Grande eastbound would leave shortly, and she'd be on it.

"Denver City," Emily said firmly to the ticket agent. "One way."

"Ain't you Will Dutcher's housekeeper?" the man asked, peering over his spectacles at her. "The one he found in the wreck?"

"Yes," Emily said.

"Why you goin' to Denver City? You leavin'?"

She thought it best not to arouse his suspicions. "I . . . uh . . . I'm going to visit my cousin. She's going to have . . . a baby, and well . . ." She tried to smile.

"That'll be four twenty-five, then, ma'am."

A few minutes remained for the train to arrive. Emily sat outside in the sun, high-button boots peeking demurely out from under her long, blue serge skirt, her hands folded around the handles of the bag in her lap. She hoped that her face was unreadable, that no one suspected the emotions rolling inside her: fear, sadness, guilt, hope. She tried not to think of Mary

and Jesse and Burke. She tried to turn her mind from
Will. She hoped he wouldn't be angry at Antonio,
blame him. Would he despise her for a thief? Would
he miss her? She was an indifferent housekeeper, a bad
laundress, but good with the kids.

She closed her eyes, bit her lip, felt moisture build
under her lids. What else could she do?

The distant sad whistle of the train came from the
west, down the broad river. Emily stood and walked
out on the platform. She stared straight ahead,
clenching her teeth so that her chin wouldn't tremble,
and felt her skirt swirl in the wind caused by the train's
passage, heard the hiss of steam and the conductor's
call.

She sat on the train like a mannequin, not really
alive inside. Her eyes saw the scenery, familiar from
her last train ride, but her mind registered little.
Somewhere in her consciousness she remembered
imagining a woman on a train dressed in clothes like
hers, but it seemed a distant, futile notion conjured up
by someone else.

The train rocked, stopped, wailed its lonely warning, backtracking her previous voyage. Emily sat,
afraid to feel or think or wonder, sat and tried not to
cry. As night fell, she dozed.

Jerking awake often, she dreamed in snatches, and
it was always of Will Dutcher. In her dreams he was
looking for her, striding down the wooden sidewalks
of Rifle, his boot heels loud. Or he was coming in
from the range, riding that big sorrel horse of his. But
most often she saw him in the parlor sitting in his pool
of light, his long legs stretched out, his face lined and
tired from a hard day's work, Shep at his feet. And his

eyes were always on her, accusing, questioning, judging.

Oh Will, she thought, *I wish it could have been different.*

IT WAS 1893 IN DENVER CITY. Emily stepped off the train that night at Union Station and knew instantly. Gaslights lit the city, buggies and trolleys and wagons choked the streets, the clothes were like those she had on. She wandered the street in mute, horrified wonder, an alien, a stranger in a strange land. *Oh, God,* she kept thinking.

Hunger forced itself upon her, and she ate in a small café, all the men staring at her. Or was she only imagining that? She asked the waitress where a lady could stay for the night, a safe place.

"Try the Larimer Street Ladies' Hotel," the waitress said. "It's safe and clean."

She had to ask directions several times, but she finally found the hotel. The desk clerk was asleep, and Emily had to ring the bell outside for a very long time. It had started raining, a fine spring rain, and she was wet and tired and without hope.

"Two dollars a night," the clerk told her. "Fifty cents more with hot water in the morning. Another two bits for breakfast."

She stayed in her room the next day, washed her clothes in the hot water they provided and waited for them to dry. She'd decided to find a job, a job in a bank, perhaps. Did they hire females in 1893? She'd decided she'd have to find a cheaper place to live, a job to support herself. Her money wouldn't last very long if she had to keep eating out.

Loneliness followed her that long day. She watched from her window the activity of downtown Denver City. There was a horse-drawn trolley and donkeys carrying loads, a mule train consisting of a dozen huge freight wagons, women in gaudy clothes and ornate hats. Young boys raced through the streets, ruffians, barefoot, with ragged clothes. Cripples and beggars and cowboys and a parade of dusty cavalry men on horses went by. Shiny hansom cabs and gorgeous coaches, rickety wagons and buckboards like Will's rolled along. Shouts and squeals and horses neighing, the clatter of hooves, the rattle of harnesses filled the air. The city smelled of dust and horse manure, garbage and bacon fat. Dandies in black suits and spats and string ties swung canes. Drab women in gingham dresses and bonnets trudged after loaded wagons. Denver City teemed with life—the life of a hundred years ago.

The next day Emily ventured forth to find employment. She went into every bank she saw and asked for a job.

The managers were polite, gentlemanly, but they didn't believe her. Oh, she could tell. What could she advise them, to send for her transcript: Wharton, class of 1988? She had no references; she simply didn't exist.

"I'm sorry, Miss Jacoby, but we have no opening at the present time," she was told, or, "We don't hire women for this position. Company policy, Miss Jacoby." Several bankers told her they wouldn't hire anyone without references. One man asked her if she realized how dangerous the job was. "We get held up once a month, Miss Jacoby. It's no job for a woman, no sir.''

She barely ate and then only in large hotel dining rooms where she felt safe. Even there the men all stared. Single women apparently did not eat alone in restaurants in 1893.

She hoarded her money. It would last a week or so. Something would happen by then—she'd find a job somewhere.

But on Friday morning, as she came out of her hotel, two boys ran down the street and careened into her, practically knocking her down. When they were gone, so was her small velvet drawstring purse and all of her money.

She walked the streets all day, searching for a job. She'd given up on banks, instead trying stores and restaurants. She got nowhere.

Panic dug sharp talons into her. She was alone, without money, marooned in the past. There was no way out, no way home, no way to her own world. For the first time, Emily became really afraid she would not make it. She was hungry, starving, tired, lost. She went back to the Larimer Street Ladies' Hotel and offered to work for her room. The desk clerk looked at her pityingly.

"Tell you what," he said. "I was supposed to keep your clothes and such to pay off last night, but I'll give 'em back to you anyway."

She was homeless, one of the street people, wandering around clutching her carpetbag. She sat on the curb in front of a shop for so long, her feet aching, her belly empty, that the proprietor came out and confronted her.

"Are you lost, miss?"

Emily looked up at the heavyset woman who stood over her. Her hair was hennaed, frizzy red curls escaping the hairpins in her bun. And pins, dozens of straight pins stuck in her bodice, a seamstress. "Yes, I am, I'm lost," Emily said in a hollow voice, still staring up into the florid face.

"Where were you going? I'll give you directions. I can't have you setting yourself down in front of my place like that. You'll scare my clients away. Now, where'd you want to get to?"

"Home," she said.

"Well," the seamstress said impatiently, "where's home?"

"Far away. Too far. I can't get there. I can't find it. I have no money." Emily was suddenly aware that she was crying, sitting there on a wooden sidewalk in Denver City, her clothes dirty, her hair matted, her only belongings in a carpetbag, and she was crying.

"Now, stop that. Can't be that bad. Where's your kinfolk?"

Emily sniffed and wiped at her eyes. "I don't have any."

"Heavens, woman, you're a sad one. I'm sorry for you, but you can't sit here," the big woman said.

"Where can I go?" Emily asked. "What can I do?"

The woman folded her arms and regarded Emily for a time. Then she went into her shop, only to return a minute later. "Here," she said, "here's two dollars. It's all I can spare, but it'll get you a room and some food. Off with you now."

Emily stared at the two crisp greenbacks through her tears. "God bless you," she said. "I'll pay you back, I swear."

"Oh, go on. I can see you're not a bad one. Go on and get yourself a decent meal."

Emily bought food at a grocery store—crackers, cheese, sausage, nothing in a tin as she had no way of opening it—and carried the food around with her in her bag. She was afraid to spend a dime on a room, afraid she'd starve, so she made her way to the Brown Palace Hotel, where she'd stayed on her way through Denver. It was there, all right, looking precisely the same but newer, and its familiarity reassured Emily. She used the elegant washroom and tidied herself up. Then she sat in one of the comfortable velvet-covered chairs in the corner of the lobby under a potted palm and tried to look inconspicuous.

It worked for a few hours; it was warm and comfortable and the hum of guests' voices lulled her. Her head nodded and...she was back in Rifle, sitting in the parlor with Will. She tried to talk to him, to tell him she was sorry, to beg him to understand, but no words came and her mouth wouldn't work. She kept trying, desperately, to make him understand, but she couldn't talk. And then Will was rising, standing over her, his eyes stormy and furious, and he was so big she was afraid. She struggled to speak, but he clamped his big hand down on her shoulder.

"Excuse me, madam," came an angry voice, "but you cannot sit here another moment."

Emily's heart gave a startled leap as she opened her eyes. "Please," she fumbled, "I'm...I'm waiting for someone. Yes, one of your guests."

The man pulled a pocket watch out and tapped it. "At one-fifteen in the morning? *Madam.*"

"I am. I'm..."

"You will leave instantly, or I will call a policeman to escort you out!"

She dragged herself up and walked toward the door, not even caring who in the lobby might have noticed her humiliation. She endured with the dull misery of one past mortal shocks. She walked, hugging herself in the cold spring night, walked all night until she was so weary she couldn't put one foot in front of the other.

It occurred to her in a moment of lucidity that she should have let the man in that hotel call the police; at least then she'd have food and a place to lay her head. Maybe she should commit a crime and go to jail—or did they have jails for women in 1893?

Maybe she'd die. Maybe she'd lie down in the dirty street and go to sleep and not wake up. It'd be easier that way.

She ate as she wandered, chewing on the sausage and cheese, dazed, wondering how she'd ended up like this, wondering at the stupidity of leaving Rifle and a warm house and food. God, how she'd taken those things for granted!

In the early hours before dawn, Emily was crossing the street in front of an elaborate hotel, its bar still open, lights and laughter and piano music spilling out into the street. She stopped and looked in over the swinging doors, envious. It was warm in there.

A well-dressed man, weaving a little, came through the doors, nearly bumping into her.

"Sorry," she muttered, turning away.

"Sorry, nothing," the man said in a jocular tone. "What a fortunate meeting, madam. Dare I inquire as to whether you're alone this fine night?"

He was making fun of her. "Excuse me, please," she said.

But he put a restraining hand on her arm. "No, no, don't leave. Just tell me how much."

"How much what?"

"Oh, so you're playing coy. How adorable. How much do you cost, my dear woman?"

Emily's back stiffened. "Listen, mister," she said, "who the hell do you think you are? Get your dirty paw off me, you creep!" And she enjoyed the shocked expression on his face so much she continued her verbal attack, with some choice, twentieth-century cuss words.

Satisfied, feeling better than she'd felt in days, Emily wandered down the cold street in the pale light of dawn, her skirt bedraggled, her hair falling out from under her hat, her carpetbag held to her breast tightly.

As she moved along the refuse-piled streets of Denver City, she thought of how good Rifle would look right now, and the ranch house with the big black stove in the kitchen crackling with heat as Antonio cooked bacon. She could smell the bacon, hear Jesse and Burke quarrel, hear Antonio singing a Spanish song, feel the warmth.

And Will. She could see Will sitting in the parlor in his collarless white shirt and black vest, his pipe lit, the newspaper in his lap and his eyes, those dark blue enigmatic eyes, resting on her.

WILL DROPPED his leather satchel onto the empty seat next to him and took off his Stetson. He tugged out his watch before sitting and checked the time. It was 7:45 p.m. Damn train should be pulling out right now.

He felt like a city dude, all gussied up in his good trousers and frock coat, his best black vest and tie. Even his tall boots were polished—Antonio had done that—and his white shirt was his last new one. Hell, he felt like a gambling man in all these fancy black duds.

And what for? Why was he chasing Emily Jacoby to Denver City?

The passenger cars finally lurched forward and headed toward Glenwood Springs. Will settled in for the long haul up over the Rockies. Damn waste of time, he told himself, frowning, smoothing his mustache. And when he did get to the city, he wondered just how he was going to find that blamed woman, anyway.

The train rumbled through Glenwood Canyon, and Will pulled out his brother's letter that had arrived that morning in Rifle.

He couldn't believe it. All along he'd thought Emily was merely touched in the head from that nasty bump. She *had* to have been the housekeeper. But Clay's letter had sure put a curious light on the identity of Miss Jacoby. The letter read,

Dear Will,

I'm very sorry about the housekeeper changing her mind. The employment agency here in Chicago did not even let me know until now that the female hadn't gotten on that train. There are some problems about the money and, of course, they are eager to procure another woman for your needs and have promised to put said female on the next train west. Do let me know your feelings in this regard. . . .

Damn, Will thought, folding the letter back up, who in hell *was* Emily then? Had she really been running from a relationship, heading to Seattle? Decent women—relationships notwithstanding—didn't run off to some wild and woolly town all alone. Certainly not. But then who *was* she? A suffragette, traveling cross-country to spread her word, afraid to tell Will the truth? Well, tarnation, if she was one of those females, he sure didn't want her around the children. Victoria Fisher had already been hinting to him that Emily Jacoby wasn't suitable for the young ones. Oh, he'd gotten her drift, all right, and resented it, too, although he'd said nothing to Mrs. Fisher. Why'd she taken against Emily? What had Emily ever done to her? *Women.*

Emily. Stupid, foolish woman. Now here she'd lied to Antonio and run off to a strange city, alone, with no money except the few dollars she'd taken from his desk. It hadn't been hard to track her down, though, because she'd left a trail, ending right at the Rio Grande depot, where Jack Rusk remembered her in great detail, down to her wild story about a cousin in Denver City.

Why *was* he chasing after the woman? He'd told Antonio and the children it was the honorable thing to do, that it was his duty to protect her from herself. He'd told himself that, too.

As smart as Emily Jacoby was about some things, she was real backward about others. He'd rescued her from that train and got stuck with her, and that sort of made him responsible for her. A man took care of a woman, that was all there was to it.

Females! He snorted and shifted his position on the seat, tilted his hat over his eyes and tried to sleep.

As hard as he tried, he had a restless night of it. He kept dreaming in snatches, bad dreams. Emily wandering the streets in Denver City, alone, accosted by strange men. Even in his dreams he was angry, though, aggravated that he had to go to all this trouble. She wasn't worth it; no woman was. All they did was put a man out.

It was dawn when the train pulled into Union Station. Will was jolted awake by the conductor's hand on his shoulder. He felt stiff and weary and annoyed. He belonged at home on the ranch, not on some wild-goose chase. Hell, she'd obviously lost her mind pulling a stunt like this. And so had he, chasing after her.

It was a miserable day, rainy and windy. Great dark clouds rolled down through the foothills west of Denver and scudded across the vast prairie to the east. Will pulled his collar up and hunched his shoulders against the biting spring wind. Damn, but this was an inconvenience.

He spent from dawn to dusk traipsing the crowded, rutted city streets, asking in every hotel, every restaurant, every shop—even the police stations—if anyone, anywhere, had seen Emily Jacoby. For his efforts he got cold and wet and frustrated.

Alone, Will dined at his hotel on Larimer Street and retired early. But it was hard to sleep knowing Emily was out there somewhere, cold, soaked, afraid, and most likely penniless by now. What if some cad picked her up off the streets and offered her shelter? Will's gut churned with irritation.

In the morning he spoke to the day clerk. "Where might I locate a young woman whose fortunes are meager?" he asked.

The man raised a brow. "Sir?"

"Oh," Will said, shifting uncomfortably, "I meant the woman is an employee of mine. A particular woman. I'm afraid she has no funds."

"Try the churches." The man shrugged. "Or maybe the Denver Rescue Mission."

"I'll do that," Will said, and tugged on the brim of his wide hat.

He checked in four separate churches, but not a single female had sought refuge in the past two days.

He tried the mission on Eighteenth Street. Nothing. Only a pathetic group of men down on their luck and a few street urchins. No one had seen a young woman with thick honey brown hair and a trim figure.

"Got some females in here," one old man told him, "but they's no lookers. No, sirree Bob, they's all old as dem dar hills." He nodded toward the distant mountains.

"Thanks, anyway," Will said, and left the establishment, deep lines of anger etched on his face.

Morning passed. Will wandered the downtown streets, poking his head into shops, banks, restaurants, hotels. It was hopeless. He stood on the sidewalk in front of the Western Union office and knew he was running out of options. About the only choice left was to telegraph Antonio and tell him he'd be back on the morning train. Maybe tonight, he'd somehow find her. If not, he'd have to let her go. His ranch, the children, his life were in Rifle.

Damn this flighty female for putting him through this. He turned to go into the telegraph office then paused. He'd try the Denver Rescue Mission one more time. Maybe she'd stopped in.

He walked down Larimer toward Eighteenth, looking at the people he passed, searching the crowds for a familiar face, a familiar figure. She had to be here, somewhere.

Ahead, he saw it, the mission. It was a horrible sight to behold. Over the door was a big sign, Whosoever Wilt May Come. Well, he for one sure wished Emily would have read that sign. God Almighty, but she was proving to be trouble. He pushed on the door and went in, smelled the same odor as last time: cooked cabbage and unwashed bodies. And there were the tables and benches with the poor, starving folks lined up spooning broth into their mouths, the lame, the blind, the sad leavings of humankind.

Standing there on the threshold, he looked up and down the tables, searching for that one familiar face, that one head of dark golden hair, that one familiar curve of cheek and jaw and forehead . . .

"Will?" he heard, and turned toward the sound. "Will?" One of the ragamuffin figures was standing, staring at him, saying again, "Will?"

His face froze in shock. "Emily?" he said, disbelieving.

"Oh, Will!" And she was lurching across the room, through the rows of poor people, tripping over feet, her arms out, her face pale and dirty.

He took a step, another. Then she was right in front of him, standing there staring up at him, tears making tracks in the dirt of her face. "Emily," he said, curiously shaken.

And then she was in his arms, burrowing like a lost puppy, holding onto his jacket with dirty hands and sobbing, "Oh, Will, oh God, Will."

His fingers touched her hair tentatively, felt the springing sun-brightened tendrils, felt a burst of tenderness that left him dazed.

"Oh God, Will, my money got stolen, and I couldn't find a job." She was sobbing. "I'm sorry, I'm so sorry!"

"Shh," he said automatically, "nothing to be sorry for. You're safe now."

"Oh, Will, I was so scared," she said in a broken voice. He patted her shoulder awkwardly, horribly embarrassed, knowing everybody in the mission was gaping.

He took a deep breath and cleared his throat. "It's all right I said," he told her, then he took hold of her arms firmly and disengaged her grasp on him.

"Will, I . . ." she said breathlessly.

"Now, now, that's enough," he said briskly. "I've come for you, Emily, to take you home."

She looked up at him, stricken, her face bleached sickly white, mottled with tears and dirt, her eyes searching, questioning. A small hiccup escaped her, and then she seemed to draw herself up a little. "Yes, Will," she said quietly, and then averted her eyes.

He did what he could for Emily after that. It was as if her sorry plight had been his fault, but it hadn't, he knew. And she was so quiet, so subdued, so damn thankful, it disturbed him in a strange way.

He took her to lunch at the Palmer House Hotel, and she ate like a starving animal. He hired a carriage after lunch and told Emily sternly that she had to throw away her filthy carpetbag, that he was buying her a new one.

"Yes, Will," she said meekly. Then, "There's one thing . . . a lady was good to me, she gave me money. I'd like to pay her back." Her eyes implored him. "Oh, Will, but I'll have to . . . borrow two dollars."

"Of course," Will said. "Of course we'll pay her."

So they drove in the carriage to the seamstress's shop and paid the woman the two dollars. Then Will couldn't help buying Emily two new outfits while they were there and a new hat. Couldn't let Emily go around in that bedraggled, torn old thing she'd been wearing, he told himself.

He took her back in the carriage to his hotel and paid for a second room, across the hall from his. And while she bathed and changed into her new clothes, he ordered the best steak in town and a bottle of French wine to be served in the dining room at eight.

Why on God's earth was he doing all this? he asked himself. Treating her as if she were Queen Victoria herself. *Damned foolishness,* he thought, lying in his room, waiting for Emily to change.

But then, it was true—he rarely got into Denver City, and since he was here, no harm done in treating himself a tad. 'Course, he was doing it for Emily, too, but only because the damned silly female had done herself a bad turn. Not that she deserved any special treatment, hell, no.

Her rap at his door came promptly at eight. He answered it and found himself face-to-face with a new Emily.

She had on a dove gray suit, fitted at the waist, flared over the hips, the skirt draped to a bustle. Her blouse was a pale pink, inset with lace and embroidered with rosebuds and ribbon. She wore kid gloves and a hat with ostrich feathers. She looked elegant, exquisite, stunning. A real big-city lady. It took him aback for a second.

But she stood there, waiting for him, as if she hadn't noticed his lapse. She was smiling, her lips parted slightly, her gloved hands clasped demurely in front of her.

"Thank you," Emily said, her voice husky, "for all this."

"Couldn't let you gallivant about in those ruined duds," he said gruffly, hating to be thanked.

She'd recaptured some of her poise, Will noticed, and he was thankful. That womanly weeping and wailing, the embracing and needing to be comforted weren't for him. Lord, no, he detested that kind of weakness. Frankly, it scared the tar out of him.

She was polite to him over dinner, speaking when spoken to, offering little, so the conversation was necessarily sparse. She ordered chicken from the long, tasseled menu. *Chicken.* In Colorado. But he said nothing, not wanting to stir things up.

The restaurant was as elegant as he could desire, red brocade wallpaper and wainscoting, thick carpeting, chandeliers, round tables with white linen and crystal and so darn many spoons and forks that he watched Emily to see which one to use. So many waiters in white jackets he couldn't tell one from the other. But he was proud, sitting there dining with a lady as proper and well dressed and pretty as Emily. Yes sirree, cleaned up, she was pretty as a picture, belonged just as well as the other fine ladies in the dining room.

"I'll pay you back," Emily said over chocolate cake, "every last cent. I promise."

"Money again," he said. "Leave it be, woman. Eat your dessert."

She stared at him for a moment, heavy silver fork poised in midair. "And to think," she said as if to herself, "last month I was making a cool seventy-eight thou a year plus perks."

He glanced at her and shook his head, bemused. She *did* come up with the oddest things, almost like she was talking some foreign language. Strange woman, different. He searched for the word and finally found it: exotic. Yes, that was it. Emily Jacoby was like an exotic bloom. Out of place but undeniably beautiful.

CHAPTER EIGHT

As EARLY MAY TURNED to full-blown spring, Emily began to marvel at her ability to survive the paradoxes of her life on Will Dutcher's ranch. She existed day after day by a peculiar and varying sense of balance that defied reality, like a tightrope walker far above the ground, moving along a swaying cable visible only to himself.

At times she accepted her fate calmly. At times she railed inwardly, tormenting herself, asking too often, why me? Had she been thrust back in time for a purpose, an as-yet-unknown reason? Or had her inexplicable passage been a quirk, a random happening? Emily didn't know. For all she really knew she was lying in a hospital somewhere, unconscious, having a particularly vivid dream because, damn it, at the time of the train wreck she'd been imagining life as a pioneer, wondering if she herself had the courage of those sturdy folk who'd civilized the American frontier.

Well, now Emily knew, didn't she? She *could* survive. She could start life over just as they had done. A heck of a way to find that out, though, she often thought.

Emily scrubbed the neck of Will's shirt on the washboard and asked herself another question that had been forming since she'd gotten back from Denver City: If indeed she was in this time and place for a purpose, just how did Will fit into the scheme? Any woman, really, could sew and mend and wash his clothes. Any woman of Will's day could clean and iron and cook and care for the children. Why her?

It wasn't as if he appreciated her, either. Squeezing compliments out of Will was near impossible. Last night, Emily recalled as she ran his shirt through the wringer and hung it in the sun, had been a perfect example of Will's indifference.

She'd helped Antonio make a stew. The children had liked it, openly telling Emily at supper. But Will. The man was impossible.

"Do *you* like the stew?" Emily had asked.

"Oh," Will had said, looking up, "the stew. It's fine."

"Not too seasoned?" she'd pressed.

"It's fine, Emily."

Emily emptied the washtub and dried her hands and wondered just what it was about Will that both drew and repelled her at the same time. He was certainly a male chauvinist—no question about that—and a surly one to boot. But he was also a man, and a darned attractive one. Too often Emily found herself surreptitiously studying Will, imagining a life with him that included intimacy. Sometimes at night, alone in the dark of her bedroom, Emily found herself listening for his footfalls, and a frightening warmth would swell and spread in her belly—what if someday those footfalls came toward her door?

Life that May took on a rhythm. There was the work to be done at the ranch house. Then there were always the evenings, a quieter time, when Will would arrive in from the range, his spurs jingling on the front porch. Shep bounded alongside him, tongue lolling, seemingly never out of energy. They'd eat their dinner, and the children would eventually settle down to bed, and she and Will would sit together in the parlor, for the most part in silence, but Emily was always aware of him.

Just how very aware of him she'd become was brought home to Emily the night she burned her hand. Antonio had been given the day off and Emily had cooked. The trouble was she'd never gotten used to just how hot the handles of the iron pots stayed when left on top of the stove. The children had gone outside to play after dinner, and Will had headed off to the barn to attend to something. Emily cleared the dining room table, her mind elsewhere, wondering just why *she* had been the one to slip through that portal of time.

"Probably to do a stack of dishes," she muttered under her breath, recalling thinking on the train just before the wreck about needing to be needed. Well, she was needed in this place, all right.

Pots and pans and dishes and only cold, hand-pumped water that needed to be heated on the stove to do them in. That's what she was needed for.

Leaving the dishes soaking and a kettle on, Emily turned to the pots on the stove. "What a mess," she said, unthinkingly picking one up by its long handle.

Searing pain held her rigid for a split second, then she let out a strangled cry and dropped the pot on the floor. Later, she would think how stupid she was not to have thrust her hand under the pump. But for a long moment she could only stare down at it weakly, the pain agonizing.

Emily never knew just when Will came in through the kitchen door. But then he noticed her, standing in the middle of the room, holding her wrist, her face waxen. "And what's the matter with you?" he began, his voice accusing.

Emily cleared her throat, the pain in her hand shrieking, excruciating. "I . . . I, ah, burned . . ."

Will crossed the space between them in an instant. He took in the whole scene: the pot on the floor, Emily's pale face, her grasp on her wrist. He gripped her wrist then and examined her hand, whistling between his teeth softly, and steered her toward the sink.

If Emily hadn't been in such acute pain, and so numbed by her stupidity, she would have pulled away from him. But she let him immerse her hand in the cold water, his arm around her waist for support.

"How in hell did you . . ." he started to say but seemed to check himself. "How did you do this?" he asked in an easier voice.

"I picked up the pan," she said lamely. "It was hot."

"Had it still on the stove, didn't you." It wasn't a question. Then he took her hand out of the water, dried it and examined it closely and led her to a chair. "Sit down before you faint or something," he said, distracted, casting around the room. "Where does Antonio keep that salve of his, anyway?"

Emily looked up at him. "In the cupboard over the sink," she said, watching him. "Why are you mad at me, Will?" she asked then. "I didn't exactly do this on purpose."

"Never said you did." He took down a mason jar filled with some sort of goo Antonio concocted for burns and cuts. All she knew was that the pain was fierce and Will was thoroughly annoyed. She wished he hadn't come home and found her like this.

Mason jar in hand, Will was saying, "Bandages? Where are the bandages?"

Emily nodded to the pantry behind the kitchen. "Bottom shelf."

And then he was back, kneeling down beside her, taking up her hand again.

A strange thing happened as Will tended the burn. His hands on hers, the feel of his warm skin, the way he held her, examined her with his fingers, soothed the pain. Her insides melted, tingled, and her pulse beat a slow, heavy cadence that throbbed along with the burn. She sat there looking down at him where he knelt in front of her and remembered his hands on the hurt mare in the barn. She'd thought then how very skilled, how very gentle was Will Dutcher's touch. And she'd been right.

She took in the soft dark curls of hair that fell down the back of his neck. And above his homespun shirt the crisp hairs on his chest just showed. . . .

Will's scent assaulted her senses. Leather, wood smoke, and sweet perspiration formed by labor. Man smells unmasked by after-shaves or soap—heady aromas, primitive and natural . . . arousing.

He was wrapping the bandage around her hand then, his head still bowed over her. "Too tight?" he asked.

"It's fine," Emily breathed.

Those shoulders. Wide, long, corded muscles spanning his back, running down his arms to those capable, strong hands...

"Can you stand up?" he was asking her, and he rose, towering over Emily, his eyes finding hers. "*Can you stand?*"

"Oh," she said, her thoughts whirling crazily. "Oh. Sure."

But still he helped her to her feet. Then, for a moment, he studied her. "I wasn't angry," he said. "I only wish you'd be more careful."

"I'll try," Emily said.

"Um," he said, and turned, heading into the parlor. And it wasn't until many minutes later that Emily noticed the pain again.

If Will was an enigma, the children were quite the opposite. Starved for affection since the death of their parents, they quickly took to Emily's touch. Especially Mary, who'd had no female companionship for many months.

"Miss Emily, what are you and Antonio going to make us tonight?" she asked, perched on the kitchen table the following evening, her legs in their thick black stockings and high shoes swinging. "That thing, what did you call it?"

"Spaghetti," Emily answered, awkwardly peeling carrots with her bandaged hand.

"Yes, spaghetti. Did you find it in the store yet? Did Mr. Tate say he'd order it for you?"

Emily sighed. "He never heard of it, honey. I know you can make it from scratch, but I don't know how and I don't suppose they sell pasta machines here."

Mary laughed at everything Emily said, especially the things she didn't understand.

"What's a boob?" she asked after Emily had so labeled Antonio under her breath.

"A boob. A person who does dumb things, you know," Emily said. Then, "It has another meaning. It's slang for a . . . a breast."

Mary looked shocked.

"Now, don't look like that. Breasts are normal, natural. All women have breasts. You'll have them someday, too."

"I will?"

"Little girls grow up and reach puberty. They develop. They . . . oh, Mary, didn't your mother ever tell you these things?"

"No," Mary whispered.

So Emily had to. Mary was absolutely scandalized. "But babies come from storks," she said.

"No, they don't. Look, you know that the cows are bred in the spring by the bulls. Then they have babies the next year. It's the same thing, only people take nine months to gestate instead of a year."

"How horrible," Mary said.

"No, it isn't. When you love a man, Mary, making love is how you show your feelings. It's a wonderful thing. It gives both partners great pleasure."

"I'll never do that," Mary stated emphatically, her legs still, their swinging stopped.

"You might change your mind, pumpkin. Everyone does sooner or later."

"Will *you*?" Mary demanded.

"Well, um, sure, when I meet a man I love and, uh, get married. Like your mother did."

Mary needed some time to think that over, Emily could see. These children were so innocent compared to the ones she'd known, the ones bombarded with sexy ads, TV, music videos, glossy magazines, computers, the vast barrage of information modern kids had to absorb. These children were simple, loving, unhassled.

Little Burke came crying to her just before supper, his pants torn, his knee bloody. She had to kiss it, clean it up and put his little trousers into the mending basket. He sat in her lap while she dabbed at his knee with her good hand, his eyes red, his face dirty, hiccuping in the aftermath of his sobs. She bent her head and kissed his mussed hair and sang him a song, "The itsy bitsy spider ran up the waterspout..."

Jesse was harder to reach, a tough little boy. He adored his uncle Will and pretended to disdain all women. But just after Will had brought Emily back from Denver City, Jesse'd had a twenty-four-hour bug of some sort. Emily had sat up all night with him, held his head when he threw up and cooled his forehead with a rag.

"It's nice you're here," Jesse had said that night, his pallid face lit by the kerosene lamp, "to keep me company."

"My pleasure," Emily had replied.

If the children were uncomplicated, not so their uncle. From the minute he would arrive home the household grew quieter. Oh, the children were comfortable enough around him, but the atmosphere just became more reserved, more careful. Emily remembered it had been much like that in her own family when she'd been a child. Still, Will's presence kept her

on edge, questioning, wondering, recalling, against
her best instincts, his nearness, the scent of him, the
way he strode out toward the barn, his long legs and
lean hips and those very broad shoulders. Sometimes
he was somber, and Emily never quite knew how to
approach him. With her he always seemed angry or
irritated. She hated him at times for that. She de-
spised him and yet there was always that craving, that
involuntary tingle along her flesh whenever he came
within ten paces of her.

As the days of May passed and the evenings length-
ened, Emily sat and either mended or read the newspaper and tried her best to accept her predicament.
She told herself that maybe she was stuck in this past
for a reason. *Accept it,* she'd think. *Wait and see.* But
then her musings would flip-flop and she'd lay down
the newspaper and lean toward Will, ready to tell him
exactly why she didn't belong in his world and that
somehow, someday, she was going to find her way
back home.

Always the moment of desperation passed, however. She couldn't tell him. Even if he didn't have her
locked up, even if he did believe her, what could Will
do about it?

Conversation with Will was like trying to drag
words out with pliers. It took a full week to get him to
tell her about his life before Rifle.

"Why does Clay live in Chicago?" she asked, setting aside Jesse's torn trousers.

Will looked up from his book and put aside his
pipe. "He stayed there when we first set out from New
York State."

"New York? I didn't know you were from New York."

"Folks died," Will said, "back in '78, and the three of us set out for the West."

"And you and Jesse came all the way to Colorado?"

"That's right." He began to bring his book back up to reading level.

"No," Emily said, "wait. Tell me about it."

"About what?" He raised a dark brow.

"About coming to the West. I mean, were you with a wagon train?"

"Yes."

"Did you get attacked by Indians?"

"Once."

"Well?"

"Well what?"

"Tell me about it," Emily said.

"Nothing much to tell. We drove them off."

"You killed Indians?"

"Of course, Emily, they were trying to kill us."

"Have you ever killed anyone else, Will?"

He shrugged, growing impatient. "Early on in Rifle there was a range war."

"And you were in it?"

"We were just settling our land. Jesse and I had to protect what was ours." He regarded her pensively. "Why do you ask?"

"Oh," Emily said, "no reason, I guess."

"Um," he mumbled, and went back to his reading.

It took forever, but eventually Emily found out a lot about Will Dutcher, his background, his present finances. And always he'd say, annoyed, "I can't see why you're so dang interested," but she'd press him, and he'd reply after a time, if only to get her off his back.

Will's finances troubled her. She knew from the newspapers that banks clear across the country were pulling in loans. She knew the local banker, Bob Bergener, was doing the same thing in Rifle, and that Will and some of his fellow ranchers were beginning to balk at the idea of increasing their payments to him. And there *was* going to be a panic nationwide. Soon. Just as soon as the U.S. went off the silver standard and lenders pulled in gold reserves. There'd be banks collapsing, people losing everything. But how would Rifle fare? And Will? Could he, too, lose everything because of a fearful banker? She could tell Will, caution him, but he'd never listen. And besides, how would she explain her foreknowledge?

What would happen to her, Emily began to wonder, if Will *did* lose everything? What would happen to her, the children, Will himself? Could they all end up on the streets? God forbid, Emily thought. She'd been *that* route already and didn't care to go it again.

"Will," Emily said one evening, "is Bergener still asking you for more money?"

He shot her a dark look. "I wish, Emily," he said, his voice hard, "you'd see to the household business and leave mine alone."

"I was only—" she began, then said no more. What good could she do by hounding him?

It happened that next evening. When Emily thought back on the incident later, she figured it was bound to occur eventually. They were turning down the lamps, getting ready to retire. Will had put Shep out as he did every night, to guard the house. He'd given him a bone to gnaw on and a pat and closed the kitchen door.

Emily went on ahead, up the dimly lit staircase, a load of mending in her arms. Behind her, Will was carrying a last lamp as he always did.

Emily tripped, stumbling across the top step, her armful scattering in the hallway. "Oh, damn... darn it," she said.

"Are you all right?" Will leaned over her and set the lamp on the landing then took her hands in his, helping her up.

"I'm fine. My ankle's a little twisted." She smiled at her clumsiness, detached her hands from his and began to pick up the scattered clothes. "First my hand," she said, "now my foot. Dumb."

"Here, let me," he said, leaning over also, the lamplight flickering on the walls and on the straight planes of his face.

"I feel so dumb," she was grumbling, accepting the clothes he was repiling in her arms.

"Anyone could have..." Will started to say but fell silent.

Emily looked up. She was leaning against the wall, her arms clutching the bundle, when her eyes met his, and she froze inside. They were close, too close in the narrow space. The lamplight played across his face, lighting his eyes. And she knew. In that instant she knew by the hot shock jolting through her that Will's indifference was a lie. It was in those deep blue eyes, in the muscle working in his jaw. It was in his suddenly rigid stance and in the hard lines of his mouth. Will was not oblivious to her.

The moment stretched out exquisitely. Will stood there unmoving, his eyes boring into hers. Emily couldn't move, either. Her limbs were on fire even while goose bumps rose on her flesh. Her belly coiled, hot and cold. She knew in a dark corner of her mind that she could drop that bundle of clothing and lean toward him and they'd both be lost. Her pulse raced—she could have Will if she wanted. She could . . .

Suddenly Emily let out a ragged breath and tore her gaze from his. *No,* her mind screamed, *no.* "I . . ." she began, clutching the bundle, "I better, ah, put these things away."

For a heartbeat of time longer Will stood in her path, the light dancing wildly around them. Then finally he stepped back, slowly, his eyes still fixed on her. "You do that," he said, his voice deep, and she had to brush past him, her heart still thudding madly in her breast. Somehow she was at her bedroom door, aware he hadn't moved, and then she was inside, closing the door, shutting him out. She took off her clothes, pulled on her long nightdress, her hands shaking, her breasts rising and falling as if she'd run a race. She sank deep beneath the covers and squeezed her eyes shut. Something had happened in that dimly lit hallway tonight. Something that both melted her flesh and terrified her. A moth drawn to a flame, she thought, and wished to God it had never happened.

After the incident Emily became as cool and distant to Will as he was to her. Sometimes she thought they'd both break and shatter like glass. At other times she clung onto the moment in the hallway, her eyes searching for Will's, her body aching, craving, and on fire for the forbidden. Her logical mind told her no, not in 1893. Women were different, they denied their physical hungers. She had to remember that, to hold it sacred. But her body, Emily was discovering, had a mind of its own. Her body yearned and cried out for release.

Emily made herself busy. Very busy. After much nagging, Antonio taught her to drive the buckboard. She never mastered harnessing the team, but she drove the rig back and forth to town, giving herself a measure of freedom and a way to escape her thoughts.

Jesse came home from school one day with a split lip. He refused to tell Emily or Will what had happened, saying only, "I got into a fight."

"You never got into a fight before," Will pointed out, frowning at his nephew.

"I did this time" was all Jesse would reply.

"Well, then, young man, I think you better go up to your room and think about it," Will said, unbending.

After some argument, Emily took dinner up to Jesse, climbing the narrow attic stairs. Her heart went out to the staunch little fellow, despite Will's objections.

"Tell me, Jesse, what happened at school? Whatever it is, it isn't so bad you can't tell me. It'll be our secret," she said, sitting on the edge of the bed.

"Nothing. I had a fight." He sat with his knees up to his chin, hugging them, and he looked straight ahead at the wall.

She sighed. "Okay, tell me when you feel like it. Eat your dinner now."

"I ain't hungry."

"I'm *not* hungry," she corrected.

The next day Emily decided to pick the children up from school and talk to Mrs. Lindley, their teacher. She might be able to find out what Jesse had been fighting about, but if not, at least she'd introduce herself and tell the woman how pleased she was with Mary's reading ability.

At lunch she found Will in the barn and told him about her plans.

"You're spoiling the children," Will said, going about his business. "Boys get in fights."

"But Jesse doesn't. It could be important. Maybe he's all bottled up inside, Will, after all, he just lost his parents and..."

"Go to the school if you want, Emily, but I wouldn't embarrass him if I were you."

"I don't plan to embarrass the boy," Emily said before stalking out to the buckboard.

The schoolhouse was located at the upper end of town, a square brick building that housed all the grades through high school. Carefully tying the reins around the brake handle, Emily climbed down and patted the horses. The children were all scrambling out of the door, free for the day, and the May sunshine dazzled Emily's eyes.

The three kids were surprised to see her. "I just wanted to meet your teacher," she explained. "So I thought I'd stop by. Why don't you all wait in the buckboard? There's a basket of muffins on the seat."

She went inside and found Mrs. Lindley at her desk in one of the classrooms, correcting papers. She was an attractive lady in her early thirties, a widow, Emily knew, with pretty features and thick, curling flaxen hair piled on top of her head.

"Mrs. Lindley," Emily said, approaching, "I'm Emily Jacoby, Will Dutcher's housekeeper. I thought it might be nice if we met."

"Miss Jacoby," the teacher said, giving her a quick, penetrating once-over, "how very thoughtful of you. Please sit down."

Emily sat in one of the small chairs, adjusting her skirt, the new maroon one from Denver that was very flattering to her. "I wanted to tell you how well Mary reads. She's into adult books and understands so much she keeps me surprised."

Mrs. Lindley folded her hands deliberately on the desk. "Did you suppose everyone out here was an illiterate dullard?"

Emily was taken aback. "Why, no, not at all. It's just that...I certainly didn't mean...what I meant was you've done a marvelous job with Mary."

"Thank you," Mrs. Lindley said frostily.

"I'm sorry, I didn't mean to imply...well, the boys are doing very well, too, but Mary seems so...well, special," Emily fumbled.

"She's a clever child."

"Yes, well." Emily cleared her throat, thoroughly intimidated. "What I came about, actually, was Jesse."

"Go on."

"He was in a fight yesterday. Uh, were you aware...?"

"I am most assuredly aware of what occurs in my school. Yes, he had an altercation with the Schaefer boy. They both sat in the corner for an hour, and that was the end of it."

"I see. Do you...ah...do you know what it was about? I'm very concerned because Jesse's never been in a fight before," Emily said.

Mrs. Lindley gestured with a hand. "Boys will be boys, Miss Jacoby. I don't know what it was about, nor do I care. I abhor fighting."

"Yes, of course, so do I. And you were right to punish him. I just wondered why he'd do such a thing out of the blue like that."

"I'm sure I don't know."

"I see." Emily was getting angry herself. Why was this woman so rude? They'd never even met before and here Emily was being patronized by a country schoolmarm from the nineteenth century! "Well," she said, putting on her corporate voice, "if you could help me understand what's going on with Jesse, I'd appreciate it. I care very much about those three children, Mrs. Lindley."

"And their uncle?"

Emily's mind raced. Did she mean to ask how Will felt about his wards or how *she* felt about Will? The nerve of the woman! "He cares very much, too. Naturally," she replied, standing. "Well, thank you for your time. It's been a pleasure meeting you."

"Likewise, Miss Jacoby."

They were both bad liars, Emily decided, walking out to the buckboard. But why should Mrs. Lindley feel such enmity for her? They were utter strangers.

Absently, Emily answered the children's questions while Jesse was allowed to drive the wagon home.

"What did Mrs. Lindley say?" Mary asked anxiously.

GET A FREE TEDDY BEAR . . .

You'll love this plush, cuddly Teddy Bear, an adorable accessory for your dressing table, bookcase or desk. Measuring 5½″ tall, he's soft and brown and has a bright red ribbon around his neck—he's completely captivating! And he's yours *absolutely free*, when you accept this no-risk offer!

AND FOUR FREE BOOKS!

Here's a chance to get **four free Harlequin Superromance® novels** from the Harlequin Reader Service®—so you can see for yourself that we're like **no ordinary book club!**

We'll send you four free books...but you never have to buy anything or remain a member any longer than you choose. You could even accept the free books and cancel immediately. In that case, you'll owe nothing and be under **no obligation!**

Find out for yourself why thousands of readers enjoy receiving books by mail from the Harlequin Reader Service. They like the **convenience of home delivery**...they like getting the best new novels before they're available in bookstores...and they love our **discount prices!**

Try us and see! Return this card promptly. We'll send your free books and a free Teddy Bear, under the terms explained on the back. We hope you'll want to remain with the reader service—but the choice is always yours!

134 CIH AJAY (U-H-SR-05/93)

NAME

ADDRESS   APT

CITY   STATE   ZIP

Offer not valid to current Harlequin Superromance® subscribers. All orders subject to approval.
© 1993 HARLEQUIN ENTERPRISES LIMITED   Printed in the U.S.A.

► CLAIM YOUR FREE BOOKS AND FREE GIFT! RETURN THIS CARD TODAY! ►

NO OBLIGATION TO BUY!

THE HARLEQUIN READER SERVICE: HERE'S HOW IT WORKS

Accepting free books puts you under no obligation to buy anything. You may keep the books and gift and return the shipping statement marked "cancel." If you do not cancel, about a month later we will send you 4 additional novels, and bill you just $2.71 each plus 25¢ delivery and applicable sales tax, if any*. That's the complete price—and compared to cover prices of $3.39 each—quite a bargain! You may cancel at any time, but if you choose to continue, every month we'll send you 4 more books, which you may either purchase at the discount price...or return at our expense and cancel your subscription.

* Terms and prices subject to change without notice.
  Sales tax applicable in N.Y.

"Um...oh, she said you were a very clever little girl."

"And me?" Burke piped up.

"Oh, you too, button." But it wasn't until they stopped along the riverbank to have the muffins and Emily got Mary aside—swearing never to reveal their talk—that Emily finally found out why Jesse had been in the fight.

"It was...over you, Miss Emily," Mary confessed.

"Me?"

The little girl nodded. "Benny Schaefer said...he said you were, well, not a proper lady."

Emily sighed, letting out a breath. "I see. And how did Benny Schaefer know that?"

"His mama told him. But," Mary said, taking her hand, "I think Mrs. Schaefer is jealous 'cause she's an old hag."

"Jealous?" Emily forced a smile.

"You know, you're so pretty."

Emily knew different, though. She realized once again how many times she'd felt the animosity of the women in Rifle. It was a small place, isolated and close-knit. She'd felt the wariness from Mrs. Tate at the Mercantile store, and from several other ladies on the street who regarded her coldly but smiled at Will. She didn't belong, and they knew it. They talked about it, too, she'd bet, gossiped at their literary club and church meetings. Emily Jacoby from Philadelphia, they'd say, with her uppity ways. Turning up stark naked in a train wreck, not even a petticoat on. A disgrace. Doesn't do womanly things, butts into men's talk. Well, if Will Dutcher's too dumb to see what she's trying to do... She was different, she was a threat to the rigidly conservative ranching community. And it didn't help that she lived with Will Dutcher, under his roof, with no chaperone but three innocent kids and old Antonio. Respectable women didn't do that—unless, naturally, they were ugly and old, widowed or dried-up man-haters.

Did Will realize how they felt?

"You swear you won't tell Jesse I told?" Mary was asking.

"I promise, honey," Emily said, then called the boys in from their romping. They finished their muffins, washed their hands in the river, talked together about school and summer vacation. But all the while Emily kept thinking, *I don't belong,* and she wanted to cry.

While Jesse drove, Emily bowed her head and felt the bouncing of the buckboard jarring her very bones. Something inside her clenched, like a fist, so hard it hurt. Oh, what had she done in coming to this time, this place? Why must innocent children suffer because of it?

I don't belong...

They followed the road that paralleled the river and the railroad tracks. Birds swooped madly overhead, feasting on the mayflies that were thick over the river. The water was turgid, muddy from runoff, and on the other side, the mountains faded into the distance. It was beautiful country, vast and fertile. Why had Emily come to this challenging land?

"See, I can drive them fine," Jesse was saying. "Will you tell Uncle Will how I did?"

"Yes, I will. You're doing a good job," she said, her mind elsewhere.

The rusted jumble of cars came up on their right, alongside the tracks. "Stop," Emily said suddenly. *"Stop."*

"Why?"

"That's the wreck, isn't it?" she breathed, staring. "The one I was in."

"I guess it is, Miss Emily."

She looked, studying the pile of cars. They hadn't cleared it away yet, perhaps because they needed heavy equipment to move it, but there sat the ornate cars, crushed, broken, faded and rusted, like the skeletons of huge, ancient creatures.

"Oh, God," she whispered, and then she found herself climbing down from the buckboard and walking toward the cars, drawn by an irresistible force.

"Miss Emily!" called Burke. "What are you doing?"

"Shh," Mary said loudly. "Let her alone."

She stood by the tracks and tried to remember that day: the snow, the mountains, the black river. It was all so different now, warm and sunny, cheerful.... She walked along the tracks, treading carefully on the ties, following some inner quest she wasn't even sure of. *Right here,* she thought, *it happened right here. I was in 1993 and then I was in 1893. If I could just...*

Was this the place, the hole in time, the crossover point? Did such a thing exist? Perhaps, like Dorothy in *The Wizard of Oz,* if she clicked her heels together and repeated, "There's no place like home," she'd be miraculously transported back. She walked on under the hot Colorado sun and closed her eyes and wished with all her heart . . .

Emily walked. And she walked. Later she would think back on it and never quite know at what point the edges of her perception began to dim and fade. The tracks ahead of her wavered in the heat and seemed to come together at a point in front of her. She felt a terrible hope grip her. *This is it,* she thought. *This is the place! I can go home!* She felt nauseous and dizzy, the way she'd felt after the accident. Her head hurt, as if it were being squeezed in a vise, and ahead of her the shiny steel rails swayed and drew her relentlessly on. She was aware suddenly of a smell, cloying, sickening, almost sweet. A roaring filled her head—a noise at the same time familiar and alien. It came to her in that haze. She was smelling diesel exhaust and hearing vehicles on the highway that would exist in the future, in *her* world.

My God, it was so close. She only had to keep going, through the vertigo and the terror, through the pain in her head. She could be free of the past. She could leave Will Dutcher and his ranch, leave Rifle and the children, if she wanted to badly enough. *She could . . .*

"Emily?"

Emily's head snapped around and the vision faded. It was Mary, tugging at her long skirt. "Miss Emily? Are you all right? Is something the matter, Miss Emily?" Mary was saying, her face pinched with anxiety.

The magic was lost, vanished into thin air at the girl's plaintive questions. Emily drew a deep breath and let it out slowly, feeling her heart settle down to a slower rhythm.

"Miss Emily?"

"Yes, Mary, it's all right," Emily said. "I'm fine."
Sadness swept her as she took Mary's small hand in
hers. Sadness and a melancholy kind of relief. She
should have gone, but she'd hesitated. Oh, God, she
should have gone!

"You were standing there so long," Mary said. "I
got worried."

Emily patted her hand. "Nothing to worry about,
honey. Come on, let's get back to the wagon. Let's go
home."

Why had she hesitated?

CHAPTER NINE

"THE GRAND VALLEY Cattleman's Association will come to order," said Ollie McCrudden, "on this fourteenth day of May, eighteen hundred and ninety-three." And he banged down the gavel.

The low hum of men's voices stopped. There was a rustle of heads turning to the front and a stomping out of cigar butts under boot heels.

"All right, men, any old business to take care of?" Ollie McCrudden asked.

Will balanced his hat on his crossed knee and listened. Thad Wooderson was still having fits about Dashel George damming up the creek—old stuff. There were the dates to set for Watermelon Days, the Fourth of July picnic, the rodeo and the county fair in September. There was a report by Tell Lister about the progeny of his new Hereford bull. Everyone listened, fiddling with mustaches, hatbands, bandannas or suspenders, but the old business wasn't important to-night.

No, Will knew, tonight there was a big turnout. Everyone for miles around had shown up. They were all here for one reason, and it wasn't to hear Wooderson gripe about water rights.

"New business, then," McCrudden boomed out. "I got a suggestion myself. Anyone want to second it?"

A rough voice called out from the throng, "Better let us in on what it is, McCrudden," and there was a scattering of laughter.

"You know what it is, Martinson," McCrudden said. He grabbed a copy of the *Rocky Mountain News* from the table in front of him and held it up for everyone to see.

Run On Gold, the paper's headlines read. Banks Pulling In Reserves.

Will shifted on the hard chair. He'd read the paper himself already, but he didn't like seeing it up there like that. It was making him edgy.

"Bob Bergener," McCrudden was saying, "is doing just what this paper says is happening all over. Now, what I'd like to know is, how are we gonna stop him?"

"We can't stop him, Ollie," came a voice from the back. "He owns the bank, he owns the money. He only lent it to us. If he wants it back, I guess he's within his rights to ask for it back."

"No, that's not right," Kelly Phelps said. "We signed papers that said when we pay and how much. Now, Bob's goin' about changing the terms. I say he ain't within his rights!"

An outburst erupted, men's voices, worried, angry. McCrudden banged down the gavel. "Shut yer traps!" he roared.

Will sat there, watching his friends and neighbors, knowing how they felt. Their livelihoods, the land they'd carved out of a brutal new territory, the cattle they'd cared for through blizzard and drought, the families they'd raised...all threatened. *It isn't fair,* he thought. *We feed the whole damn country, the fat*

*politicians in Washington, too, and they're letting us
bear the brunt of this mess they got us into.*

"We gotta stand together," someone was saying.
"We all just pay what we're supposed to, no more. Let
Bergener stew."

"He can lose the bank," someone else yelled out.
"Just plain shut the doors, lock it up, and our money's in there. Sure, we borrowed some from him, but
he's got every cent of real money I got on deposit.
Ain't you all in the same boat?"

More grumbles, nods of agreement, a flurry of
whispered comments.

Will listened, reserving judgment. He wasn't a man
to go shooting his mouth off. If he came up with
something, it would be well thought-out. Tonight, he
was just listening.

He already knew, as did every man in the room, that
a lot of problems with the U.S. Treasury had begun a
few years ago when Congress had passed the Sherman Silver Purchase Act. Oh, sure, it had been healthy
enough at first for the West—especially for the silver
miners in the Rockies—because the government
promised to purchase fifty percent more silver from
those miners to stimulate growth in the West. But now
the piper had to be paid, because the gold reserve, due
to the purchase of all that silver, had fallen to a
frighteningly low level. Everyone was scared. Reports
of runs on banks were beginning to crop up, warnings
of hard times, bank failures and evictions were on everyone's lips. And Bob Bergener was just as scared as
anyone else.

The gavel banged again. "So, out of all you razor-sharp financiers," Ollie McCrudden was saying sarcastically, "anyone got a real suggestion?"

"Sell your cattle," Phelps said. "Sell heavy. Get hard cash and hold on to it."

"If everyone does that, Phelps, the price of beef will go so low you'll end up shooting 'em," Martinson growled.

"And if the bank closes, that won't save what's in it, anyway," someone put in.

"So, we all go and get our money out. Tomorrow, first thing," Tell Lister shouted.

Will couldn't help it then. "That's called a run on the bank, Tell," he drawled. "Then Bergener loses his shirt, calls in our loans and the bank fails. I can't see the sense in that."

"What's the matter, Dutcher," someone called out. "You gettin' advice from that there new housekeeper of yours?"

Some chuckles were to be heard, some muttering.

"Who said that?" Will asked, starting to get a little hot under the collar. "You men know I'm not likely to take advice from a woman. Of all the dang stupid things to say."

"Heard she's pretty smart," Abner Fisher called out. "Real education. Not bad lookin', neither."

"What in God's name does my housekeeper have to do with this?" Will asked, his voice hard, his brows drawn as he scanned the crowd, meeting every set of eyes in the room, challenging them. Most looked away first.

"Not a damn thing," Ollie McCrudden said then. "Let's discuss something worthwhile. We got more important things to decide than what kind of house-keeper Dutcher's got, you damn fools.''

The low rumble of voices started again until Mc-Crudden stopped it with the gavel. It went on like that for another half hour, angry men, frightened men, searching for a way out. By the time seven o'clock rolled around, every man there was ready to spit nails, and no solutions were forthcoming.

''Okay, men,'' McCrudden finally said, ''we're not going to linger on this anymore. It's time to push the chairs back for the dance. The ladies, no doubt, are waitin' on us, and the food's on the fire. We'll take this up again next month. Meetin's ended.'' *Bang* went the gavel.

''Seconded!'' yelled someone, and there was a ten-sion-relieving ruffle of laughter as the men began readying the room for the annual Cattleman's Association dance and barbecue.

THE MEN SEEMED QUIET, Emily thought, as she entered the schoolhouse with the three children. But she knew why. She'd seen the headlines in the *Rocky Mountain News* and knew they must have been discussing it. Oh, how she'd like to stand up in front of that cattleman's meeting and tell them what to do! As if they'd listen to her!

She carried her basket of rolls, a pie and a dried fruit compote to the long tables being set up against the wall in one room. Outside, the women had already started the barbecues, where slabs of beef, ribs, steaks and chops sizzled, filling the air with a mouth-watering aroma.

''Can I have some pie?'' Burke inquired.

"No, not yet, after dinner, kiddo. You know that," Emily said, searching the room for Will.

"There's Uncle Will," Mary said, pointing.

It was ridiculous, Emily thought, but she'd been nervous about this social outing. It was the first one she'd attended, and she was afraid she'd be uncomfortable, knowing how the women of Rifle felt about her. She was glad to have the children to bolster her confidence, glad to have Burke hanging on one hand and Mary on the other. Everyone else seemed to know one another, to be related, old friends, business partners or something.

She wished Will could have come in with her, but he'd simply told her to meet him there, as he had to attend the Cattleman's Association meeting first. And she was too embarrassed to say, "Will, I'm nervous about meeting all those people. Do you think you could go in with me?"

There he was, across the room, his dark head bent, talking to someone.

"Come on, Miss Emily, let's go see Uncle Will. Come on," Mary was saying.

The crowd thinned for an instant, and Emily saw who he was talking to—Mrs. Lindley, looking radiant, her pale blond hair a riot of curls and velvet bows. A flush stained Emily's cheeks. "No, hon, he's busy. Uh, let's put our food out, all right?"

Jesse came out of the crowd, tugging on Will's hand a few minutes later. "See," Jesse said. "Miss Emily made pie and this fruit thing."

"Hello, Will," she said stiffly.

"Emily." He nodded.

"There sure are lots of people here," she said lamely.

"Uh-huh, sure are." He smoothed his mustache. "Have any trouble with the harness?"

"No, uh, Antonio helped."

"Been out to get a plate at the barbecue yet?" Will asked.

"No, not yet."

"The young ones all here? Let's go, then, before the line reaches from here to Glenwood."

A lot of people said hello to Will, chucked Mary under the chin, told Jesse and Burke how much they'd grown or how much they looked like their papa. Will, correctly, introduced Emily, "And this is my house-keeper, Miss Emily Jacoby from Philadelphia." The men gave her a close once-over and smiled, tipping their hats, but the women offered forced pleasantries or nodded with distaste.

Emily decided she had no use for these women, and she wasn't going to let them bother her. After all, they were nobodies, uneducated, a hundred years out-of-date. So what if they had families and friends, hus-bands, children, a community to which they be-longed? So what? It wasn't *her* world.

Emily held her chin up and her back straight. She smiled graciously at everyone, male or female, and complimented their homemade dishes. She didn't let down for a moment.

After the food was gone, the band from Glenwood Springs struck up a tune. It took a song of two, but soon couples started dancing, fathers with daughters, sons with mothers, sweethearts, cousins, sisters. There was no style to their dancing, no steps, but they were all having fun, laughing and twirling. Mrs. Fisher danced with Doc Tichenor, whose face glowed red above his white goatee. The Tates waltzed sedately, Ollie McCrudden danced with his wife, Reba.

And Will...he spoke to people, his foot tapped, he took another cookie from the dessert table. He asked no one to dance, didn't even look around to see who was available.

"Aren't you going to dance, Uncle Will?" Mary asked ingenuously, as if she could read Emily's mind and had asked the question for her.

"Aw, Mary, I don't know how to dance so well," he said. "No one ever taught me."

"*I'll* teach you. Come dance, please, Uncle Will," she cried, excited.

"Oh, Mary, I don't know..."

But he swung her up off the floor and whirled her around to the tune of "Dixie." Mary was ecstatic, giggling, her blond braids flying out as they turned. Emily couldn't help noticing how well he moved, narrow hipped, broad shouldered, his legs long and slightly bowed, his dark jacket stretched across his back as he held Mary. And he was smiling, a rare occurrence, his teeth white beneath his mustache, a dimple, yes, a *dimple* in one cheek. Emily had never noticed that before, and she marveled, a dimple.

"Miss Emily, look, they're dancing. Isn't that funny!" Burke said, his face smudged.

"Yes, hon, it's funny, all right."

She turned and met a pair of eyes that were fixed on her—Mrs. Lindley. Emily lifted her chin, made eye contact and smiled right at the woman.

Will and Mary came back when the song ended. He was perspiring, and Mary was red cheeked. "Oh, did you see us? That was fun, Uncle Will!" she said. "Why don't you dance with Miss Emily? You won't have to hold *her* up, will you?"

"Yes, Uncle Will, dance," Burke said, clapping his hands gleefully.

Emily felt the mood change; the very air around them froze. She glanced at Will quickly and saw the smile disappear from his face and a flush rise up his neck.

"Oh, button," Emily said swiftly, "I think your Uncle Will's tired, and I don't really, well, I don't know how to do this dance."

"That's what Uncle Will said," Jesse pointed out, "but he *does* know how. It's easy."

"Oh, I don't think..."

"Oh, please, come on," Mary said. "You have to dance. Everybody's dancing, Miss Emily."

"Well, Mary," Will began, "I don't..."

"Come on, come on," the three children chanted, jumping up and down like little jack-in-the-boxes. "Dance, dance!"

The band struck up "My Darlin' Clementine," and Emily and Will stood there looking at each other, hearing the children's piping voices. Emily held her breath, paralyzed, helpless to do or say anything. The lamenting, familiar notes pulsed in her head, pounded in her heart. "Oh, my darlin', oh, my darlin', oh, my darlin' Clementine. You are lost and gone for-ever..."

Slowly, reluctantly, his arms came away from his sides. He pinned her with his dark blue gaze, as if to say, "I'll do this only if I have to," and waited.

She had to—there was no avoiding it, no turning away. She went to him, stood facing him. His right hand touched hers, and his left hand rested lightly on her waist. She stared straight ahead over his shoulder and moved woodenly with him, at arm's length.

Her breath came short and shallow, as if she couldn't bear to draw in his scent. Her heart beat madly in her breast. *Stop!* she cried inwardly. *It's only a dance.*

Not a word was spoken between them, nor a smile exchanged. Once when she stole a glance at Will's face, she saw that it was hard as oak, congealed into an expressionless mask. The song seemed to go on and on endlessly. Her feet shuffled clumsily, feeling as if Will could hardly endure holding her.

And yet, where his big, work-hardened hands touched her, there was a kind of heat, a flame licking at her skin even through her shirtwaist and petticoats, a warmth that made her knees watery and her limbs weak and shaky.

The dance would never end. They moved around the floor, among the laughing, careening couples, set apart—an island of silent awkwardness in the midst of gaiety and clamor. Emily was aware of people looking at them, the men with interest, the women with rancor. And Mrs. Lindley—her blue eyes were fixed on them with fierce resentment. *I don't want him,* Emily thought, *you can have him. I don't belong here.*

The music ended at last, and an echoing silence fell
between Will and Emily. She tried to smile. "Thank
you," she murmured, looking down.

"My pleasure," he said quietly, lying.

After that, the evening was torture to Emily. Even
when Abner Fisher, one of the wild Fisher clan, asked
her to dance, she was stiff and awkward, so tense she
felt like screaming. She sensed the young man's disappointment and tried to put a good face on it.

"Where are you from again, Miss Emily?" he asked
as they swept past the band, the knot of glaring, hard-
faced ladies, the laughing men dipping into the punch
bowl, the children playing hide-and-seek in the crowd.

"Back East, Philadelphia," she replied.

"Is that there a big city?"

"Pretty big, yet, but not like New York or L.A."

"L.A.?" he asked, puzzled.

"Uh, Los Angeles, in California." *Oh God,* she
thought, *L.A. was a small tourist center in 1893. Few
people had ever heard of it!*

"Oh," he said. "Los Angeles. Funny name."

"You'll be hearing about it. It's going to grow a
lot," Emily fumbled.

Abner, a strong ranch lad with rolled up sleeves,
pulled her closer. She felt claustrophobic and tense.
She felt sorry for Abner, and only too aware of Mrs.
Lindley and her cohorts watching her with hostility.
*There she is, the forward woman, leading another man
astray,* they were saying.

And Will. Once in a while she saw him leaning
against the wall in the corner, smoothing his mustache, or speaking to someone, never once looking in
her direction.

Abner left her after one dance, and she was relieved. She simply couldn't deal with him. It took all her energy to paste a pleasant expression on her face and pretend nothing was wrong.

But everything *was* wrong. Herself, Will, the women accosting her with their glares. She debated asking Will if they could leave, but that would be a victory for the respectable biddies of Rifle, and Emily was not quite ready to concede them the field. She'd see it through no matter what it cost her.

"Aren't you going to dance some more?" Mary asked, towing Burke by the hand.

"Oh, no, I don't think so, sweetie, my feet hurt. Guess I'm just too old."

"You're not old," Mary said. "Why aren't you talking to Uncle Will?"

"Oh, for goodness' sakes, Mary, stop asking questions! Now, look, your braids are coming out. Let me redo them for you," Emily said, flustered.

"I'm having *fun*," Burke told her, a hard candy jammed in one cheek, another clutched in his dirty first.

"That's good, button. Where's Jesse?"

"Oh, he's outside playing with the boys. They're too wild," Mary said disdainfully.

By the time the dance was breaking up, Emily felt drained. She trembled with fatigue and tension and gladly went to fetch her plates, bowls and basket, as well as the children's jackets for the ride home.

Will's first words to her since their one awful dance were purely practical: "I'll see to the team."

"All right," she said, "I'll get the children together."

Relief swept her. They'd be out of here soon, and she could settle down, relax and forget the whole ordeal. *Never again,* she vowed, *never again will I ever put myself at this town's mercy.*

Basket over her arm and children in tow, Emily made her way through the thinning crowd toward the door. People were hugging and kissing, saying their farewells and talking about the next time they'd meet. The kerosene lamps were being extinguished, one by one, the tables cleared, the band was packing up.

Thank heavens was all Emily could think. *It's over.*

Outside, she drew in a breath of the chilly night air. A breeze cooled her face, and the stars shone in the immense black sky above. She could go home now, where it was safe and the children, at least, loved her and needed her. Thank heavens.

"Excuse me, Miss Jacoby," came a voice at her elbow, "but could you step inside for a moment? You've forgotten something."

It was Mrs. Lindley. Emily sighed. "Go on, kids. Uncle Will's over there with the buckboard. I'll be there in a minute, okay? Here, Mary, take the basket."

She went inside the nearly empty, dim, echoing hall with the schoolteacher, not suspecting a thing. Not too bright, she would think later. "What did I leave?" she asked pleasantly. "I'm so forgetful sometimes."

She should have known. The women were there, waiting for her, the social register of Rifle, Colorado, the town matriarchs—Mrs. Lindley, Mrs. Tate, Mrs. Fisher and a few others whose names she didn't know but whose faces were familiar.

"Oh," she said, stopping short. "Is there...?"

"Miss Jacoby," said Mrs. Lindley, "we wanted a word with you."

"Well, I really do have to go. Will and the children are..."

"Will? You mean *Mr. Dutcher?*" Mrs. Tate asked.

She knew then, knew with a cold certainty that sent a shiver down her spine. "Excuse me, please," she said, and turned to leave.

Mrs. Fisher put a hand out and held her arm with a steely grasp. "Just a minute, missy."

"We all feel a sense of responsibility," Mrs. Lindley said. "This is a small town, a very close community. We have to take care of one another here."

"I don't quite understand what I have to do with that," Emily said stiffly, looking coldly down at the hand still on her arm.

"We have to see to our morals here. We have to be very careful," Mrs. Tate said self-righteously.

"Let go of my arm," Emily said abruptly to Mrs. Fisher, "this instant."

Mrs. Fisher let go.

Emily faced them, her back ramrod straight. "I've done nothing wrong, and I won't apologize. How dare you insinuate—"

"We have our standards," interrupted Mrs. Lindley. "Plain and simple, Miss Jacoby. We don't like servants at our social functions. They have their own, you see."

Emily drew in a shocked breath. Fury flooded her with heat, and she put on her corporate voice. "I am no more a servant than you are. I take care of Will Dutcher's house and his children. Don't you dare touch me again or presume to speak to me like that, do you understand, *ladies?*'' She glared at them, one after the other, with a look she'd used effectively on the Mafia accountant who'd come to her bank with a money-laundering scheme. Then she turned, her skirt swirling, her head high, and strode swiftly out into the night.

CHAPTER TEN

EMILY KEPT IT IN the whole ride back to the ranch. She swallowed and bit her lip and felt her blood boil but said not one single word to Will. But she would. *You bet,* as soon as the children were tucked in, Mr. Will Dutcher was going to get an earful.

It was *his* fault. He should have known the rules. For God's sake, Emily thought as she bounced along, he should never have told her to meet him there with the children. This was his town; Will knew the rules.... Of course he did. Or...had he, could he actually have asked her there to humiliate her? *Oh, God.*

"That was the best time ever," Mary was saying from the back, "wasn't it, Miss Emily?"

"Oh, the absolute best, honey."

While Will put the team in the barn, Emily climbed the stairs to the attic with the children. One by one faces were washed, clothes hung in the closet, prayers said by the children on their knees at bedsides.

"I'm not sleepy," Burke said after his prayers.

"Shut up," came Jesse's older voice.

"I hate boys," Mary said loftily.

Emily sighed and pressed Burke down onto his bed. "It's late, kids, can we please hang it up until morning?"

Mary giggled and Jesse looked at Emily oddly. "Hang what up?"

"Never mind," Emily said, going to turn down the lamp. "Sweet dreams, you little monkeys."

"'Night, Miss Emily," they chorused.

She found Will in the parlor, lighting his pipe, one leg crossed comfortably over the other knee. So casual. So... so oblivious. Her temper churned and seethed—he had to have known the rules.

He gave her a curt nod. "Children settled?" Blue smoke lifted from his pipe and encircled his head.

"The children are in bed," Emily said stiffly, wondering just how she was going to get back at him. She put her hands on her hips and eyed him. "Tell me something," she said, still standing in the doorway, "am I what you'd call a *servant?*" *Control,* she thought, *don't lose your cool now.*

Will's eyes lifted slowly to hers. "How do you mean that?"

"Just like I said it. Am I?"

"I suppose a housekeeper might be called a servant. Of course, Antonio is more..."

"Okay," Emily said, her lower lip starting to tremble, "then what are the rules about servants attending a town dance?"

"Well, I'm not sure..."

"Oh, yes, you are!"

"What are you..."

"You had me show up at that dance tonight when all along you knew I'd be humiliated!"

"I never..."

So much for her cool. Emily stomped her foot. "You did, too! And I want to know why! What have I ever done—"

"Someone humiliated you?" Will put down his pipe and leaned forward.

"You know damned good and well they did."

"And just who is 'they'?" Now there was an edge to Will's voice, a reaction to Emily's challenge.

"The women. *Your* Mrs. Lindley, in particular, but the whole town was behind it. Why, Will? Why in hell did you make me come?"

"That's the second time you've sworn at me in the space of a minute, Emily, and if you think I'm going to sit here and—"

"Screw you," she got out, her head pounding with her fury.

Will came slowly, purposefully, to his feet. "Now, I'm just guessing that's one of your highfalutin insults," he said, taking a step in her direction.

"You got that straight, buster," Emily said, her chin thrust forward.

He stood there, a frown on his face. "You want to tell me what you're talking about, this business about insults and you being a servant?"

She clenched her fists and tried to fight down her fury. "As if you didn't know!"

"Tell me," he said harshly.

"Those...those women. Mrs. Fisher and Mrs. Tate and *Violet* Lindley. All of them! They told me I was a servant and wasn't welcome at their parties. 'Servants have their own,'" she mimicked.

"They told you that?"

"Yes. They told me that. They did it deliberately, and you should have known! You put me in an impossible situation and didn't give a damn about how I'd feel!" She was breathing hard, hot, prickling with self-righteous anger. "How dare you treat me like that?"

"Those women," Will muttered under his breath. "Look, Emily, they get carried away sometimes, I guess."

"Carried away!" she exclaimed.

"Pay no mind. They're just trying to cause trouble. Nothing better to do."

"Oh, I suppose they do this to every newcomer in town! No, it's me. They hate me! They hate me, and I never did anything to them. Those old hags!"

"Now, Emily..."

"Don't pull that 'now, Emily' on me," she said.

Will watched her for a long moment then said, "Look, I think you should turn in. You've got some crazy notion in that head of yours and a good night's rest—"

"Right," Emily bit out, "how did I know this was somehow going to be *my* fault? Right."

"Go to bed," he said, his voice now hard and commanding.

"Don't order me around, Will Dutcher!" she cried. "I'm not your servant!"

"You'll keep a decent tongue in your mouth while you live under my roof," he said warningly, his eyes dark with anger.

"I'll say whatever I want," she cried, knowing she was egging him on childishly, but not caring.

"Go to bed," he said again, his tone deep and threatening.

For a minute she stood her ground, watching him carefully. She'd go to bed, good idea, but not in retreat. No way. She picked up the lamp in the hall and started to head toward the steps. "You knew," she said, loud enough for him to hear. "Either you knew, Will, or you're so dumb it's pathetic."

Satisfied, she climbed the stairs, her knees still weak with her rage. But she felt vindicated somehow. She'd faced him and told him just what she thought of him. Maybe she was wrong; maybe Will really had never thought of her as a servant. But he damn well should have. Maybe he'd learned a lesson tonight and...

"Emily."

His voice from behind startled her, and she whirled, almost dropping the lamp.

"You think you're better than us," he stated. "You think mighty highly of Emily Jacoby."

"Maybe I do," Emily whispered.

"And maybe you're just a woman scared, running from a past that—"

"That's none of your business."

"Isn't it?" Will moved along the hallway in her direction, his steps slow and menacing.

"No," she whispered, "it's *my* business. You don't know anything about me."

"I know all I need to," he said, and kept coming, growing bigger in the lamplight. Much bigger.

Emily's heart pounded. She'd gone too far, pushed him over the line, and now there would be consequences—this was not 1993, where a woman was protected by laws....

Sudden fear gripped her with sharp talons while she stood facing him in the dimness. But there was something else inside her, too, a kind of wild anticipation that defied explanation. It was as if she were readying herself for the explosion that was certain to come. If he touched her, if he dared lay one single finger on her in anger, she'd fight back.

Will took another step toward her, his hands tightened into fists at his sides.

"Don't you dare," Emily whispered, pressing down the fear.

He still came forward, slowly, a step at a time. His face was demonic in the flickering light, one side shadowed darkly, the other swathed in amber. The muscle worked furiously in his jaw. He took another step and the distance closed.

"If you dare to..." Emily got out, but then he was there, towering over her, his dark blue eyes boring down into hers.

Emily sucked in a breath, ready, every fiber of her being taut and alert as his hands came up and gripped her arms. She twisted abruptly, trying to free herself, her eyes shooting a warning.

"Don't," she hissed. "Let me..."

And then it happened. Before she could turn away, Will had crushed her body to his and his mouth was on hers, twisting, forcing her head and body back until the wall stopped her. Her mind reeled as she got her hands up between them, but Will was too strong, his lips bruising hers, his hands going around to the small of her back and half lifting her, his body shuddering as he pressed her to the wall.

And then something shifted inside her, something wild and utterly out of control began to stream through her body, and she was shaking, trembling, as if flames ran in rivers through her veins. She felt herself begin to give away, her muscles starting to sag, her lips responding beneath the pressure of his mouth. Her mind cried *No, this can't be happening,* but her body was beginning to sing a tune of its own.

Abruptly Will ended the kiss then and stepped back, his face contorted in a kind of pain Emily had never seen. The back of her hand went to her bruised mouth and her eyes held his in wonder while her limbs trembled and her chest rose and fell as if she'd run a race.

Emily knew then. While they stood only inches apart and faced each other shakily, she knew: she wanted Will. She wanted him to press her against that wall again until they were both sagging and panting and...

"Don't you realize," he was saying, a low throaty groan, "don't you know I could never hurt you?"

"Will," she breathed, leaning toward him, "oh Will, I...I want you so much. I..." She lifted her hands to his face tentatively, her fingers barely touching his whisker-stubbled cheeks. "I want you," she breathed, and then his head was descending toward hers, and their lips were coming together, slowly, uncertain, on fire.

Emily melted in his arms, her fingers locking behind his neck, her breasts pressed to the wall of his chest. Never had she known such a consuming hunger as then, when Will's hands moved up and down her back, crushing her to him.

Later Emily would know that it was she who led them toward his room. That it was she who had first begun to tear at the buttons on his shirt and that Will had been unsure, even as his own fingers began to pull at the buttons on her blouse. But Emily kept the flames raging, her hands and mouth on his neck and exposed chest, her fingers working frantically as she pulled his shirttail from his trousers and tugged the material aside.

Will was equally frantic to expose Emily to his hands and naked body. Piece by piece, with a searing desperation, he pulled off her clothes and flung them aside until they both stood in the patch of moonlight, gloriously unclothed, their bodies pulsing with desire.

Only once did Will hesitate. His voice a deep, coarse rasp, he asked, "Are you sure, Emily?"

"I've never been more certain of anything," she replied, breathless, pulling him to her.

Together they sank to his mattress, hands swift on thighs and bellies and hips. In a far place in Emily's mind it occurred to her that time and space had no meaning to a man and woman in the throes of love. She could have been a cave woman or from some far distant future. And Will. A man was always going to be a man, with the same aching needs and hardness to his loins no matter where or when. There were no questions between them, only the wild hot yearning and desperate drive to become one.

Will kissed the pulsing throb at her throat and each breast in turn, sucking her flesh deep into his mouth hungrily, his hands gripping the softness of her hips as he poised above her. And then their eyes met for a moment, the unspoken message singing between them. *Yes.*

There was never a question, either, when he found the warm damp entrance to Emily's womanhood and he glided upward, deep inside her while Emily clutched his shoulders and thrust her hips against his.

It was man to woman, woman to man, rocking, sucking in panting breath, heat to heat, connected as one entity, a pulse clenched within moist hotness.

They reached their pinnacle quickly, urgently, pounding flesh to flesh, cries muffled in shoulders and necks, fingers entwined in the coarse sheets.

Afterward, Emily lay next to his long damp body and ran her fingers across his chest, back and forth, until he shivered to her feather touch.

"What happened?" Will asked, turning toward her, his hand cupping her chin till their love-drowsy eyes met.

"What was bound to happen, Will. We both knew it."

"Did we?"

"Yes," Emily said with a sigh, "we did."

They lay together for a time, the silver light from the moon gleaming on their nakedness. It ran through Emily's mind that at least the time of month had been safe for her. Still, she knew, it didn't matter; she would have taken him to her despite the danger. *Oh, God,* she thought, how could such heaven be wrong?

Somewhere outside, a coyote howled at the moon, and the warm spring wind soughed through the branches of the awakening trees. Emily propped herself on an elbow and ran a slim finger along his jaw. "Will, I...I want you so much," she whispered, and it happened again, that red-hot pulse of her blood, the urge in her stomach. But this time they came together slowly, taking precious moments to explore each other. Emily allowed herself the delight of touching those hard, corded muscles that ran beneath the skin of his back and stomach, along his thighs and narrow hips where his skin was pale, untouched by the sun.

Their mouths met and held as they drank each other in. Will's hands cupped her heavy breasts and teased at the peaks until they grew rigid, his eyes never leaving her.

Emily's entire body felt engorged with need, straining against itself as she pressed her hips to his, urging him, asking him for release with her body, a message as old as time, as new as the moment.

And then she was atop him, her legs straddling his hips, guiding herself down to him, taking him in, deep, hot, filling her until she arched her back and moaned in pleasure, his hands on her breasts, lifting, kneading, his hips thrusting upward to fill her with his desire.

Her climax came grudgingly, slowly, building and receding as she labored to breathe, emptying and filling her until finally she was swept along with the rising tide and cried out softly into the night. Moments later Will, too, groaned in blissful agony and pulled her against him hard and long as the pulsing of his blood abated.

That night they slept little. There was scant talking. Before dawn Emily kissed his sleeping form and gathered her clothes, slipping down the hall, a smile playing at her lips.

EMILY'S BUBBLE BEGAN to burst that afternoon as reality settled back into her love-dazed brain. What had she *done?* Despite the joy in her body, her mind was working again, plotting, conjuring, questioning. Over and over she had to remind herself that this was neither her time nor place, and Will Dutcher could never truly belong to her nor she to him. They could never fit.

Okay, Emily told herself firmly as she helped peel potatoes in the kitchen, it had finally happened between them, an inevitability, she supposed, that had been brewing since her first day on his ranch. Well, she thought, it wasn't going to happen again. She wouldn't let it. And, Emily knew, she'd been darned lucky the chances of a pregnancy were slim. No, it couldn't happen again.

The children arrived home at four. That morning had been awkward, Emily deathly afraid her happiness was an open book for all to see. But they hadn't seemed to notice the flush in her cheeks or the smile on her lips, or Will's barely concealed embarrassment. Antonio, if he'd noticed, had gone on about this business—just another day.

Emily *was* happy. Even as her brain churned with doubts, her happiness seemed to override all else. She was falling in love and *that* she couldn't ignore.

Will rode in at five. She heard the jingle of his spurs, and her heart pounded giddily against her ribs. Will. Tall, beautiful, silent and distant yet so wonderful. *Will.* Nothing mattered at that moment—not her crazy entrapment in the past, not the gossip or the cold stares and acid words she'd endured from the women of Rifle, not her tedious chores or even the life she'd left behind. Only Will mattered and it felt good.

"Hello," she said, smiling. She opened the door for him, taking his hat and work gloves and jacket.

"Hello, Emily."

He was so handsome, his dark hair curling around his ears, the shadow of whiskers on his sun-browned skin, and those eyes, so blue, so deep . . .

"Have you got a minute?" he was saying, then he looked past her, toward the kitchen, and began pulling on her hand, leading her into the parlor. "We have to talk, Emily," he said.

"Of course, Will," she said, following him, her hand gripped in his large, callused one.

He pressed her down on the sofa then began to pace the rug, back and forth, one hand unconsciously stroking the sides of his mustache.

"What is it?" Emily began, wondering. *Something* was wrong.

"Look," he said, turning toward her abruptly, "in the morning I'm going to send Antonio into town to get Reverend Shumaker. We'll marry, right here in the parlor. The children can even . . ."

But Emily was shaking her head. "No," she said, "no, Will. We . . . I *can't*. I thought . . ."

"What *did* you think?" he asked, incredulous. "You couldn't possibly have thought we'd . . . behave like that and go on as before. Emily," he said, "I *want* to marry you."

"I . . . can't." Her voice was very small, unaccountably afraid.

"Listen—" he began.

"No, Will," she interrupted, "I just can't. I . . ."

"But," he sputtered, "but what about your reputation? You couldn't possibly have expected less, Emily, not after what we . . . did."

She looked up into his bewildered face, a deep sadness suddenly drifting over her like a shroud. "Please," she said, "please try to understand, Will. But . . . but this isn't my . . . my home. I mean, someday I'm going to have to . . . leave, Will, go back where I truly belong. You must know that. In your heart, Will, you have to know I don't really belong here. . . ."

"Emily—" he began.

"No," she said, holding up a hand, "don't. Nothing you can say will change my mind. I . . . I do wish we could work it out. I honestly do, but—" And abruptly she was on her feet, tears burning wretchedly behind her eyes. How could she have thought they'd go on as before? She knew Will; she should have known he'd expect marriage, even if he didn't love her. He was an honorable man, an honorable Victorian man. How could she have failed to see this coming? "Oh, God," Emily cried, running from the room, bursting through the front door and rushing down the dirt lane.

Emily ran. She ran until she thought her lungs were on fire. What was he thinking? But she didn't care. She couldn't allow herself to care. She knew only that she had to get away. Somehow she had to run and keep on running until she found her way home.

Her mad dash became a walk, and the tears finally slid down her cheeks. The sun was still up, pressing warmly on her shoulders as she left the beaten road and began heading diagonally across a field, diagonally in the direction of the railroad tracks, even though they were miles away. If she could just get to that spot and slip back through that portal to her own time.

I can't stay here, her mind cried. *I'll ruin both our lives, even the innocent children's.*

Emily plodded on across the never-ending field, her skirt snagging on clumps of silver sage, her boots slipping into holes, her ankles twisting. If she just kept going...

The sun began to dip lower in the evening sky, illuminating the surrounding mesas in reds and golds and rich purples. Emily wiped at her tears with dirty fingers and drew in deep, quivering breaths. She had to keep going—if she gave up, went back to Will and smothered herself in his strength, she'd be lost forever. But worse, far worse, she might somehow alter the future, create that paradox that could destroy the world she'd come from.

I have to get home, home....

She could see it now up ahead, the fence that still divided Will's land from his brother's. Past that barrier was the road. Then, in a mile or so, the bridge across the stream. She could make it. Then the road to Rifle and down to the river. She could follow the path alongside the tracks, find that spot, that illusive door. She *could* do it. And she'd never look back, never....

Emily hitched up her skirts and climbed the fence, holding on to the post for balance. *Rest,* she thought, if she could just rest a minute. She sat perched on top of the fence, gripping it with her hands. A few minutes' rest, that's all she needed. She was going to make it this time....

It was as if an invisible force turned Emily's head, twisted it so that she was no longer looking forward but was, instead, turning back to see the past. And that was when she spotted him, coming across the range on his horse, the last rays of sun gilding the puffs of dust that rose up from the horse's hooves.

Emily's heart clutched. She shouldn't have looked. Like Lot's wife, she felt as if she were turning into a pillar of salt, frozen in that piece of time and space, held inescapably in the moment. *Run,* her brain commanded, but she was immobilized, wanting Will to snatch her off her perch yet dreading she'd be lost all over again.

Then he was there, his horse's nostrils flaring, the beast's sides heaving. In that cloud of dust Will swung down off his mount and let the reins trail out of his hand. Emily watched him, unmoving, afraid and deliriously elated, tears vying with the joy she felt that he must truly care about her—perhaps even love her a little.

His hands were at her waist, lifting her, pulling her down to him so that her breasts were to his chest.

"You crazy, foolish woman," he was saying, his warmth searing her, his voice gruff and irritated despite the care with which he held her. "Where in hell did you think you were going?" he asked in that hard voice.

"I... Home, Will, I was going home," Emily began, knowing she could never explain.

"Your home is with me. With the children."

"No," Emily whispered, but her reply was lost as his lips claimed hers in hunger, branding her once again.

CHAPTER ELEVEN

WILL KEPT HIS COUNSEL the whole next day, avoiding Emily by staying out on the range. He was thoroughly bewildered by the woman's behavior. How in the name of God could a man and woman fit so danged well together yet still be apart?

It was Emily's doing, though. He'd offered her marriage, and she'd not only turned him down, but she'd run off, to boot!

If Will lived to be a hundred, he'd never understand women.

It took the whole afternoon for him to figure out how he could approach her again on the subject of marriage. She must just have been confused and upset last night. Still, every time he formed sentences in his mind, the things he'd say to her, he couldn't seem to make the words come together properly. 'Course, he never was one to go rambling on.

On the ride back in from the range another notion seeped into his bemused thoughts: he wondered if he loved the woman. He'd never been in love, so how was he supposed to know? He wanted her—like a fever in his blood. Was that love?

Will once again broached the subject of marriage in the parlor that evening, clearing his throat several times, as nervous as a cat in a tree. Why hadn't she just said yes the first time? Were women put on this earth to torment men? "Now don't go runnin' off again," he began, putting down his paper, leaning toward her, "but I'd like to talk some."

Emily merely put aside her sewing and nodded as if she knew what was coming.

Goldang, but this was hard. "I...I, ah, want you to reconsider my proposal, Em," he said, looking at the floor. "I think we, ah, we make a suitable match and..."

But Emily was shaking her head. She sighed. "Will," she said, "I just don't belong here. It could never work."

"Is it, ah, someone else? That fella in Philadelphia you mentioned?"

"No, honestly, Will, it isn't. He was my fiancé, that's true, but it's over. It isn't him."

"Is it Rifle?"

"Partly, I guess. I don't fit. I never could. Maybe," she said, "maybe I'm really a big-city girl at heart."

"And maybe it's the reception you got from the women here. I'll be damned if I can understand why they'd..."

"*I* understand, Will," she said.

"So it's the women," he stated darkly.

"No. It's a lot more. I, I guess I just belong in a city."

"Yes, ma'am," he said dryly, "I surely did notice how you enjoyed yourself in Denver City."

"That...that was different. I had my money stolen and..."

"*My* money," he put in.

"Yes, *your* money. But, Will, I'm used to handling my own affairs, having my own money. I can't live like this."

"I'll *give* you money, if that's all it is. Lord God, woman, it seems like you got money on the brain. I'm talking about marriage, and you're talking about *money*," he said, exasperated.

"I'm sorry. It isn't about money, you're right. That's just a symptom. Sometimes...love isn't enough," she said sadly.

"Then what *is* enough, Emily?"

"I don't know. Getting home, maybe."

"I'll buy you a ticket to Philadelphia. You go on back home, take care of things. We'll wait," he said. "I'll take you on any terms, married or not. Just don't run away from me again," he blurted out.

"I wish it were that simple. I can't go back. There's nothing there for me, nobody. It's all gone."

He looked at her, baffled. "Then stay here."

"Oh, Will! It's crazy, it's impossible. It wouldn't work. Trust me on that. But I will promise you one thing, I won't run away. When I can figure out where to go, I'll tell you, and I'll make plans. And you and the children can see me off at the station. I'll kiss you goodbye, Will, as if we were good friends, and then I'll go."

"When is this going to happen?"

She looked down at her clasped hands. "I don't know, not yet."

"Well, Emily, I'm not a man to beg, and I figure I've already done enough of that. I won't force you. You know your own mind."

"Thank you, Will."

"So, for now, you're still my housekeeper, is that it?"

"Well, a little more than that, maybe. Your friend," she said.

"My friend!" He gave a short, harsh laugh. "And just how long do you expect us to remain 'friends' with you here under my roof, sleeping just down the hall?" He turned away from her and stood there stiffly.

"Will," she said, but then she stopped, as if there were nothing she could say.

He turned back to face her, his temper rising. "You and your modern ways, Emily! You won't marry me, but you don't like what people say. Make up your mind, woman!"

She stared at him, her face stricken, and he felt his anger evaporate. Whatever misguided notions Emily had, she was a woman and he...

"I'll leave, Will. I'll go somewhere," she said abruptly.

"You tried that," he said harshly.

"But, I'll do it, I'll go...."

He stepped up to her and grabbed her arms, wanting to shake her. "Where's your sense, woman?" he asked. "Damn it, what in God's name do you think...?"

It happened without forethought. One second he was boiling in anger, and the next moment he was bringing her close, putting a hand up, running his fingers through her hair, pulling a pin out, then another. She raised her head, quivered as if in pain and closed her eyes.

"You're no young maiden, Emily, who doesn't know her own mind," he said hotly.

She shook her head, eyes still shut.

"Look at me."

She opened her eyes, and there were tears in them. "Damn it, but I do want you for my own woman," he said, pulling her against him, pressing her mouth with his.

Her arms went around his neck, and she melted against him, opening to him. She felt like silk dragged across his fevered skin, smooth and cool and narcotic in her sensuality. Not like any woman he'd ever known, so free with her body, giving from a deep store of love. Nothing in his life had ever equaled the feel of this woman in his arms; nothing had prepared him for these sensations. Will knew now why men got married, why they chose a woman and settled down. Now he knew. And just when he'd found out, the knowledge was going to be snatched from him.

He found her mouth again. Her response made white-hot shafts of need pierce his belly. His tongue met hers, and his body remembered the feel of her surrounding him, taking him in, loving him. He held her face in both hands, kissing her eyelids, her nose, kissing away the tears that swelled under the closed lids.

"No, wait," she said breathlessly. "The children..."

They went upstairs, hand quivering in hand, all the way to the attic, and stood, arms entwined, watching the three sleeping children. Then they went down to his room, shut the door quietly behind them and turned to each other.

She took him by surprise. He needed a moment to recover, but then he returned her kiss, working his mouth over hers. They clung together hotly, painfully, with an urgency that startled them both. Grinding, seeking a new angle to satisfy their hunger, they searched each other's lips.

Plunging his hand into her hair, Will held her head still so that he could plunder her mouth selfishly. But she only moaned and accepted his tongue into her mouth.

Later, they were in his bed. He hardly remembered how they had arrived there. She was naked, the way he'd seen her that first time, and he stopped for a moment to look at her, just to look, to stamp her image into his brain so that he would remember when she was... But he wouldn't think of that.

She glistened like alabaster in the moonlight, slender and curved, with heavy breasts. She lay on her side, facing him, her features soft with passion, her body a temple at which to worship.

"I'll always remember you like this," he said, running a hand along her thigh and feeling the flesh quiver.

"I'll always remember you, Will. The first man I ever loved," she said. "The only one."

He felt heat in his innards, the desperate need to join their bodies more closely. He moved, felt her touch his hardness and moan. *Oh, Lord,* he thought, as her legs moved in invitation.

He felt himself nudge the center of her womanhood, and blood coursed through his veins, making him dizzy. She opened to him, guiding him into her body. He slid into her warmth, and a million splinters of feeling exploded in him, making him plunge deeper inside her. He heard her voice, felt her hands and knew he was pleasuring her. *Not too fast,* he cautioned himself.

He thrust and felt her move against him. He slipped his arms under her and burrowed his face into her neck, giving himself up to pure sensation.

He felt her breath on his neck, the small sounds she made, the pulsing inside her. Their rhythm became faster, frenzied, and he knew he was losing control, losing...

She bucked under him, crying out, and he thrust harder into her, again, and yet again, knowing the joy of giving her pleasure, knowing they had each other in every way they could, holding this time in his memory to savor later—later, when he was alone.

She cried afterward, a small sniffling in the dark.

"What's wrong?" he asked.

"Nothing," she said. "I'm sorry, Will, I never used to cry so much. It seems lately, everything makes me cry."

He put his arm around her and drew her close, so that her head rested on his shoulder. *"Women,"* he said softly.

"Oh, don't be like that, Will," she said, starting to get angry. "You *wish* you could cry. You're just too uptight."

"That's right, Em," he said into her ear. "You're right." He could feel her relaxing against him and turned his head to kiss the corner of her mouth. "Go to sleep, now."

"What's going to happen to us, Will?" she asked in a little voice.

"Shh, don't worry. Things work out. Somehow things always work out," he said confidently, but inside he wondered, knowing he'd never love another woman the way he loved the strange and wonderful Emily Jacoby.

THE NEXT EVENING WAS HOT, and they sat on the porch after supper, watching the sun set behind the mesas. Emily watched Will, watched his face, his hands, the way his legs bulged with muscle at the thigh and were just a bit bowlegged. Oh, yes, she loved him. Her body was heavy, sated, drowsy. She almost didn't care anymore. She could stay here with Will, she thought, just give up and stay and love him, have children with him, raise them on his ranch along with Mary and Jesse and Burke. The normal things a woman did, the things that fulfilled her best.

But then she weighed the other side, and it frightened her. Emily Jacoby had never existed in 1893 Rifle; therefore, she couldn't have children. She'd bring ruin and misery to Will and everything he knew and valued. She loved him too much to do that, far too much.

He dropped the newspaper impatiently onto the porch and said something under his breath, angrily knocking embers out of his pipe onto the sole of his boot.

"What?" she asked.

"Nothing."

She picked up the paper and looked at the front page. Ominous headlines were printed in black across the top of the page. *Rocky Mountain News*. May 20, 1893. Treasury Secretary Denies Rumor That Gold

Has Fallen Below $100,000,000. Public Outcry For Repeal Of Sherman Silver Purchase Act.

Details tumbled into place in Emily's mind. The Silver Panic of 1893, that's what it would be called in history. The Sherman Silver Purchase Act would be repealed, and the government would no longer deplete its gold reserve to purchase silver. But by then it would be too late, turning into a precursor to the Great Depression of 1929, with brokerage houses and banks failing. All the silver-mining towns of the West would suffer. Aspen would be a dusty backwater until it turned to skiing in the 1940s. Thriving mining camps would turn into ghost towns overnight. But what had happened to Rifle, Colorado?

And here she was in the middle of it, with her knowledge of the future and her degree from Wharton. But what could she do? No one listened to her and if they did, what could they do to halt the panic?

"Will," she said, letting the paper fall to her lap.

"Um?"

"You're worried about this, this problem, aren't you?"

"A man'd be plain stupid not to be worried," he said.

She thought hard, not wanting to sound like a crackpot. "I've been thinking, Will. You can't really get hurt by this silver thing except in one way— through Bergener's bank. Am I right, Will?"

"Look, Em, I've told you. It's my problem. Don't worry yourself over it."

"But, Will, wait, listen for a minute. If his bank fails, you could be in trouble."

"Yes, I could, but Bergener's pretty solid. He's a real careful man."

"Then, really, the worst thing that could happen would be a run on the bank."

"Maybe."

"If there was some way to stop a run on the bank..."

"Emily." He reached over and took her hand. "Forget it. It's not your problem."

"It is...I care about you and the children. I don't want anything to happen to you, to this ranch."

"We'll manage," he said.

"But maybe I could help," she said. "I could—"

"What?" he asked. "With all your fancy schooling and your working in that bank in Philadelphia, what could you do? Could you stop people from trying to get their money out of Bergener's bank?"

"No," she said quietly.

"I never did see such a stubborn, meddling woman," he said, shaking his head. "I don't know, maybe that's why..." He hesitated, then, "You're different than any other woman I ever met."

"Different?" she asked. "How?"

"Don't press me so."

"Come on, how?"

"Ah, hell, Emily," he said, his voice gruff, "you get a man to talking is how."

"You mean talking to a woman, don't you?"

"If you say so."

"Come on," she teased, "admit it, Will, you *like* having me to talk to."

"If it makes you happy," he said nonchalantly, "then sure, I just enjoy myself to no ends, woman."

But for all his harshness, for all his mocking, Emily knew he didn't hate talking to her as much as he'd like her to think. She smiled and raised his hands to her lips. The children came running from the barn in the warm, fading twilight.

"Guess what, Uncle Will?" Jesse cried. "We saw Daisy's new foal!"

"She is the prettiest baby," Mary said.

"She fell over," Burke added, "like a silly thing."

"Not *silly*," Jesse corrected, "she's just young and her legs aren't strong yet."

"She was *too* silly!" Burke insisted. "Like Antonio when he comes home Saturday night."

"He means drunk," Mary said disparagingly. "Oh, Burke."

"I'd love to see her," Emily said. "But I'll go later. It's bedtime for you three."

After the children were in bed, Emily walked with Will to the barn where the mares ready to foal were kept this time of year. He carried a lantern, and Emily walked beside him, a thin wool shawl drawn over her shoulders. Shep romped at Will's side, his stump of a tail wagging, his whole body quivering with excitement at the outing.

"I've never seen a newborn foal," she said.

"Never?" Will asked, astonished. "For the love of God, they have horses in cities back East, don't they?"

"Oh, sure, they do, but not *baby* horses," she hastened to say.

The barn was dark, filled with the pungent smell of horse and the sweet scent of hay. Emily could hear horses moving about, the soft thud of a hoof and the rustle of straw, the brushing of a heavy body against wood stanchions. A tortoiseshell cat came out of the darkness to run against their legs and hiss at Shep. Will strode to the end stall and held the lantern high.

"Hey, Daisy, old girl, how are you?" The mare came to him and nosed the hand he held out. "Well, what do you know," he said, "a lump of sugar."

"Where's the baby?" Emily whispered.

He moved the lantern and there, in the corner, a dark shadow lay curled up. As if disturbed by the light, the newborn foal stirred and tried to rise. It struggled, its long, gangly legs untried. Finally it walked splay legged to its mother and started to nurse.

"Oh," said Emily in wonder.

The barn cat meowed, as if in agreement.

"I know. I never get over it," Will said. "Every year."

They leaned on the wooden partition and watched the foal. She wobbled on spindly, knobby-kneed legs and flicked her little brush of a tail as she nursed.

"Daisy throws me a good one every year," Will said. "She's a fine old mare."

Emily heard that curious gentleness in his voice, the tone he used for those he loved. She leaned her head against his shoulder and felt his arm slide around her waist. She was utterly content. She could be just like old Daisy and throw Will a good one every year, and they'd grow old together and . . .

No! It was seductive, that idea, but dangerous. It wouldn't work, and one day she'd grow tired of this life. Hadn't she told Will that enough times?

But in the darkness she put a hand on her belly surreptitiously. It was empty, had always been empty. Would the time come when she'd ripen and carry a child for someone she loved? Would the time come when she'd be as content as she was that very moment?

They strolled back to the house and into the dark kitchen. Will held her close and kissed her. "I won't press you," he said. "I promised. But I can't bear this closeness...."

"Yes," she said. "I know."

"Will you...?"

"Yes," she breathed.

They came together in urgent hunger. Standing, they clung together, half-dressed, his shirt open, her blouse unbuttoned. He covered her face with kisses, her neck, the place in her throat where the pulse beat. She plunged her hand into his dark hair, caressed the back of his neck. Their breath mingled.

"You taste so good," Emily whispered.

"You taste like sunshine," he answered.

He tugged at her shirtwaist, and she shrugged out of it. He loosened one of her breasts from her chemise, bent down and kissed it. She gasped with the exquisite agony of the sensation.

She was filled with the glory of her love, bursting with it. She couldn't get enough of the feel of him, the taste, the smell. The world receded, and there were only the two of them in the universe. A century was a mere speck of time, insignificant, and their love overcame its puny impediment.

THERE WAS A Cattleman's Association meeting the next afternoon, called due to the mounting tensions in town. Rumor ran riot. Bergener was going to close the bank. No, he was going to call in all the loans and take cattle where there was no cash. He was out of gold, his deposits were worthless. He was hotfooting it out of town, gone bust. He was hiring professionals to guard against a run on the bank—gunslingers, trigger-happy gunmen who'd shoot to kill anyone trying to get inside the bank.

Will had to leave early to ride into town.

"Don't be rash," Emily said, hanging on to his stirrup. "Try to calm everyone down. Panics are caused by fear half the time, not real shortages. If everyone stays calm and no one threatens Bergener, it'll blow over, Will, I know that."

The day had turned blustery, ushering in a spring storm. Dust-laden wind flew across the corral, molding Emily's skirt to her legs. Wisps of hair flew into her eyes, making her squint up at him.

He smiled down at her and shook his head. "Full of advice, aren't you, Emily?"

"Will, listen to me. I'm serious. I *know*. Don't let them do anything crazy. Sit tight and wait this out."

"And if Bergener *has* sent for gunmen? If he *does* close the bank?"

"Negotiate. Don't give ultimatums. There's always the possibility of compromise."

"I hear you, Em, but I'm not so sure how much of an influence I'll be."

"Try, Will, okay?"

He leaned over and kissed her upturned mouth. "You care so goldarn much, Em, don't you?"

"Yes," she said fiercely.

She waited the long, windy afternoon as black clouds scudded in from the west. She helped feed the children and then waited some more. The rain began to fall, lightning splitting the sky and thunder reverberating from the mountains standing sentinel over the Grand Valley.

God, what she'd give for a telephone! Then Will could just call her and let her know what had happened at the meeting! But, no, she had to sit and wait it out, chewing her fingernails, her stomach in a knot.

Another worry occurred to her: Will had called her meddlesome. Could her meddling here create a paradox? Maybe, in the course of history, it was somehow necessary for Bergener's bank to fail, for Rifle to go bust, for Will Dutcher to lose his ranch.

But—she remembered—Rifle had still existed in her time. It had been on the map and in the tourist book. *Someone* had saved Rifle. Why not her?

The storm crashed outside, and she alternately worried about the meeting and Will riding home in the bad weather. The wick of the kerosene lamp wavered even in the glass chimney when gusts sneaked in the windows.

She picked up one of Mary's books and tried to read it, but soon, it sat unread in her lap, and she waited, biting her lips, straining to hear his step on the porch through the storm's turmoil.

It came at last, the thump of boot heels, the opening of the door, the patter of rain and boom of thunder.

"Will!" she cried, running to him.

He stood, wrapped in his duster, his hat dripping, a puddle at his feet.

"Will? Are you all right? I was worried . . . it's so late . . . you're soaking wet. Oh, Will, the storm was so bad . . ."

"Hush, woman," he said, divesting himself of his wet duster and hat, sitting in a chair to pull his boots off. "Sometimes you just plain have too much to say for yourself."

"Here, let me," she said, taking his wet coat, his boots. "Are you hungry? I saved you some chili and bread. Would you like . . . ?"

He smoothed his mustache and shook the drops of water off his fingers. "Not now, Emily, I'm all done in."

"You aren't hungry? Did you eat in town?"

"Let it rest. I'm not hungry," he said wearily.

She stood there, holding his wet clothes, afraid to ask, terrified of his answer yet driven to know. She studied him sitting there, wet, tired, dejected, and she hesitated even as her mind screamed inside her head— *what happened?*

He ran a hand through his wet hair. "I'd like a whiskey, Em," he said finally.

"Oh, sure, just a sec."

He drank it in a gulp. Deliberately he put the glass down then looked up at Emily. "Everyone in town demanded their deposits in gold," he said tiredly. "Bergener refused to attend the meeting and threatened to shut his bank. Something's gonna blow soon. It can't go on like this."

"Oh, Will . . ."

"There'll be an explosion. Some damn trigger-happy fool will set it off." He put his head in his hands, elbows on his knees. "You'd think we'd know better in this day and age."

Emily stared at him, her heart aching, her brain whirling. If only she could do something to help, anything.

"Damn," Will muttered again, "it's going to be bad."

Worse than you know, Emily thought in silence, but maybe, maybe somehow, she could change that.

CHAPTER TWELVE

WILL CLOSED the barn door and pulled his bandanna out of his back pocket. He wiped the sweat from his brow and neck, then leaned down to give old Shep a pat on the head. The dog was panting like a steam engine. Tarnation, but it promised to be a hot summer coming up. He only hoped a drought wasn't going to follow on the heels of this late May heat. What with money already so scarce, that was exactly what the valley didn't need.

He headed across the yard toward the house, across the hot, dusty yard, his work for the day done. Several of the hands were standing in front of the bunkhouse washing off their grime from the range. In a couple minutes Will planned on doing the same— maybe Emily would even heat up some bathwater. Lord, but it was hot out.

Will had reached the front porch steps and was kicking the dirt from his boots, when Shep started barking his head off at the sound of hooves galloping up the lane. *What now?* he thought, swearing under his breath.

The horse and rider came into view, and he could see it was Johnny McCrudden, the boy's face flushed in the heat. "Mr. Dutcher," he called, "wait up!"

Will sighed and went back down the steps.

"Mr. Dutcher," the boy breathed, his mount sidling and turning, well lathered, "my pa sent me on over to tell you the bank's closed up."

"'Course it is, Johnny, it's past four already."

"No," the boy panted, "it's *closed*."

"For good?" Will's stomach fell to his feet.

"Yup. And Pa says you gotta all meet. It's real bad, Mr. Dutcher, town's going crazy."

"I imagine so," Will grumbled. Ever since that meeting last week he'd been expecting this. They all had, but still the news came as a shock. "Tell your pa I'll be at the schoolhouse as soon as I can. An hour, got that, son?"

"Yes, sir, Mr. Dutcher. I'm headin' on out to the Farleys' place now, then on home. I'll tell Pa." The boy gave his mount a hard kick and disappeared in a cloud of dust.

"Oh, no," Emily said when Will told her, her brow furrowing, "it's really *closed?*"

"Guess so." Will splashed water on his face and neck and took the towel she handed him. "I've gotta ride on into town right now," he said, trying to act casual in front of her, "'cause the men are going to meet and talk it over."

Emily sank down onto his bed, her face troubled. "This is awful," she said, "terrible. What's going to happen, Will?"

"Nothing's going to happen, Em. We're just going to talk things over."

"But don't you realize..."

"Emily," he said, "you're drivin' me crazy with this. Let it lay, woman, it's men's business."

She walked with him to the barn while Will resaddled his mare. And then she began it all over again, that female talk of hers, and Will could find no other way of silencing her but to take the woman into his arms and cover her mouth with his. For a moment she struggled, knowing what he was doing, but then she gave in, as always, her supple curves and hollows molding against his body, her mouth opening to his. Will was surprised at his own response. Hell, he needed to be on his way. But somehow his body wasn't listening to his head.

Breathing hard, he pulled back after a time and held her at arm's length. "Em," he said, "how long you going to keep this up?"

"Keep what up?" she asked, her eyes half-closed, that smoky tone to her voice.

"Keeping yourself from me, that's what, woman. You know we both—"

But she pressed a slim finger to his lips. "It's the wrong time, Will, I told you. Maybe...maybe soon."

"And maybe not at all," he said under his breath, knowing she heard him but not caring.

It tortured him, having Emily so close and not being able to possess her. Tortured him more than he was willing to let on to her or admit to himself. He knew she was right to be careful and cursed the part of him that hungered for her ceaselessly. He wanted her, all of her, her mind and heart and body. And it seemed he couldn't have her. She was here, under his roof, for a short time, lent to him by a curious fate, but she wasn't his to have and to hold, and the truth of it brought black moods down upon him. The only reaction allowed to him was anger, but even that didn't daunt

Emily. She seemed to understand his brooding and his moods, and that was even more frustrating.

"I'll keep supper hot," she told him as he pulled away from her and swung onto his horse.

"Don't know how long I'll be," he said curtly.

"I'll have supper waiting," she repeated. "Good luck, Will."

He turned the sorrel mare, kicked her and loped off down the lane, feeling Emily's gaze on his back like a red-hot brand.

The town *was* up in arms—maybe not crazy like Johnny'd said, but the men were steaming mad when Will got to the schoolhouse—steaming and afraid, too. So was Will. Though he'd be hog-tied and dragged through the streets before he'd shoot off his mouth like some of them.

"Can we please have some order in here!" Ollie McCrudden shouted, banging his gavel over and over until the windowpanes shook. "Come to order!"

"I'll blow any man's head off who comes on my land to take what's mine!" yelled one irate rancher.

"To hell with the land," called another. "I say we break down the bank's doors and take what's ours!"

"...lynch that Bergener! Why, he's not better than a goldang horse thief!"

"Lynch him!" came a chorus.

"Order!" shouted Ollie. "Order!"

On it went. Will listened in silence, one foot crossed over his knee, his hat balanced on his leg.

"Will," came Ollie's voice over the din, "Will Dutcher, will you come on up here and talk some dang sense into these men?"

Will did it. But, Lord, he hated speaking in public. Words were hard enough for him as it was. He mounted the two steps to the podium and cleared his throat. "Men," he said. Then "Men! Listen, this isn't gettin' us anywhere tonight. Be reasonable. Storming the bank isn't going to help, and lynching Bob is gonna make it worse. This is 1893, gentlemen, and we're a civilized..."

"You a coward there, Dutcher?" shouted a man from the rear of the room. "That housekeeper of yours gettin' to you?"

McCrudden banged the gavel hard. "Leave the blamed housekeeper out of it, men!" he shouted.

"I don't need that line of bull from you, Lonnagan, no, nor anyone else," Will said in a steely voice. "You know me, men. I'm no coward, and I'll go outside with any of you to prove it."

"Apologize, Lonnagan," somebody said. "Go on, man."

"Sorry, Dutcher," Lonnagan muttered.

"We got a problem here," Will went on, "and we have to do what's best for all of us."

"So what's that?" someone asked.

Will cleared his throat once more. "I say we wait a few days and see. Could be Bob might get himself straightened out, and all this wild talk is pure horse bunk."

"Well," Ollie said, standing next to him still, "I did hear Bergener's sent to Denver City for some hired guns."

There was an apprehensive rustle among the men. They'd all heard it, too.

"Could be rumor, Ollie," Will said.

"Could be."

"You know it ain't, Dutcher," Tell Lister called from the crowd.

Will looked out across the angry assembly. "Listen," he said, "I still say we wait this out for a time. We aren't going to fix a thing by forming a mob. We can talk to Bob, for one thing and..."

"And string him up for another!" came a thundering voice.

Will gave up. They'd settle down once they all got back to their homes that night. As a crowd they were getting dangerous, but dispersed they might come to their senses. For a little while, that was....

"Gentlemen," he called over the noise, "I'm heading on home. I gotta sleep on things, and I sure hope you all do the same. Let's call this meeting to a close." He looked at Ollie McCrudden. "How about it, Ollie?"

"Sure, Will, sure. But," he said so only Will could hear, "I reckon we can't keep them down for long."

Will rode on back to the ranch slowly, dejected, a whole lot more concerned than he was letting on even to himself. He remembered the bloody range war of '80. He wondered if anyone else did, though, or was the whole valley about to erupt again? He felt as if he were watching a violent summer storm racing across the mesas, a storm he could see coming but one he couldn't stop.

And that business about Emily. People were talking, saying things about her. His hand tightened on the reins, and his horse tossed her head, feeling his tension. His whole body went taut at the thought of gossip, the invasion of his privacy—his and Emily's. They had no right.

That night at the barbecue... She'd taken the brunt of the people's fear and anger so far, but now Will could see it heading toward him, the storm racing, black clouds all boiling and seething. Emily and the Silver Panic and the bank closing all mixed up together in a ferocious swirling wind that would level everything in its path.

Always, Emily—at the center of everything. It was as if her coming had caused these things to happen, although he knew that couldn't be.

And yet, would he give her up? Would he choose not having known her? *No,* he told himself, *never.*

As promised, Emily had the children all tucked in and supper waiting. But Will had no appetite. He forced down food anyway, trying to put on a good face, and smiled faintly at her talk, thanking the Lord she wasn't pestering him. But Emily knew, Will thought. There never was hiding a blasted thing from that female. She always knew.

The following morning dawned clear and brilliant, streaks of golden light touching the distant peaks and making Will feel that maybe things weren't as bad as they seemed last night. Maybe they could meet in a group with Bob and somehow sort things out. Sure. The trouble was, what if Bob really had sent to Denver for help? He sure as hell hoped not. 'Cause if Bob had gone off half-cocked and done a stupid thing like that, blood was sure to spill on the streets of Rifle.

He ate breakfast with the children and listened in amusement to their talk of getting out of school for the summer.

"I'm not going back in the autumn," Jesse announced, "not if I gotta do all that arithmetic."

"You're just dumb," Burke said, spilling honey all over his bread.

"You're *both* dumb," Mary put in loftily.

But Emily. Emily wasn't anywhere to be found once breakfast was put on the table. And when Will finally located her out back of the kitchen—she and Antonio dragging some kind of contraption across the yard— she scolded Will and told him not to peek and to head on out to the range. "Go away," she called, "you'll see everything tonight. Go away!"

It was another scorcher, though some clouds finally drifted in after lunch and cooled things down a tad. Still, Will rode in hot and tired again at four, his thoughts on the herd and his land—if things got worse he could lose it all. And then there was Emily. If three months ago someone had told Will he'd be mooning after a female before summer set in, Will would have called that person a damn liar and a fool.

He turned the mare out after a good rubdown and closed the gate, giving the old girl a last pat on her neck. The mare's muscles rippled warmly beneath his familiar touch.

He strode toward the house, across the hot, dusty yard, Shep at his side, and his thoughts, as always, turned to Emily.

Damned woman. She had her hooks in him good, so that they hurt, digging at his insides. As if he didn't have enough troubles. But when he thought of her gone…that hurt even worse, a sick twisting in his gut, an emptiness.

If she stayed . . . if she stayed, he'd try to make her happy, do everything in his power to keep her here.

He'd never thought he'd feel like that about a woman, but he did, and he'd do his best for her. Problem was, right now his good intentions didn't seem to be getting him anywhere.

Emily Jacoby wouldn't have him.

She kept saying she was going to leave—but when and where to? Would she go back to that man in Philadelphia?

Oh, sure, he'd do everything in his power to keep Em with him, short of grovel. He wouldn't plead, not anymore. A man had his pride, and if he lost that, no woman would want him anyway, especially not Em. He'd survive without her, although it would hurt like goldarn hell. And the young ones—it'd be mighty hard on them, too, but they'd all make it somehow.

It didn't seem to matter—the trouble she caused him. Her running off to Denver City, her nagging, her different ways. And what the other ranchers thought about her, like Lonnagan yesterday. A man had to be out of his mind, begging for trouble with a woman like Emily. And yet, when they were alone, none of that seemed to matter.

Damn, but that woman had turned his life upside down. He just never could stop thinking of her, not for a minute. She tormented him, infuriated him, fascinated him . . .

"Oh, Will!" Emily exclaimed as he strode into the kitchen, "it works!"

"Um. What works?"

"My invention, silly. I'm an inventor!"

"Guess we better take a look then," he said, and gave her one of his grudging smiles.

Emily's invention—or contraption—was about the strangest thing Will had ever seen. Somehow she, the children and Antonio had been working on the thing for a couple of weeks. It was big and heavy looking, a mass of iron and pipes stuck to the side of his house out behind the kitchen. Beneath the ugly tub-shaped contraption was the old stove from his brother's place. One pipe was sticking into the kitchen wall and another went to the well.

"What in tarnation..." Will began, hands on hips as he studied the thing.

The children giggled.

"It's a hot-water heater," Emily said, practically leaping out of her skin with delight. "You pump water into the tub and light the fire and voilà, hot water in your sink and tub! Antonio even found the right valves at the blacksmith's and..."

"But what's it for?" Will asked, bemused.

"I told you. *Hot water.* Year-round, automatic hot water! And I figure if you collected oil shale you could practically heat the water for nothing." She beamed and snapped her fingers. "And you, Will Dutcher, are going to be the very first to try it out!"

"Oh, no," he began, frowning.

All evening, those golden hairs escaping their pins, Emily went about her work cheerfully, if tiredly. Everyone took a bath—except Antonio who bathed once a month whether he needed to or not—and Emily delighted so much in her invention that Will finally had to ask, "You done impressing yourself, woman?"

Of course, Will had seen contraptions like this in the fancy catalogs, but he'd never really seen the need for one. Still, he said nothing to Emily, even when she announced she might just apply for a patent.

They were sitting on the porch, the cooler evening air carrying the scent of apple blossoms, the children playing tag out near the corral. "Yes," Emily was saying, rocking in her favorite chair, "I might just apply for a patent. And then if I could figure out how to get a road up onto Burning Mountain and haul some of that shale, I could even sell it to..." She cocked her head. "Will? Are you listening?"

In truth he hadn't been. Earlier it had been easy to fall into the mood of happiness Emily's invention had brought to his household, but now, well now, Will guessed, it was time to think of other things, to wonder if Bob Bergener really had hired himself some guns from the big city.

"Will?" Her voice nudged him gently. "What is it? Please. Please tell me what's happened. Ever since last night when you rode into town, well, you've been so distant. You didn't even...kiss me good-night last night," she whispered. *"Please."*

But he only reached over and took her hand in his and continued staring out across the darkening land. His land.

THE ATMOSPHERE IN TOWN was just as Will had described to Emily—tense. She was surprised that even Mrs. Tate in the Mercantile store seemed too preoccupied to snub her that Saturday morning—preoccupied with the news that had come over the wire from Glenwood Springs: there were gunmen on the 12:33 p.m. westbound ticketed to Rifle.

"Will that be all, Miss Jacoby?" Mrs. Tate asked, packing up the box of supplies for Emily.

"Yes, thank you," Emily said stiffly, recalling all too well the insults she'd endured at the dance. She turned to Mary. "Have you got everything you need, honey? The lace for the doll's dress? Buttons?"

"Yes, Miss Emily," she said, and Mrs. Tate gave her a lollipop. There was nothing, of course, for Emily. Mary tugged on Emily's hand. "Let's go on over to the blacksmith's and find Uncle Will. I want to see the bad men on the train. Let's hurry."

Emily wasn't at all sure the children should be allowed to go to the train depot, though it seemed the whole town planned on turning out for the event. For a place where there were no phones, word had certainly spread fast enough. It could only have been two hours ago that the wire from Glenwood had arrived. Now the streets were bustling with the news, ranchers, farmers and businessmen alike were heading down to the tracks.

"Come on, Miss Emily," Mary urged, pulling her along toward the blacksmith's.

They found Will and the boys still waiting for Mr. Crowley to finish the repairs on one of the springs on the buckboard. And even Jesse and Burke, though they couldn't have had a clue as to why everyone was heading to the depot, were bubbling with curiosity.

"You'd think the circus was coming to town," Will told Emily, frowning.

"Let's just go on home," she suggested. "What if there's trouble, Will? I mean, the children and all."

But he shook his head. "First, if won't harm the children to see it. They gotta learn and grow up sometime."

"And second?"

"I wouldn't miss this for the world."

The station was jammed. The throng subdued a bit as men checked pocket watches and women and children strained to see ahead on the tracks. Down by the stockyard, carriages and buckboards were parked, crowding the street where cattle and horses would be unloaded.

"It's a zoo," Emily said, tugging on Will's shirtsleeves. "I think we should go, Will. If there's trouble . . ."

"Won't be no trouble," Ollie McCrudden said from behind them. "Not today, ma'am, not till the gunslingers park themselves in front of the bank or try to round up someone's herd. *Then* there's gonna be trouble, all right."

"Amen to that," Will put in grimly.

"Bob Bergener's a fool," Emily said, for all to hear, and Will shot her a look.

They heard the whistle long before the train rounded the bend in the river and came into sight. The crowd moved down along the tracks, spreading out to get a better view of the gunmen. Emily kept the children close by, scolding them when they tried to weasel into the front of the crowd. Finally Will set young Burke on his shoulders.

"Baby," Jesse said, standing on tiptoe.

The train reared, braking, steam trailing behind it in a long billowing cloud. The whistle blew twice more, clearing the tracks, announcing its on-time arrival. The crowd held its collective breath.

"Do you think there are really gunslingers on it?" Emily asked, still not quite able to fit her mind around the reality of real, live western gunmen coming to town.

"Wouldn't have gotten that message from the stationmaster in Glenwood if there weren't," Will said as he watched the train pull into the station and roll to a shrieking, jerky stop.

The conductor got off first, setting the steps in place for the debarking passengers. Then, through the cloud of steam came two ladies and their children, a few men and a couple of cowboy types lugging saddles, probably seeking work. Two more women. A young man and his wife, carrying a baby in her arms...

The passengers wove their way through the crowd with questioning looks, but all eyes were on the passenger cars, watching, waiting. After a moment or two, when no one else seemed to be getting off, a small murmur rose from the townsfolk, a nervous hum. Maybe, Emily thought, maybe there weren't any hired guns coming to...

But then her racing mind suddenly ground to a halt. There was one of them. Her heart began a heavy, frightened beat in her breast.

There was no mistaking the man. He stood in the doorway for a moment, surveying the crowd, a thin smile splitting his lips like a slash.

Though danger seemed to emanate from him, the stranger had the look of an Old West dandy. Perhaps in his late thirties, the dark-headed man was tall and slender and dressed in black. Black coat and vest and trousers and boots. A black Stetson pulled menacingly low on his brow. Dark eyes, deep set and penetrating, viewed the throng casually. Emily couldn't help but notice the two pearl-handled pistols showing at his sides. She took Mary's hand in hers and squeezed it.

Then came the next man, a twin of the first though he was terribly young and fair headed. One by one, all packing lethal hardware at their sides, the gunslingers emerged, stepping down onto the platform, steam billowing up around their legs. The crowd grudgingly parted to let them through.

They were all ages and proportions, but the one thing they did have in common were those cold, expressionless eyes, the eyes of killers.

"I count twelve," Will said, turning to Ollie. "Bergener must really be expecting an uprising."

"And well he should," Ollie said, still staring at the men.

The crowd was silent for the most part, all heads turned to watch the army of gunmen head down along the platform toward the cattle cars.

Emily, too, watched, her mind reeling. This wasn't really happening, she kept telling herself. This was a scene from a movie, for God's sake—it couldn't be real. In a minute she expected to see Billy the Kid, for Pete's sakes, his old clothes baggy on his skinny frame, his face childlike, his weapons lethal.

The crowd followed the hired men along the platform, slowly, quietly, expectant. Emily held fast to the children and followed Will. "Where are they going?" she whispered at Will's broad back.

"Getting their mounts off the cattle car, I suspect." He stopped then and turned for a moment and gave her a reassuring look. "It's all right, Em, they're just men."

The gunmen moved in a file, a couple of them toting rifles slung over their shoulders. The steam still hissed out from the engine, and moved with the crowd along the platform, wet and metallic smelling, obscuring Emily's view at moments. But always it parted, and there they were, the gunslingers, awaiting their horses.

Some of the crowd finally dispersed, but Will, it seemed, was staying. Emily wanted to go, too, yet she knew he'd be angry. Will wasn't one for backing away from trouble. He'd stay and watch and judge until he was satisfied. "Just men," indeed.

"Listen," Ollie said next to them, "I'm gonna head on over to the schoolhouse. We all got some figuring to do here, Will. You joinin' us?"

"I'll be along," Will replied, but his gaze was still riveted on the twelve men who were just now leading their horses down the wooden ramp, hooves echoing dully, rump and flanks twisting nervously, scattering folks aside.

"Wow," Jesse said, freeing his hand from Emily's, "you get a look at those pistols on that tall one?"

"Oh," Mary said, shivering, "he scares me."

"Me, too, button," Emily whispered.

But Will didn't seem in the least intimidated as the men with their horses methodically parted the crowd and headed on up the street toward town. No. Will just stood his ground, refusing to move aside for one of the men as he passed. Will even tipped his hat and smiled coolly.

"What are you *doing?*" Emily whispered in his ear.

"It's our town, Em," he said, "and someone's got to let them know it."

While the women and children were relegated to their wagons and buggies out in front of the school-house, the men trudged on inside, faces grim.

"Can we go now?" Mary asked from the rear of the buckboard.

"Not yet," Emily said, "but they won't be long." From where she sat, Emily could see the gunmen gathering in front of the bank down the street. She thought she could make out Bob Bergener, too, pulling up in his fine black buggy. *Figures,* she thought. He didn't have the gumption to meet his thugs at the station—afraid the crowd would turn on him, no doubt. But now he was a big man, surrounded by those killers. Emily's stomach knotted.

Voices from time to time could be heard coming from inside the school—loud, panic-stricken voices of irate men.

"I say we shoot it out with them right here and now!"

"It's *our* gold in that bank, men, let's go get it!"

"I'm arming my ranch hands, fellas, they ain't taking what's mine!"

"Order! Please!" Ollie's voice could be heard over the rabble.

God, how she longed to march herself inside and explain to them, tell them all there was only one way to save the town—negotiate with Bergener and promise not to make a run on their deposits if he'd reopen the doors to his bank. But they'd never listen. No, they'd stone her for opening her mouth. There was a chance, though—a slim one. If she could persuade Will to talk to them . . .

Emily sat and waited with the other women, her nerves raw from expecting the doors to the schoolhouse to burst open and the men come pouring out into the street, guns ready. She was only vaguely aware of a few feminine glares shot in Ker direction. Much more important than the women's coolness to her was Will's welfare. He couldn't, he *wouldn't* be so blind as to join a mob, would he?

She held her breath and spoke calmly to the children, explaining the situation as best she could.

"Is Uncle Will going to get in a gunfight?" Jesse asked, fidgeting in the back.

"Oh, of course not," Emily said with a lot more assurance than she was feeling.

Eventually the men emerged from their meeting, growling and muttering. Emily could have reached out and touched the aura of anger and fear that hung around them. As one, the ranchers turned to face the gunmen in front of the bank down the street. They stood there, as still as statues but throbbing with an awful expectancy, staring at the knot of black-clothed men around Bergener.

The gunmen must have felt the tension. They became aware of the scrutiny, and one by one, they turned to face the ranchers. The two groups of men remained like that, frozen, staring, silent, quivering with readiness, the hot air vibrating with hate.

"No," Emily whispered to herself.

Time passed by with unbearable slowness, every woman holding her breath, every man on the brink of violence.

Then there was a movement, the faintest shift of mood. A muffled voice reached Emily's ear from down the street, and she saw that Bergener was opening the door of the bank, ushering his hired guards inside. Her eyes pivoted to the ranchers. They were still, electric in their intensity, waiting.

One by one, the black-garbed gunmen disappeared inside the bank. The door closed, and the street was empty once again except for the glare and eddies of dust kicked up by the hot breeze.

A sigh went through the crowd in front of the school, a kind of groan; there was movement, voices, quiet then louder, the gruff bravado of men who'd faced an enemy and prevailed.

Emily slumped on the seat of the buckboard, drawing in a deep breath. It had been so close, so horribly close.

That night she went to bed miserable. Will had barely spoken to her the whole afternoon. He was preoccupied, worried that Bergener would turn his hired guns loose on the whole countryside, rounding up cattle, looting, even burning. It was as if a pestilence had been let loose on Rifle.

At seven that evening Will had ridden out with his ranch hands to post them at various positions for the night. "When will you be back in?" Emily had asked him, catching him in the barn.

"Don't rightly know" was all he'd said, then he'd swung himself lithely up onto his horse and ridden off down the lane. Shep's black-and-white form followed him, as always.

Emily lay in her bed and prayed. She prayed no harm would come to any of the townspeople, but especially Will. If anything happened to him . . .

He tapped on her door long past midnight. "Emily, you awake?" came his hushed voice.

Her heart raced. "Yes, oh yes, Will, come in." And she held him to her as he lay down on her bed, his long form stretched out next to hers, his body warm, smelling of sage and dust and his own masculinity.

Slowly, his strong arm encircling her waist, Will pulled Emily against him and touched her lips with his. She could feel his hardness and his weariness and embraced him, wanting him, pressing her body to his until her nipples grew rigid beneath the cotton nightdress. A warmth spread in her belly as his mouth moved with more urgency over hers and a hand cupped a full breast.

"Oh, Em," he whispered against her lips, "I need you, woman," and his hand slid up beneath her clothing and stroked her smooth hip and belly and took her breast, pressing it, cupping it until her body swelled with desire.

"God," he groaned again, his voice rasping, deep, hungry, and his mouth found her nipple and drew it into its damp warmth.

Abruptly Emily stiffened. "Will," she breathed, barely in control of herself, "I . . . we can't. The time's wrong. I . . ."

And just as suddenly he withdrew his warmth from her, coming to a sitting position in the moonlight, raking his callused hands through the thickness of his hair.

"Will," she said, "please. I can't get pregnant. I just *can't*. Don't do this to us."

"I *want* to make you pregnant," he ground out, turning to pin her with his gaze, "then maybe you'll let me get the preacher out here."

"I . . . can't," Emily repeated, averting her gaze as she tugged her nightdress down, ashamed.

For a long moment he continued to stare at her darkly, as if he hated her. Then he came to his feet and took his hat from the bedpost, shoving it down low over his brow. "Have it your way," he said harshly, "I gotta head on back out anyway. Pleasant dreams, lady," he finished hotly, and then he was gone, banging her door too loudly.

Emily held back her tears. Crying again wasn't going to solve a thing. What she needed to do was gather her strength. Somehow she had to help Will. Oh, she knew tonight more than ever that her time in the Grand Valley with Will soon had to end. They couldn't go on torturing each other this way. But before she left—before she somehow found her way back to a world she could survive in—she had to know in her heart Will and his children would be safe.

Yes, she needed her strength. Because Emily knew it was going to take every ounce of it to leave this man, this hard man she'd come to love with every fiber of her being.

CHAPTER THIRTEEN

WILL RODE UP the lane toward the ranch house slowly, unenthusiastic about facing Emily. The news from town was all bad, and she'd ask questions until she got it all out of him. It wasn't her place to demand so, but she did. That was Emily, he guessed.

He dismounted in front of the barn, unsaddled and watered his mare, putting off the inevitable a few minutes longer.

"All right," he said to himself, pushing his hat up with the back of his hand, "time to face the music."

Emily was waiting for him in the kitchen, pulling something out of the oven as he opened the door, her face flushed from the heat.

She wore that old blue skirt, but she had on a blouse he hadn't seen, a candy-striped one, and it was so warm in the kitchen she'd rolled up the sleeves and unbuttoned the high neck. She had a look about her, Emily did, a flair, a special grace, and the thought of her leaving him was a knife in his gut. They didn't discuss it, ever, but it was there, hanging over them like a storm cloud. Sooner or later, Emily was going to leave.

She straightened and smiled at him. "Oh, there you are, just in time for these fruit tarts."

She struck him as she always did, as if the sun had come up, radiant and beautiful and life-giving. He'd tried to resist this reaction to Emily, and he'd never admit it to a soul, but there it was—anticipation, excitement, thankfulness. Every damned time he saw her.

"Have a good day?" she asked.

He grunted, threw his hat onto the table.

"Oh, *that* kind of day," she said.

"Emily..."

"Here, have a glass of water and sit down and tell me."

He sighed but he sat. The water was cool and clear, and she waited with folded arms while he drank it.

"Well?"

"Nothing's changed. The men are there, around the bank, in shifts. No one's seen much of Bergener. Word's out that he's given Ollie McCrudden notice. Pay a thousand dollars toward his loan or Bergener will take his cattle. Ollie's got the biggest debt of anybody around here, so I guess he's the first to get put on notice."

"A thousand dollars?" Emily said. "Does Ollie have that kind of cash?"

"Lord, no. Nobody does. Bergener knows that, too."

"What's going to happen?"

He ran a hand through his hair. "I'll be damned if I know. Nothing good."

"Oh, Will..." She sat down across from him at the table and put her hand on his. "Maybe...maybe you could talk to Bergener, negotiate. The man has a stake in seeing you ranchers succeed, not fail."

"I tell you, Emily, the man won't talk. He's holed up in his bank, and no one can reach him without getting shot. It's past talking now."

"It can't be. There must be something we can do."

"Didn't they teach you what to do in that fancy school of yours?" he asked dryly.

"They taught us to negotiate," she said slowly.

"Well, I'm real afraid the only negotiating around here's gonna be done with a gun."

When it came, Will thought later, he wasn't really surprised. It was a warm, pretty day of full-on summer with a blue sky and fleecy clouds when Tell Lister rode by with the news. "They're rounding up five hundred of McCrudden's cattle," he said, "and shipping 'em off."

"I'll be there," Will said grimly.

He strode inside and went straight to the desk, opened a drawer and pulled out his gun and holster.

"What are you doing?" Emily asked.

"Going to McCrudden's place. Those gunmen of Bergener's are taking his cattle," he said shortly.

"Will...? A gun? I've never seen you with a gun," she said, her eyes wide.

"Haven't needed one for years. Now I do."

"What...what are you going to do?" she asked, shaken.

"Defend McCrudden."

"Will. Oh, God, will there be shooting? Oh, you can't do this...it doesn't solve any problems. Not like *this*, Will!"

"Let it be, Emily. A man does what he has to do."

He checked the cylinder, spinning it, then took a handful of bullets from a box in the drawer and loaded the chambers, one by one. He was aware of Emily watching him anxiously as he strapped on the holster, put the six-shooter in place then drew it out a couple of times, the leather stiff and protesting after years of no use. "Needs saddle soaping," he said to himself, trying his draw once again.

"I don't believe this," Emily was saying, horrified. She put a hand on his arm, stopping him. "Don't go," she said. "What if...if..."

But Will shrugged her hand off. "I'll see you later. Take care of the young ones," he said gruffly.

"Will, oh my God..."

"I best be going now, Emily."

The ranchers were drawn up in front of Mc-Crudden's, a band of angry, frightened men, each one with a six-gun strapped around his waist and a rifle sheathed on the saddle.

"They're out on my west section," McCrudden said, "and they gotta pass by here to get back into town."

"I say we ride out and shoot every blamed man jack of 'em," said someone in a hard voice.

"Teach Bergener to mess with us."

"Wait till tonight and get 'em."

"Hold it, men," Will said. "Let's be sensible about this. If Bergener has a legal right, if there's papers says he can take the cattle, then we can't stop him. He'll just get the sheriff from Glenwood on us."

"Papers be damned!" Martinson yelled.

"I can't let him take my herd," McCrudden said. "Hell, I offered him two hundred in gold. What's the man want, blood?"

In the distance they could see the cloud of dust raised by the herd that was being driven closer to them; they could hear the lowing of cattle and the soft thud of thousands of split hooves. It silenced them for a minute, made them take stock of the situation, but just for a moment.

"Ambush 'em," Dashel George growled.

"No, we talk first," Will said.

"What is it with you, Dutcher? You gettin' soft?" Thad Wooderson sneered.

Will ignored him.

The gunman riding point came over to them, cantering slowly. "Howdy," he said. "Mind clearing the path, men? We're bringing the herd through here in a short while."

"I wouldn't be so sure of that," Ollie McCrudden said darkly.

"Now, hang on there, Ollie," Will said, then he turned to the point man. "Do you have a legal right to these cattle, mister?"

"Bergener's got a court order," the gunslinger said, his dark eyes darting from man to man, weighing the possibilities.

"Can I see it?" Will asked.

"Don't have it. Bergener kept it. But this here drive is legal, and I'm bringin' the herd through."

"I tell you what," Will said, trying to defuse the tension. "Let's wait until Mr. McCrudden here can see the court order. As it is, we only got your word for it."

"You doubtin' my word?" the gunman asked coolly.

"No, this isn't your land, though, and I think it'd be a sight better if we all saw those papers. Why don't you send someone into town for them, and we'll all wait here."

"My orders are to take five hundred head to the stockyards, and that's what I aim to do," the man said. "I wouldn't try to stop me, were I you."

"Says who?" Ollie said, his horse dancing under him.

"Says me," the man replied coldly. "Now, if you gentlemen will excuse me." The man turned his horse and loped back toward the slowly moving herd.

"I ain't gonna let him do this," McCrudden growled. "You men with me? You're next, you know."

There were cries of "Yes, you bet, let's go!" There were mutters, curses, and the nervous sidling of a dozen horses. The tension could have been cut with a knife.

Will wished he knew the truth of the matter. If Bergener had a court order... But the man could be lying—and then the ranchers had to defend McCrudden's herd to the death. And the gunman's manner wasn't conducive to neighborly feelings. Besides, Will couldn't sit there on his duff and think about it, because the other men were already moving toward the herd, their faces set.

The herd moved ponderously, relentlessly. Gunmen with bandannas tied over their faces ranged along the sides of the cattle. McCrudden kicked his horse into a gallop, pulled his gun from its holster and waved it in the air, shouting something Will couldn't hear. Then it struck Will. Sure, Ollie was going to stampede the cattle, send them all over kingdom come. *Not bad, McCrudden,* he thought, kicking his own horse

into a gallop. That'd sure stop things long enough to
see if this really was legal.

More shots. The other men were following Ollie,
firing, galloping straight at the cattle. There was a
slowing of the momentum of the herd, a milling of the
lead animals, the plaintive lowing of frightened cattle. Yes, it would work.…

In the tumult, amid the noise and dust and gun-
shots, Will wasn't sure who took aim at Ollie Mc-
Crudden and pulled the trigger. One second
McCrudden was racing, shooting his Colt, yelling his
head off, the next he was slumping, sliding from his
saddle, a red stain on his shirt.

The tableau was frozen for a split second, all the
ranchers paralyzed with shock, fury, horror. *Shot, a
man had been shot in cold-blooded deliberation!*
Their resolve bled away, and they pulled up around the
still form on the ground, muttering.

Will galloped up and pulled his horse to a sliding
halt, jumped off and knelt next to Ollie. He felt for a
pulse, found one, saw the bullet hole in the man's
shoulder.

"Thank the Lord, he's alive! Someone help me
here. Tell, go get Ollie's buckboard. Someone get his
horse. We better get him to Doc's pretty quick," he
said.

Reba McCrudden insisted on going into Rifle with
her husband. The ranchers accompanied the buckboard, a parade devoid of gaiety, an honor guard of
sorts, and Will Dutcher drove McCrudden's team.

They waited in the saloon for word of Mc-
Crudden's condition all afternoon, quiet, thoughtful,
furious, self-righteous by turns.

And not one of them gave a thought to Mc-Crudden's five hundred head that were still making their slow and ponderous way toward the stockyards. No one did—not until the herd passed straight down the main street of Rifle, right past the saloon, kicking up a choking cloud of dust, filling the air with the noise and smell of their passage.

The ranchers sat in the saloon, helpless, useless, and glowered down into their shot glasses of whiskey the whole, endlessly long hour it took McCrudden's cattle to make their last journey.

WILL FOUND that he was getting into the habit of relating to Emily everything that happened. He always told himself he wasn't going to, but she wormed it out of him anyway—or was it just getting easier for him to let it all out?

This time, however, she'd already heard.

"The children told me. They heard in school. How bad is Ollie McCrudden, Will?" she asked, her face pinched and white.

"He'll live. Gonna be laid up for some time, though."

"He did a foolish thing."

"Could be. Also, could be he did what he had to do to live with himself. You ever consider that, Emily?"

She looked at him with those beautiful blue eyes for a long time. "No, no... I guess I didn't look at it that way," she finally said. "But I suppose... if someone came to take the children, I'd...I'd have to do a thing like that. I'd have to do something."

He nodded, weary beyond belief. "The trouble is," he said, "there really was a court order. We all saw it afterward when we were in the saloon."

"So Ollie *was* in the wrong," she said. "Still, shooting him . . . What did the sheriff say?"

"Sheriff's up in Glenwood," he told her, "not about to make the trip when no one's been killed and taking the cattle was legal."

"I see," Emily said, and Will felt suddenly old and tired in the aftermath of today's violence.

"I've kept dinner warm for you. Please eat something, Will. Would you like a bath?"

He ate—a little—and smoked a pipe while Emily filled the bathtub for him. The children were in bed and Antonio was cleaning up the kitchen, mumbling to himself. Will looked around at his peaceful, comfortable house and wondered if it could all be taken from him on Bob Bergener's whim. He'd promised his brother Jesse he'd take care of the children. Was this what he'd promised, that the three innocent children would lose their inheritance, be thrown out of their home as paupers? God forbid.

If a man couldn't take care of his family, if he couldn't hold on to the land that he'd carved out of wilderness, well then, he wasn't much of a man.

"It's ready," Emily said, disturbing his reverie.

The hot water was soothing, and Will tried to relax, to forget. And after a short time, Emily slipped into the bathroom, one of those odd, forward things she did and thought nothing of.

"Antonio's gone to bed," she said. "So I . . ."

"Emily, it's not decent."

"Will, it's not as if I haven't seen you naked. For goodness' sakes, don't be a prude."

She sat on the edge of the tub and soaped his hair then rinsed it off. "Did your mother's father keep his hair when he got older?" she asked.

"What?"

"Well, if your maternal grandfather was bald, you might be, too."

"Now, how in blazes do you know that?"

"It's some kind of genetic law." She soaped his shoulders and back, her hands slipping across him sensuously. "Well, was he bald?"

"Good Lord, woman, how should I know?" The water slid like silk across his skin. "He died in Scotland before he came over here."

"Did you ever see any pictures of him?"

"They had no cameras and such then, Emily. It was too long ago," he said lazily, leaning back, his eyes closed.

"Oh, right, I knew that," she said hastily.

"Sometimes, Emily, you're daft."

"It's just that you have such nice hair. I'd hate to see you lose it." She ran her fingers through his wet hair, snagging them on a tangle. "And a nice neck." She ran her fingers down his throat to his collarbone.

"You starting something you can't finish?" Will asked, taking her hand and pulling her down toward him.

"Will, my dress'll get wet."

"Damn your dress, woman."

THE TOWN AND ALL the surrounding ranches lived in a fever of expectation from day to day. May moved into June, the land greened then dried to brown under the hot Colorado sun, and still Bergener's gunmen guarded the bank. Rumor had it that Lonnagan was next on the banker's list. Either he paid up or his cattle got collected and sold off. The town held its breath, waited, wondered and gossiped endlessly. All the ranchers in Garfield County took to wearing their guns every day, Will included. And all over the country, that late spring of '93, businesses went broke, banks failed and people lost their homes. The silver-mining towns emptied out, and in Colorado, only Cripple Creek, a gold-mining boomtown, held on to its prosperity.

"Hard luck," the ranch hands said, worrying about their jobs. "Hard times," the merchants said, unable to withdraw money from the bank to restock shelves.

"They're calling it the Silver Panic of 1893," Will said, tapping the paper with a finger. "Already got a name."

"Um," Emily said, biting her tongue as she darned a sock. She cut a thread, put the sock down and looked straight at him. "Can I go into town tomorrow, Will? You've kept me a virtual prisoner out here for days. I've got cabin fever."

Slowly he knocked his pipe ashes out. "Emily..."

"I know. It's dangerous. You've told me. But I'm going to go crazy soon if I don't get into town."

"Something's going to happen sooner or later, and I'd sure hate for you to be in the middle of it," he said.

"I'd just like to go by the Mercantile. There're a few things I need. It wouldn't take long. I won't go near the bank, I promise. And, Will, you'll be right there with me. What can happen?"

"Those gunmen are all over town. Emily, they accosted the Zimmerman girl the other day. Insulted her. Right in public. It almost started a war right there and then, but Hank Henderson calmed Zimmerman down, and the stranger backed off."

"Disgusting," Emily said.

"You could call it that. And I don't want anyone in my family to be the start of anything. 'Specially since I've been talking peace and negotiation." He shook his head, considering. "Better you stay here, out of harm's way."

But she kept it up, wheedling and hinting for two more days, until Will gave in. Emily got all dressed up for the trip: her gray Denver suit and blouse and the hat with ostrich feathers. "I want to give those old biddies something to talk about besides those gunmen," she said, pulling on her gloves.

Emily. Headstrong, stubborn, strange in so many ways. Tough as old leather one minute, melting in his arms the next. A beautiful bundle of contradictions. But not the marrying kind. Or so she said.

Will drove into town, aware of Emily beside him, so pretty, so proud, so goldarn classy. He wanted to pull her close right there under the noonday sun and kiss her lips until they were bruised and pouty looking. Damn woman was in his blood, like a sickness.

Rifle was ominously still that hot June day. The dust barely had the energy to rise from the streets, and everyone was inside or lurking in the shade. Everyone except the gunmen who stood sentinel, rifles over shoulders, in front of Bergener's bank.

"Jerks," Emily hissed, glaring down the street at them.

"Now, you stay clear, Em. I don't want any trouble," Will warned.

"I promise. But they're jerks," she repeated.

"They're men just doing a job, Em."

"Some job!"

He drove down the street toward the train station. "I'm going to pick up the feed at the depot first," he told her, "then we'll go back up to the Mercantile."

"Can't you drop me off?"

"I'd rather you stay with me."

"How chauvinistic of you, Will," she said dryly.

Funny how Emily used such big, odd words. But he always knew exactly what she meant by her tone, and this was one he didn't like. He looked sideways at her, but she seemed to accept his decision, so he let it drop.

He was loading the bags of feed onto the wagon when Jackson Rusk came out to pass the time of day.

"Bad times, Will," Jack said.

"It'll improve," Will replied.

"Hope you're right."

He noticed Emily climbing down from the buckboard. "'Scuse me, Jack," Will said. "Em! What're you doing?"

She called over to him. "Will, I'm going to run up the street to the store. You're busy. Pick me up there, okay? Good day, Mr. Rusk."

"Hold on there, I'll only be a minute."

She smiled sweetly at him. "I don't want to hurry you. I'll just go on up the street."

"Emily!"

"Bye, Mr. Rusk, it was nice seeing you," she said, then she turned and walked with her usual long stride toward the Mercantile store.

He should have stopped her, he would think later. He should have run after her, grabbed her and put her across his knee. But it was hot, and he was embarrassed in front of Jack Rusk, and it just didn't seem worthwhile to kick up a fuss.

It took him all of five minutes to finish loading the feed. He had a strange feeling—something wasn't right. Em—she shouldn't have gone off alone like that, stubborn female. He hurried, barely knowing he was doing it. He was short with Jack Rusk, and he slapped the reins too hard on the horse's back. Damn woman.

He got as far as the saloon when he saw her. Sure as hell, one of the gunmen was there, right in front of her. He should have known!

He threw the reins over the brake and jumped down from the seat. There was no one else on the sunbaked street, not another soul. It was as if it were only he and Emily and the gunman left alive in the world. He ran. He could hear snatches of words as he got closer, the man's sinister grin, the tautness of Emily's stance.

Then the tableau cracked like a mirror broken into flashing shards. He saw Emily move, knee the man in the groin, heard a yell and saw the man's contorted face. Then Emily whirled and was running back toward Will.

"Will," she cried, scared, relieved.

But the man was cursing, pulling his gun, pointing it directly at Emily. Will reached out and grabbed her, swung her around behind him, pulling his own gun simultaneously. He was aware of Emily's panting, of the heat, the danger, the man's pearl-handled Colt pointed straight at him. There was no time to think,

only time to act. He fired. Behind him, Emily cried
out. The man staggered, dropped his gun and clutched
at his arm where a red stain showed. He sagged to his
knees.

And then everything slowed down again, back to
normal, and there was time to weigh, to realize what
had just happened.

"Come on, Emily," Will said harshly, "I think
you've done enough harm for one day."

She stood, horrified, her face pallid, a hand over her
mouth. "I'm sorry," she breathed. "Oh, Will, I..."

People came out into the street, one, then two, then
five, then a crowd. Faces appeared at windows, in
doorways, in alleys.

And the other gunmen had heard the shot—they
came running, a group of them, all in black, their eyes
blazing, their boots kicking up puffs of dust in the hot
street, their guns glinting dully in the sun's harsh glare.

"Come on," Will repeated, tugging at Emily's arm.

"Hold on there, pardner," the lead gunman called
out.

"Will..." Emily started.

"Let's go, Emily."

But it was too late by then—the phalanx of hired
guns was there, in front of him, blocking the path to
the wagon. He swung his gun up and pointed it at the
leader.

"Get your friend here and get out of my way," Will
said in a steely voice.

"Now, wait a minute..."

Will gestured with his gun. "Move. Me and the lady
are leaving."

Hard eyes looked back at him, measuring his resolve. They slid to Emily, gauging her, too.

"Now," Will said.

The leader stared back, cold obsidian to icy cobalt.
Muscles quivered, hands clenched whitely over gun
grips. The air was hot and metallic, tainted with violence. The sun stood stock-still overhead. The man in
black relented, moved in some imperceptible way that
signaled Will he'd won. Will took a step, the men
moved aside, reluctantly, but they moved.

Will kept his gun out, felt icy fingers of fear raise the
hair on his neck. He had to pull Emily, half drag her,
and she stumbled. Sweat trickled down his temple,
tickling. His eyes burned, his arm trembled with tension.

Then they were at the rig, the gunmen behind him,
the townsfolk silent and apprehensive, back farther.
No one said a word as he boosted Emily up to the seat
then swung up himself. He took the reins, stared
straight ahead, gun on the seat between him and Emily, and slapped the reins on the bays' backs, raising
dust.

The buckboard creaked and lurched forward, part-
ing the crowd. He kept the team to a walk through the
throng of familiar faces, but not a person acknowl-
edged him. No one tipped his hat or called a greeting
or smiled.

He knew why, too. Trouble had begun in Rifle: war
had been declared. And Will Dutcher had started it—
him and his foolhardy troublemaker of a housekeeper, Emily Jacoby.

CHAPTER FOURTEEN

IF THE SHOOTING IN TOWN had been a scene from hell, the ride home was purgatory. To her dying day Emily would never forget Will's face on that ride—coldly furious, frighteningly hard. She couldn't say a thing, either, because his rage was justified. Will knew it; Emily knew it. The incident lay between them, a chasm, an unamendable breach. She knew Will was never going to discuss it, and Emily also knew there was no way she could apologize. The damage was done. Because of her impatience, God knew what was going to erupt between the town and Bergener's men. Why had she been so impulsive? Will had asked her to wait for him at the depot. But no, Emily Jacoby, modern 1990s woman, could handle herself....

It was her fault. She couldn't be the demure, simple woman Will needed in his life. She couldn't stay. She'd known that for many weeks now. But how was she going to leave? If she couldn't find her way home, where would she go?

As talk of all-out war raged across the valley like a prairie fire, Emily went about her daily existence with that terrifying dilemma eating away at her. She had to leave Will, yet she couldn't muster the courage to go.

She tried to tell herself that she had to see Will's ranch safe before she left, but she was powerless to do anything to help him, it seemed. No one would listen to her, especially now, and even Will must have been wondering about her judgment. And all the time the terrible questions faced her: where to go, what to do? She couldn't stay and she couldn't go. And she was afraid that she'd cause another awful incident, put Will in danger, make another fatal error that would get them all in trouble. Even the children, the poor innocent kids would suffer because of her.

Worse was the silent treatment she was getting from Will. Oh, she didn't blame him if she thought about it objectively, but just when she needed him the most, just when she was scared and miserable and lost, he'd turned cold toward her. Cold and distant like he'd been at first.

He hated her. He couldn't wait to get rid of her. She'd caused nothing but trouble. She knew that's what Will was thinking.

When the subject of the annual June rodeo and picnic came up, she told him she wasn't going. Hadn't she promised herself never to get into that situation again? And it was even worse since the shooting. She just couldn't face those people.

"I won't," she said. "I can't."

Will Dutcher fixed his dark blue gaze on her and settled his hat on his head. "You'll go, Emily, and that's that. No Dutcher ever backed down. Where's your pride, woman?"

"I'm not a Dutcher," she said. "I don't need your kind of pride."

"You live under my roof, and you'll go and put a good face on it or I'll drag you there," Will said.

"You wouldn't dare!"

"Don't count on it, Emily" was all he said before turning on his heel and heading out to work the range.

She fumed. For two days Emily fumed and swore she wasn't going to put herself through that nightmare again just because Will commanded it. But in the end she decided to go. Not because of Will. Not because it was 1893 and women did as they were told. She decided to go because of something he said one evening, something surprisingly astute for a Victorian man.

"If you don't go to the picnic, Emily, they'll have won. I can't see a strong female like you givin' in so easy." He shook his head and strode on out of the kitchen.

He was absolutely right.

So Emily prepared for the town gathering. She and Antonio—who actually bathed for it—baked two pies and made a large pot of beans, Mexican style, that flamed with Antonio's special chili peppers. The boys got their hair trimmed and their ears scrubbed and donned their best shirts and short trousers. Emily suspected they'd be filthy five minutes after they got to the picnic, but she'd be darned if she was going to arrive with ragamuffins at her side—wouldn't the ladies just love *that* ammunition?

They left for the affair before noon. It was Saturday, the first weekend in June, and the day was idyllic, cloudless, the Colorado sky a deep flawless blue. The striated mesas were brilliantly delineated against that sky, their red and gold and ocher hues seeming to shimmer in the air, and beyond in the high country, snow still glistened on the craggy peaks.

A perfect day. And for the children's sakes Emily tried to act cheerful. They'd been so looking forward to this outing. Inside, she was taut as a stretched wire. She could face down the Rifle matriarchs if she had to, but it wasn't going to be pleasant.

"Am not! I am *not* a baby!" Burke was yelling at Jesse in the back.

"That's enough of that," Emily roused herself to say. Oh, God, who was going to raise these children, she wondered once again. Who would love them and help them grow up? Could Will manage it alone?

She glanced over at him where he sat holding the reins, his hat pulled low against the sun, his profile strong and handsome. A wave of sadness swept her—Will would probably be much better off without her. He needed a woman of his own time, perhaps another housekeeper, maybe a local widow or someone young and innocent and very pretty. Will deserved that. But it made Emily want to cry at the injustice. What cruel hand of fate or vindictive god had sent her into this past to survive and then demand she leave— leave the first man, the only man, damn it, she'd ever loved?

The Rifle fairgrounds were already crowded by the time the Dutchers arrived. Emily and Antonio unloaded his pot of chili beans and carried the pies to the log trestles set up near the barbecue pits. Children raced and yelled and women tittered and clucked tongues. The men spread out, some heading toward the rodeo arena to place their bets early, others organizing the baseball tournament. It was only noon, but already dust rose around the fairgrounds, and the hot sun caused brows to bead in sweat.

Emily looked for Will. He was nowhere to be seen. She wandered around aimlessly, eyeing some of the homemade goods on sale at a row of tables set beneath a cottonwood tree. Quilts, canned jellies and jams, pies, sunbonnets and tablecloths, lace doilies and hand-stitched pillowcases. Mostly there were women picking over the items, exclaiming with oohs and aahs, asking prices, tasting sample jams with plump fingers.

Emily wandered, ignored, through the tables, but she could feel the eyes of the women boring holes in her gingham dress. God, how she wanted to hate them! Yet Emily knew it was she who was at fault— she didn't belong.

She found Mary with a group of her classmates showing off their dolls and dresses. "Hello, button," Emily said, kneeling down with the group, "have you seen your Uncle Will?"

"He's at the rodeo," Mary said. "Wants to watch Jeb Akers get his hind rear busted."

"Mary," Emily began.

"That's what Uncle Will said, honest, Miss Emily."

"Well, okay." Emily rose. "I'm going to join him, honey," she said, "but maybe we can all eat lunch together in a little while. Okay?"

"Okay." Mary went back to her friends.

Emily wandered off again, a pariah. No one really needed her, she decided, feeling sorry for herself. Oh, she'd find Will and hang out nearby, but she'd probably make him mad.

A pack of dogs came streaming by as she walked toward the arena, nearly tripping her in her long skirt, and she swore aloud at them, not caring anymore who saw or heard. This was not her world. It never would be. Why, Emily wondered for the umpteenth time, why had she been thrust into it?

She found Will with a group of his peers watching a cowboy being bucked off a nasty brown bull, the young man's hat flying, trampled in the dust by the snorting beast.

"Damn!" yelled a man. "Russ didn't make it ten seconds!"

"You owe me a buck, Phelps," laughed another.

Emily saw someone hand Will a silver dollar, grudgingly. "Hello," she said, "I thought I'd see if you want some lunch."

Will looked a little embarrassed. Obviously Emily was the only woman in the crowd. She noticed one of the men quickly hiding a silver flask in his pocket. "Maybe later," Will said. "That suit you?"

"Sure," she said, "fine. I'll just go... ah... check on the children."

"You do that," Will said, and she thought she detected a note of relief in his voice. Then, as she was turning to go, Will put a hand on her arm. "Bergener's here," he said, nodding to a spot in the bleachers across the arena. "He's got a few of his men along with him. Stay clear, will you?"

"Of course I will," Emily retorted, smarting at how dumb he thought she was.

"All right," he said, and she felt his eyes follow her as she threaded her way through the crowd.

For a time Emily watched the first baseball game, ranchers versus farmers, and she marveled how nothing had changed in a hundred years—not with baseball, anyway. The second baseman yelled at the umpire and kicked dirt on the man's shoes; the pitcher spit in his mitt, and almost to a man they all let loose on the diamond with streams of tobacco juice. She smiled to herself when the batter stepped up to the plate and "adjusted" himself before setting his stance in the dirt. The few women sitting in shaded benches looked at their feet.

She found Burke with a group of boys his age challenging Jesse's peers to a game of Capture the Flag down near the river, and Mary was still sitting in the shade not too far away with her own friends. Emily stopped and checked with each of them, telling them not to wander off too far because their Uncle Will was going to join them for lunch soon.

"Okay, Miss Emily," the boys said then raced off.

At last, Mary joined her, bored with her dolls. "Let's go to the river and look at the fish," Mary said, taking Emily's hand, dragging her doll with the other.

"You can see fish in the river?"

"Oh, yes, Miss Emily, lots of them. I know just where, too."

So they strolled through a meadow of tall grass lined by cottonwoods and aspens until they reached the banks of Rifle Creek. Mary's braids gleamed in the sun, and freckles stood out on her upturned nose and shiny cheeks as she settled herself down on the soft bank. Emily sat, too, retying the red ribbons on Mary's braids, dusting off the child's doll.

"Are you enjoying the picnic?" Emily asked.

"Oh, yes." Then the girl frowned a little. "But last year Mama and Papa were here, too. Do you think they're in heaven, Miss Emily?"

"I'm sure they are, sweetie. Do you miss them terribly?"

Mary nodded. "Uncle Will's nice, but he's not as much fun."

"He's learning," Emily said. "He's used to being a bachelor, honey, and it takes time for some men."

"Do you have children, Miss Emily?"

Emily laughed. "Not yet, button. Someday, maybe."

"With . . . Uncle Will?" the girl ventured.

Emily sighed. "Probably not. We're . . . not married, you see."

"You won't ever get married?"

"Well..." Then Emily decided. "Listen, Mary," she said, staring into the slow, rolling water, "I may not always be here with you. I...there's some place I have to go to."

"Where?" Mary frowned.

"Well, my own home. You see...never mind," she said, "I just thought you should know that someday I'll have to go."

"Will we ever see each other again?" Mary asked, her eyes wide.

Emily thought. "Well, maybe. I mean, I kind of think that somehow we will. I know that's silly, but I can't imagine never seeing you again."

"Why is it silly?"

"It's...ah...you'll just have to trust me on that one, sweetie."

"Oh," Mary said, pointing now, "there's a fish!"

"Where? Oh, I see it. A trout. Amazing. If we had a pole I swear I'd—"

"Well, well," came a voice from behind, startling them. "If it ain't the little lady."

Emily was on her feet in a flash, her blood pounding. It was him, the gunman Will had shot!

"Get out of here," Emily said, smelling the alcohol on him, looking around quickly for help. "You have no right..."

"I got all the rights I need, lady," he said, taking a step toward them. "Now, why don't you just send the little brat off, and you and me can make up real nice."

Emily slowly pushed Mary behind her and glared at the man. "Get out of here," she hissed. "You're drunk."

His countenance darkened. A big man, Will's size or better, though a few years older, he was obviously not to be trifled with. He took another step forward and reached out toward her.

Suddenly Emily reacted. "Run, Mary," she whispered harshly, fervently, shoving the child away. *"Run!"* And then she blocked the man's path. "Don't you dare lay a finger on me," she warned, her cheeks flaming as she saw from the corner of her eye Mary darting away, back toward the fairgrounds.

The man, too, half followed the little girl's flight but his attention was still on Emily. "I think you owe me, lady," he was saying, and abruptly he snatched her arm and yanked her toward him.

Emily lashed out. With both hands, she reached for his face and raked her nails across a cheek before he could twist her arm painfully, forcing her to her knees.

"Hellcat, ain't ya?" he said, grinning, blood welling from the marks she'd made. "But I think I'm gonna tame ya, lady, I think you'll soon be begging me to—"

"Go to hell!" Emily spit out. "I'd rather die first!" and she twisted free, stumbling, trying to scramble away, but he was too quick, grabbing her around her waist with his good arm, half lifting her.

Emily fought. She got in a painful punch to his wounded shoulder that made him yell. Still, he was winning, pulling her against his chest, his mouth searching for hers while she frantically twisted her head.

Suddenly she was free. She stumbled backward, breathless and confused, her blood pounding furiously. And the man . . . it was as if he'd been lifted straight off his feet.

It was Will. His fist bloodied, he was pushing Emily aside, moving swiftly toward the man again, his face contorted in rage. The next thing Emily knew, Will had reached down and drawn the gunslinger's pistol from its holster and was flinging it into the river. The man made a scurrying move on his knees toward the gun, but it was gone in a white splash.

"You son of a . . ." the man swore, holding his jaw.

But Will was ignoring him. He turned to Emily. "You all right?"

"I'm . . . fine."

"Then get the children. We're going home."

"Will . . . I . . ." she began.

"Get the children, Emily," he stormed, and turned back to the man.

IT WAS THE WORST AFTERNOON of Emily's entire life. It wasn't just Will's anger. It wasn't the children's disappointment—there would be other picnics. It was her. She simply could not function in this role into which she'd been so insanely thrown. If it had been any other woman in Rifle, Emily realized, the confrontation with that hired gunman would not have occurred. It was *her*.

Marry him? she thought, lying on her bed as dusk fell over the valley, what a joke! He knew she was different, he'd said so dozens of times, so why then didn't he realize just how different? Why didn't *he* send her away?

Emily wept. It wasn't Will's way to turn her out. If she left it up to him he'd storm at her and hate her and meet her sadness with stony silence. But another part of Will would love her and cherish her and keep her prisoner forever.

So I'll go, Emily told herself. She'd go and leave Will and the children and try to find her way home. But first . . . first she'd do everything in her power to save Will's land for him. Maybe that was why she'd been sent to Rifle, Emily thought, maybe she'd been sent, not as a test of her own survival but, as some sort of a guide. She'd been sent because she was a banker, she knew her history. . . .

Emily sat up, and pushed the loose strands of her hair behind her ears. Okay, she thought, she'd hurt Will enough. Now it was time to help him.

Purposefully Emily walked down the stairs and through the silent house. The children were in bed; Antonio hadn't returned from the picnic. But Will was there all right, sitting alone on the dark porch. Through her open bedroom window she'd heard his rocker creaking back and forth for the past hour. He was there, brooding alone in the night.

She opened the door quietly and stood before him. "Can I . . . join you?" Emily said softly.

"Suit yourself." He stopped rocking, and all Emily could see was his strong profile and the half glow from the embers in his pipe.

She sat on the steps, facing the moonless sky and rangeland, her skirts spread beneath her. There was so much she wanted to explain to Will—if he could be made to believe where she'd really come from, then he'd understand. But Will wouldn't believe her. No one would. Still, if she could just make him listen about the town's banking troubles, if she could tie him down somehow and make him listen to reason . . .

"Will?" Carefully.

"Um."

"You know I never encouraged that today."

"Of course I know that."

"But you're angry . . . at me."

"I'm angry. Yes. But not at you."

"You're lying."

The rocker creaked under him.

"You know I don't . . . fit, don't you?"

"I don't know who you are, Emily," he said in that husky voice.

"I guess you don't," she breathed. "But you *do* believe I'm knowledgeable about some things, don't you?"

"Some things. Maybe."

"About banking? Finances?"

"Maybe."

"Then will you listen to me, really *listen,* for a minute?"

"Emily..."

"Please, Will. I can help you save the ranch. I really can."

He made a doubtful grunt.

Emily ignored him. "You have to call a meeting," she said, "and you've got to convince the men to negotiate with Bergener. It won't be easy, I know..."

"That's for sure."

"Don't be a defeatist," she said, still staring across the land, Will's land. "It can be done. If the men promise to leave their money in Bergener's bank, then I'll bet he can be persuaded to hold off calling in his loans. It'll be tight for a time, Will, really tight. But no one will lose. If things go on the way they are, everyone's going to suffer."

Will laughed without humor. "Is that another one of those things they taught you in your fancy school back East?"

"Yes. As a matter of fact, they did."

"Um."

For a long time they sat in silence, the quiet broken only occasionally by the distant howl of a coyote and a growl from Shep. Emily hugged her knees in the stillness and wondered if Will had heard a word she'd said.

"They'll never listen to me," he said after a while. "Why should they?"

"Because," Emily said, her heart quickening. "Because you're a strong man, Will Dutcher, and you're smart."

"Am I now?"

"Yes, you are. They'll listen," she said ardently, feeling his eyes on her back. "They'll listen because you'll be a voice of reason in a sea of chaos."

"You sound pretty dang sure of that."

"I am." Slowly Emily turned to find him in the darkness. "Will you try this? Will you?"

"Maybe," he said, and the chair groaned as he leaned forward and tentatively, uncertain, his fingers touched the back of her neck.

CHAPTER FIFTEEN

WILL CURSED Emily many a time over the next few days as he rode his sorrel mare under a blistering sun trying to persuade the ranchers to meet and negotiate with Bergener. But he found he had a surprising knack for convincing men, even the most obdurate ones who wanted to lynch Bergener. They listened to him.

The only time he ran into trouble was when a couple of the men snidely brought up the subject of his housekeeper. Then and only then did he lose his temper. "Mind your own business," he told them, glaring, his hat settled low on his head. They shut their mouths.

He rode under the hot sun and talked himself dry. He got the stubborn, scared, angry ranchers to promise to meet once more at the schoolhouse. And he wished to hell he was as sure this plan would work as Emily was.

"So it's tomorrow night?" Emily asked, serving him a pile of mashed potatoes.

"Tomorrow night," he grumbled. "Tomorrow I'm gonna be the laughingstock of the whole town. I can see it now, standing up in front of those bloodthirsty boys and tellin' them to lay down their weapons."

"You're going to *tell* them not to make a run on the bank, Will, and then you can approach Bergener and negotiate with him. He'll listen. What choice does he have?"

"Plenty," Will growled. "He can keep sending his gunslingers out to the ranches, for one."

Emily cocked her head. "He's a reasonable man, Will. He'll see the light. You just have to keep your head."

"Easy to say."

A short while later, Emily turned from hard-nosed banker and nag into a soft, languorous woman who leaned over him where he sat on the porch, brushed his hair with her lips and whispered that they could make love again—it was all right.

Oh God, his loins tightened and goose bumps rose on his skin. A tremor of expectancy went through Will, unwanted, unplanned, but as uncontrollable as the changing of seasons.

Emily.

He sat on the porch and watched the hot red sun sink behind the cliffs and waited, his heart pounding with the sweet, aching delay of fulfillment.

"Will," came her voice through the growing darkness, "do you...do you really hate it when I talk men's stuff to you? Tell me the truth."

He made a snorting sound.

"The truth," she said.

"No," he got out, moving restively in his chair, "I don't hate it, Em."

Later, she stood in the center of his bedroom in her nightgown, and she smiled when Will closed the door behind him. But when he went to turn down the lamp, Emily said no and shook her head, her golden hair falling softly to her shoulders.

"Leave it on?" he asked.

"Yes," she whispered, "I want to see you, Will, see us together."

"Well, I'll be..."

It was an experience wholly unique to Will, undressing in the light. But he was barely paying any mind to his own nakedness; rather, he couldn't tear his gaze from Emily as she stood there and let the white cotton gown slip slowly and enticingly off her creamy shoulders. First one breast seemed to burst free and then the other, rosy and pert. His hands formed fists at his sides, trying to bide their time. Then Emily's nightgown slipped lower, exposing the soft swell of her belly and hips. Lower still, until she was gloriously naked before him, the coppery triangle below her belly exposed, her round thighs...

Will stepped slowly to her until their chests touched and his lips found hers. Then, before he could stop himself, he was crushing her to him, lifting her toward the bed, breasts pressed to hard chest, belly to belly, his manhood stiff and pulsing where it met the soft curls below her abdomen.

Lying next to him now, Emily opened like a flower to the blaze of his perusal. He couldn't help himself. He took in every inch of her with a hunger and desire he'd never known. His body ached, painfully, pleasurably, as he touched her nipples with his fingers in wonder, watching them rise while Emily moaned softly. Breasts, belly, hips, thighs, Will stroked and teased until his fingers sought the warmth between her legs.

Emily gasped, her head lolling back, her fingers twisting in the sheets beside her as Will's hand continued its journey. Warm, soft, clinging, damp, Emily's body accepted him and rose against his touch. His mouth sought her neck and collarbone, his tongue tracing a hot path down to her bosom. Gently he drew a peak against his teeth and tasted the honey salt of her flesh. She moaned, her body swollen with desire, pulsing against him, aching to his own needs.

"Oh, Will," she breathed, "oh, quickly..."

He mounted her, and Emily rose up to meet his urgent thrust, her legs wrapping around his hips, accepting all he could give her. She cried out, arching her back, straining, and he watched her face as she bit her lip and twisted her head, and he withdrew himself and then plunged again.

"Oh, Will," she was saying, over and over, and he held her back as long as he could, moving slowly, taunting her, making her draw her nails across his back until he knew they were both at the brink, heat to heat, their bodies reaching a crescendo, arching, twisting, plunging.

Once more that night Will made love to his woman. It seemed he could never get enough of Emily Jacoby. She *was* different. Innocent yet coy, naive yet knowledgeable. She was a bundle of so many contradictions it was hard for him to imagine another like her. And again, as they lay together in the warm aftermath of their love, Will wondered if she hadn't just sprung naked from the earth and landed on that train for him to find. It was a ridiculous notion, but whenever it crossed Will's thoughts it gave him pause.

"Who are you, Emily?" he whispered against the softness of her hair.

But she moved, cuddling against him and drifted off to sleep in his arms, and Will knew—without knowing how he knew—that this remarkable creature was only lent to him to succor and comfort and instruct him in the way of love, and when she had finished, she'd be gone.

"YOU MEN GONNA COME to order?" Will's words boomed over the raised voices of the crowd in the schoolhouse.

"Where's Ollie McCrudden?" called one of the businessmen.

"He ain't gonna be up and about for weeks!" shouted another.

"Order!" Will demanded, frowning, frustrated. Damn that Emily and her wild notions. "Order, men! This'll just take a minute!"

An hour was much more like it. But slowly, grudgingly, a few of the cooler heads began to see the reason in Will's proposal.

Will let out a long breath and banged the gavel on the podium. "Come on, fellas," he said, tiring, "who here really wants a war? I say we give my plan a try. Either Bob goes for the deal or he doesn't. We haven't got a thing to lose." He looked around at the faces. "Hell," he said, "you want to see your boys shooting it out with those gunman? Or how about you, Fisher? How old are your sons? They'll want to fight, too. I say we try to deal with Bergener like sane men. Let's see some hands."

"You gonna talk to Bob yourself there, Will?" came a voice.

"I plan on it. Now let's see some hands, men, all those in favor of me approaching—"

But the hands never had a chance to be raised. Suddenly the door to the meeting hall burst open and all twelve of Bergener's hired men piled in, six-shooters raised.

"Jesus," Will said, his own hand, like everyone else's, going for his sidearm.

For a full minute the room pulsed with silence, the tension flying in the air like venomous projectiles. The townsfolk and ranchers were on one side, the gunmen on the other, both camps frozen, waiting, the ranchers' hands hovering over their guns, the hired men with black hats pulled low over their brows, fingers twitching at their triggers.

Then Will saw him move, the man he'd shot in the arm, the same one who'd accosted Emily last Saturday at the picnic.

"Dutcher," the gunman said, breaking the palpable silence, "Will Dutcher! You're first, mister. You and me got some unfinished business." He took another step forward and the crowd shifted fluidly, like water, blocking him.

Will met the man's determined eyes. "You want me?" he said. "Then I'm yours. I got no problem with that. But not in here."

"No!" someone shouted abruptly. "Don't do it, Will!"

But Will wasn't listening. If he had to face this killer, there was no point in dragging the rest of the men into it with him. They'd take their trouble outside, where no one was likely to get caught in the path of a bullet.

A flash of surprise and regret brushed Will, but it was a distant, removed thought that flared only for a moment: he was too old to be pulling a stunt like this, he had responsibilities. How had things come to this pass, how had he got himself into this damned ridiculous situation?

Emily, a small voice whispered back to him. *Emily.*

He squared his shoulders, settled his hat firmly on his head, took a deep breath and stepped down off the platform. "Let's go," he said in that deep, rough voice. "Let's get it done with."

Everyone followed the two men, shoving, crowding one another to get a frontline view of the showdown. If Will hadn't been so pumped up, he might have laughed. As it was, all he could think about was survival. He hadn't practiced with his pistol for years; he sure as heck wished he'd kept up. Still, he hadn't been bad, pretty darn quick, in fact, at one time. Maybe...

Will positioned himself with the setting sun to his back. Not a big advantage, but something in his favor. The crowed gathered, a wide respectful circle around the two men who stood ten paces apart, stockstill now, eyes locked. Will noticed the man grin. But then he saw something else, something that gave him pause. The gunman's shooting arm was wounded. His sling was off, but still, it put him at a hell of a disadvantage. *Stupid,* Will thought, *the stupid...*

Will knew suddenly. This was about the man's pride. Will, twice now, had humiliated him, and most likely his comrades had been at him real good, at him to get even.

Think, Will commanded himself. He didn't know if he could take the man down, but whichever way it turned out, it still wasn't going to defuse the situation. It would only lead to more bloodshed. How to find an honorable way out for both of them?

Will sighed inwardly. Lord, but he hated to do this in front of half the town. "Listen," he said, letting his shoulders relax a little, staring into those steely eyes, "I'm a rancher, not a sharpshooter." *Lord Almighty.* "I don't want any more trouble, mister. In fact, I didn't exactly plan on dying today. Did you?"

The man eyed him warily.

Then some dang fool yelled out, "Take him down, Will! He's got a bad arm! Take him down!"

Will turned his head and gave the taunter a scathing look. "You want to spill some blood, come on out here and spill it. If not, shut up." He turned back to his opponent. "What do you say? I'm for getting Bergener on over here and settling our differences. They aren't your problems, mister. They're between us and Bergener. You're only getting paid to do a job."

For a long moment Will was sure the man was ready to go for his gun. Will's body tensed. He'd given him an out, for God's sakes, why wasn't he ... ? Then the man grinned again and shrugged. "You know, Dutcher," he said, "I figured ya for a coward, guess I was right."

Will smiled thinly, holding his temper in check. "You bet," he said slowly, keeping the man's gaze. "Now why don't we back on down and one of you boys go and collect Bergener?" Carefully Will turned away and began heading back toward the schoolhouse, and that was when he saw her, a small face in the crowd—Emily. He locked his jaw and headed into the building.

It took the man fifteen minutes to get there, but eventually Bob Bergener did come. He looked pinched and nervous, and his hired men stood sentinel at the door. Still, he listened as Will spoke from the podium again. He listened and nodded once or twice and then finally moved toward the platform himself.

"What do you say, Bob?" Will asked him. "Are you going to try to help resolve our troubles or are you going to let the whole town go to ruin, yourself included?"

Bergener came before the crowd, his back ramrod straight, his belly protruding beneath his brocaded vest. He cleared his throat twice. "I don't want trouble," he began, and a few jeers rose from the men. "I only brought help in because of all the runs on the banks clear across the country. You fellas know that."

"Why didn't ya come to us, Bob," someone yelled, "ask us to cooperate?"

"We're neighbors, Bergener, and you got Ollie shot!"

"Yeah! What about Ollie?"

"Settle down," Will said, still standing next to Bergener, "there's nothing we can do about Ollie right now. But we *can* prevent more bloodshed."

Bergener coughed into his fist. "Will here's right, boys. Like I said, I'm only protecting what's mine."

"How about it, Bob," Tell Lister called out, "you gonna open the bank?"

Bob looked tensely around the group. "You fellas going to make a run on my bank and close me for good?"

Silence hung in the air.

Finally Will spoke up. "I think we can all give our word that it'll be business as usual, Bob. But we gotta have a guarantee from you you'll ease up on calling in the loans."

Bergener looked at him, weighing Will's credibility. "I want to see a show of hands," he said. "I want to know that if I reopen tomorrow no one's going to come barging in demanding gold deposits."

"How about *your* word, Bob," Will said. "How about you promise to lighten up on calling in payments?"

"I . . . ah . . . I'll do that," he said at last. "Yes. I'll promise you folks to go easy if I get that show of hands." And then finally, after weeks and weeks of bitterness, a few hands came cautiously up.

Will glanced around. "Come on, men," he said, "give it a try. You got nothing to lose here. Let's see those hands." Slowly, after another few minutes, every hand in the room was raised.

Turning to Bob, Will said, "The bank'll be open in the morning, we assume?"

"In the morning," Bergener said, and stepped down off the platform.

"And get rid of them killers!" someone called out.

Bergener nodded nervously as he made his way through the crowd, the gunmen following him out the door into the night.

"Then that's it," Will said, holding the gavel in his hand. "We gave our word, men. Meeting adjourned." *Bang.*

For a time, some of the men gathered outside and talked over helping out Ollie McCrudden until their neighbor got back onto his feet. Will listened, approving, but he was searching for Emily. How in blazes had she gotten to town? The buckboard, most likely. And alone. Would she never learn?

The men slowly began to disperse, heading home, and Will saw her then, sitting in the wagon alongside the schoolhouse near where he'd tied his own horse. At least, he thought, no one else seemed to notice her. Heck, she was the only woman who'd ventured out that evening. It figured. But he guessed if he were being honest with himself, he couldn't really blame Emily for her impatience and curiosity. No. It had been her idea in the first place. In fact, Will decided as he strode up to her, Emily had all but saved the town. He just wished she hadn't seen that confrontation out in front. Will had backed down. Sure, on purpose. But he wished it hadn't come to that.

"Hello," she said.

"Hello, Emily. See you couldn't wait."

She shook her head and patted the seat next to her. "Can you tie your horse to the back and ride with me?" she asked.

"So you can ask a hundred fool questions?" Will stood looking up at her through the darkness, hands on his hips.

"Yes," she said, smiling, "so I can nag you."

He raised a hand and smoothed his mustache and finally nodded. "Guess I owe you," he said, "we all do," and he began to head toward his horse.

It was then that the wounded gunman rode up, kicking a cloud of dust into the night air. He tipped his hat to Emily, his horse sidling next to the buckboard, and then he addressed Will. "My arm ain't always gonna be stiff, Dutcher," he said, controlling his mount.

Will led his own horse toward the back of the buckboard and began tying her up. "Tell you what," Will said easily, "you name the time and the place and I'll be there."

The man eyed Will for a long moment then finally grinned and tipped his hat at Emily once more and rode off.

CHAPTER SIXTEEN

THINGS CALMED DOWN after that. Bergener's hired
guns left town quietly—they were there one day and
gone the next. The bank reopened, and people didn't
mob it to withdraw their funds. Money was tight,
loans were next to impossible to get, and a few ranchers would go under before 1893 was over.

But not Will Dutcher.

"You're *sure* you'll make enough from the cattle
this fall to pay Bergener?" Emily asked one June
night.

"For the love of God, Em, I told you already. Quit
your bellyaching," Will replied.

"Even if beef prices go down?" she pressed.

"I'll even have some cash to spare. Does that satisfy you?"

"Yes." Emily sighed. Will would be all right. Thank
God, she'd seen to that. Will Dutcher would keep his
ranch. She looked out over the darkening land that
stretched to the foot of the cliffs, saw the vague dark
humps of cattle grazing under a sliver of a moon and
realized that she loved this land, too. It was a harsh,
severe place, plagued with extremes of weather, but
there was always a stream cutting through it, coming
down from the mountains, for blessed relief. Fruit
trees flourished all over the Grand Valley. Grapes rip-

ened. Potatoes and strawberries and vegetables and wheat grew. Bees made honey.

People had to be tough. They had to endure physical and psychological danger—cold, hunger, brutally hard labor, boredom, loneliness—but they'd made it work.

Emily had endured it, too. She stared out over the Dutcher spread that night and hugged herself, smelling the dust and the sagebrush and Will's pipe smoke, feeling the hot, dry air on her skin as she rocked gently in a chair that pressed a loose board on the porch and squeaked with every pass.

Soon it will be time to leave, she thought. She didn't know how or why or when, but she knew, sensed it in some profound way. Soon, but not yet.

"Em?" His voice came negligently out of the hot, scented darkness.

"Um?"

"I never told you...I've never really said it." He cleared his throat. "You were right about the bank thing. I owe...we all owe you a big thank-you."

"Oh, Will..."

"I just wanted to set the record straight."

Oh, how she loved his voice, rough and low pitched, his words few and so much more precious for their sparseness. "It's all right, I..."

"They think it was my idea, Emily."

"That's all right," she murmured. "It doesn't matter."

"I...I'd like everyone to know that it was your doing, the whole thing," he said quietly.

She shook her head in the darkness. "No, Will. And if you think that would make them accept me any better, you're wrong. They'll still hate me, even more for meddling in men's business."

He was quiet for a time. "Maybe," he finally allowed.

"It's all right, Will. I don't care what they think."

They sat together for a time, wordlessly feeling each other's nearness, and she knew he was thinking about something. Quietly, at peace, she waited for him to speak. Somewhere a coyote howled, and Shep raised his head from his paws to peer into the darkness and growl.

"You'll be fixing to leave soon, won't you, Emily?" he finally asked.

Her heart caught, suffused with pain. She stopped rocking. "Will..."

"It's like I know it in my bones," he said.

Tears pressed against her eyelids but she blinked them back. "You'll be relieved," she said. "You won't have to listen to me nag you anymore, and..." Her voice broke and she swallowed. "And Violet Lindley can probably cook much better than I can, and she'll..."

"Violet Lindley can't hold a candle to you, Emily," he said harshly.

"She's crazy about you, Will."

"You're the one that's crazy, Em."

"No, no I'm not," she said sadly.

"When?" he asked after a pause. "How long?"

She hung her head. "I don't know," she whispered. "Soon."

He rose abruptly, angrily, and walked to the porch rail and stood with his back to her. She knew he wouldn't beg or plead or ask, not Will Dutcher. He'd said he wouldn't and he was a man of his word.

"I'm sorry," she said to his back.

He moved impatiently but said nothing, one hand toying with his mustache.

Emily rose and went to stand silently next to him. She could see his silhouette, silvered by the moonlight, a strong profile, its lines clean, harsh almost, brows drawn, mouth hard, a muscle ticking in his jaw. Slowly she reached out and touched his hand.

He turned then, swiftly, and took her in his arms, held her tightly, fiercely. "Damn you, woman," he growled.

She put her arms around him and laid her head on his chest. His heart beat heavily beneath her ear. "You know how I feel about you, Will," she breathed. "Never forget it, never doubt it."

He groaned. She turned her face up to him, and his mouth descended onto hers. They clung together, hip welded to hip, chest to chest, knee to knee. How could she leave this man? How could she give him up?

They went upstairs together, not even bothering with a lamp. They undressed silently, stepping out of their clothes, coming together with sighs and soft murmurings and desperate passion. *It could be the last time,* she thought, and she knew he was thinking the same thing. *The last time to feel his arms around me, to hear his breathing so urgent in my ear, to taste the salt of his sweat and feel him inside me, making me whole.*

She loved him with her body, giving him all the pleasure she could, wanting him to be utterly satisfied. She loved him until they were both sated, lying entangled, the sweat cooling on their fevered skin. She loved him as he lay in her arms, sleeping restlessly, his body heavy against her. She watched over him all night, lying there awake in the warm blackness, not wanting to waste a moment, a precious moment of the time she had left.

SUNDAYS WERE FOR CHURCH. Emily had never gone, but this Sunday Mary begged her to go with them because the children were being given awards for their Sunday school classes, and Mary was going to win one.

"Please, Miss Emily, please come! I'm going to get a bouquet of flowers and a white Bible of my own, and I want you to be there. Please!"

Emily looked at Mary's earnest little face, her neatly plaited braids, her pale freckles and the new white dress with a flounced skirt beneath which peeked out high-button boots. For a split second she wondered what Mary would look like when she grew up, and despaired because she'd never see it. "Of course I'll come, Mary," she said. "I can't miss that, can I?"

"Oh, good, oh, I'm so glad!" Mary cried.

The boys were already dressed in their best—black shorts and knee-high socks and starched white shirts, as was Will in his trousers and jacket and black bow tied at the starched collar.

"You best hurry and get ready then," he said, wiping his mouth on a napkin and pushing back his chair. "Reverend Shumaker gets real angry when anyone's late."

So, she thought as she changed hurriedly into the gray suit, she'd go and sit in church—for Mary's sake.

She hadn't been since she was a child, since she'd won her own Bible. Where had the time gone?

They could have been a model family that Sunday morning: handsome father, well-dressed blond mother and three lovely children riding on a buckboard behind two shiny bay horses.

They could have been, but they weren't.

The Reverend Mr. Shumaker greeted everyone at the open door, his thin face cracking into a smile with effort. Emily thought he looked like a dour Abraham Lincoln. Will introduced her and she nodded and said, "I'm very happy to meet you, Reverend."

"This is your first time here, isn't it, Miss Jacoby?" he asked, unsmiling.

"Yes, it is, and I'm so looking forward to your sermon," she said sweetly, and went past him into the small, unadorned church.

Someone had put a huge vase of late, high mountain lilacs on the pulpit, and the sweet, cloying scent permeated the air as people filed in, filling the pews. The Dutchers went to their pew and Emily followed. It was quiet in the church, a little stuffy on this warm summer day. There were whispers, rustling, a few louder children's voices and overlaying it all, that choking perfume of lilacs.

The day was a special one, the graduation of the Sunday school classes, and before the Reverend Mr. Shumaker spoke, the ceremony took place. There was a prayer, led by Mrs. Fisher, a psalm read by Mrs. Tate, a song, "Rock of Ages," sung by everyone. Will sang quite well, Emily noticed, his voice a strong baritone. As for Emily, she mouthed the words, only recalling a few of them.

Then the children were awarded their prizes. Mary sat expectantly, but Burke and Jesse fiddled and whispered and swung their legs. Will paid no mind, but Emily kept shushing them. She was hot in the church, perspiring in her underclothes and blouse and suit jacket. It wouldn't do to take her jacket off, either. And those flowers. They sent their sweet, heavy scent out to fill every corner of the church.

Mary was called. "Miss Mary Dutcher, winner of the sixth-grade class, for memorizing the Twenty-Third Psalm, letter-perfect. Here you are, Mary."

Mrs. Fisher handed her a bouquet and a white Bible, just as Mary had said, and Emily was so happy for her, so thrilled and proud, just as if Emily were her very own child. She glanced at Will. He was smiling at Mary, smiling genuinely.

"Good girl," he said as Mary sidled back into the pew with her flowers and Bible.

"Thank you, Uncle Will." And Mary blushed and grinned, brimming over with joy.

"Mary, hon, I'm very proud of you," Emily said, kissing the child on her pink cheek.

"I'm so glad you came," Mary said. "This is the very best day of my whole life."

But everyone was quieting now, and the Reverend Mr. Shumaker was climbing up to the pulpit. He adjusted his spectacles and peered over them at the churchgoers.

"Good morning," he began, "and God bless you all. We are gathered here to worship the Lord on his holy day. We are gathered here to put our minds and our hearts in order so that we can receive the word of the Lord."

Emily settled back, her mind only half on the sermon. She fanned herself with the songbook, as other women were doing, and the scent of lilacs came to her in waves, alternately sickeningly sweet and then as fleeting as a half-forgotten memory.

It must have been some time after that when she noticed the change in the atmosphere. Her mind clicked in to the tone of the minister's voice, the way the people shifted and moved on their hard seats. She listened then, and at first she couldn't believe what she was hearing.

"Those who break our Lord's commandments will be punished," the man was saying. "And there are those commandments that are not law but tradition. We are here on the frontier of our great country, trying with our hearts and minds to follow those traditions, to be pure in the eyes of God. It is hard out here, isolated as we are, and so we must try harder than our city brethren. Yes, harder! We cannot let ourselves fall into sin or we'll be damned forever. We must root out evil wherever we find it!"

Oh, thought Emily, he was *that* kind of preacher.

"We are men and women, Oh Lord, weak sinners out here on the fringes of civilization, but we cannot fall, we cannot let ourselves descend into the depths of sin, of, yes, I'll say it, of *fornication!*"

Every person in the room drew in his breath, a sibilant hiss of air like a snake ready to strike. Emily stiffened, heard the whispers, the murmurs, the word repeated, echoed around the small, bare church: *fornication.*

"Save us, Oh Lord, save the sinners among us. They must stop their transgressions and ask forgiveness of

Thee now, yes, right now! Or they must—'' and he pointed with a stiff quivering finger ''—go!''

The finger was pointing directly at her, Emily knew. Every head in the room turned in a rustling whisper, a prolonged turning that would never end. Every eye was on her, baleful, accusing.

The Reverend Mr. Shumaker was talking again, his voice full of anger, cajoling the worshipers, threatening them, but Emily heard little of it. She sat there cold as ice, stiff, so full of pain that she felt she was sweating crimson drops of her life's blood.

''Yeah, though I walk through the valley of evil, I will fear no sinner!'' Shumaker said, perverting the text, but no one noticed. ''I shall cast out evil from my house!''

It was then that she felt Will's fingers close on hers. She almost broke down and cried, but Will's grasp kept her resolute. She sat throughout the entire sermon, staring straight ahead, gripping his hand tightly, her heart swelling with love for him, the cloying scent of lilacs assaulting her nostrils.

They left quickly when it was over. Emily bustled the children out, her eyes blinded by tears that she let no one see. Will helped her up to the seat of the buckboard and looked questioningly at her. ''Emily, do you . . . ?'' he began.

''Please,'' she whispered, looking down, ''let's just go, Will.''

She didn't want to break down in front of the children. They were confused enough as it was, knowing some strange ''grown-up'' thing was wrong, but not understanding what or why. The boys forgot it quickly, but Mary, sensitive, loving Mary, deserved an explanation. *Not now though,* Emily thought, *not just now.*

She went up to her room the minute they reached the ranch house. Behind her she could hear Mary's tremulous question, "Uncle Will, what's wrong with Miss Emily?" And Will's evasive answer, "She doesn't feel well, Mary."

He came to her as soon as he'd taken care of the horses, still dressed in his black suit. He came into her bedroom without knocking and sat on the edge of her lumpy mattress so that it sagged.

"Emily," he said softly.

She rolled over to face him. Her eyes were red but dry. She'd done her weeping.

"Emily, they aren't bad people," he said.

She sighed, lying there and looking up at him. "I know. It's me. I'm bad."

"No, Em, never."

"To them I'm bad. Nothing will change that. It's too late now. Even if..." She hesitated.

"Even if what?" He reached out and pushed a wisp of hair back from her forehead, and she thrilled to his touch, closing her eyes.

"Nothing," she said, rolling her head away from him, one last, treacherous tear sliding out of the corner of her eye and down her temple.

"Emily." He cleared his throat. "I said I wouldn't beg. I said..."

She touched his lips, stopping him. "Then don't, please don't."

He looked at her, and their eyes met and locked. No words were needed. She saw that he knew. And he was in torment.

"I have to go, Will," she whispered, but she didn't need to say it, not really.

"When?"

"Today. Now."

"You'd let them run you out of town like that?"

She sighed again, a quavering intake of breath. "Let them think they won. It doesn't matter."

"What'll I tell the young ones?"

She laid a hand on his arm and tried to smile. "I'll tell them."

"Emily..."

"Oh, Will...kiss me, one last time, Will."

He leaned forward and scooped her up off the bed. She wound her arms around his neck and breathed in his scent, moving her mouth under his, feeling his mustache against her skin. It was a lingering, sad kiss, one of love and regret rather than passion.

When they drew apart, he gripped her shoulders hard and stared into her eyes. "I've never told it to a woman," he said roughly, "not ever. You're the only one, Emily Jacoby. I love you."

She searched his face. "You know I love you, too," she breathed. "Don't forget me."

"How could I? I'll remember you forever. I'll grow old remembering you."

She shook her head. "Marry someone, Will. Violet Lindley. Or someone else. Have children. Be happy."

He smiled crookedly. "You're some bossy housekeeper, woman."

"I know. I can't help it." She sat up on the edge of her bed and straightened her skirt, tucked some stray wisps of hair up. "Let me be now, Will. I'll pack and be down soon. You can drive me to the station then. All right?''

"If that's what you want..."

"Yes," she said with determination, "that's what I want."

"You know," he said, as if to himself, "from the first day I laid eyes on you I knew it wasn't...right."

"What wasn't?"

"You, Emily. I guess I always knew in my bones you didn't belong here."

"Oh, Will," she began.

"No," he said, "you told me, but I didn't want to hear it. I still don't," he muttered darkly, and left her alone in the silent room.

Emily gathered the children in the parlor later that afternoon. They looked back at her with solemn expressions, knowing something was wrong. The three of them—Mary, Jesse and Burke—were in order of height, just as she'd seen them the first time, when she'd awakened from the accident. Three precious blond heads, three orphans who'd needed her love.

Her throat closed, and for a moment she was unable to say a word.

"Miss Emily," Mary began, "Uncle Will says you're going away."

Emily closed her eyes. He'd told them. "Oh, Mary, honey, I'm sorry it has to be so sudden." She took the little girl's hand. "You see, I'm not really the housekeeper your Uncle Clay sent, and I have to leave now. You know, I told you that, hon."

"Why?" Jesse asked.

Emily took a deep breath. "I have to go back to my own life. I don't belong here. I have a job somewhere else and friends and . . ."

"Don't you like it here?" Mary asked.

Oh, God, this was hard. "Yes, hon. I love you kids. I even love Uncle Will. But . . . but sometimes grown-ups have to do things . . . things that they don't like, that're hard."

"Why?" Burke asked.

Why? Emily thought. *Yes, why?* "They just do. Like you have to go to school. Because it's important and later on in life it will be even more important."

They stared at her with wide blue eyes, confused, upset, not comprehending. Oh, Emily thought, what had she done?

Wordlessly she stooped and gathered all three children to her and hugged them. She buried her face in Mary's hair and felt the three firm, sweet, small bodies against her breast. *I can't,* she thought, *I can't do this. I . . .*

"Will you come back to visit us?" Mary asked in a choked voice.

"I . . . remember when I said I had a feeling we'd see each other again? I still believe that. I don't know where or when, but . . . somehow. I think we'll see each other again somehow, darling."

When she stood up, Will was there. He must have come in without her noticing, and he'd been watching. Her gaze met his over the children's heads.

"We'd best be on our way," he said quietly, his eyes dark with buried emotion.

"Yes," she replied, then she turned to the children again. "I have to go now. Mary, you'll have to be the lady of the house for a while, until Uncle Will gets another housekeeper. Honey, keep up your reading, okay? And make sure the boys wash their hands before supper. Jesse, you're the oldest boy. You take care of Burke and don't fight with him.'' She paused. "Burke, be good, button. Someday you'll be as big as Jesse, I promise. Take care of yourself.''

"Emily,'' Will reminded.

"Yes, I'm coming.''

She put on her gray suit jacket and picked up the carpetbag Will had bought her in Denver. She took a deep breath. "Let me say goodbye to Antonio. Just a second.''

She went into the kitchen where the old man was peeling potatoes for Sunday supper.

"Goodbye, Antonio,'' she said.

He turned rheumy eyes to her. "Boss says you leaving, Miss Emily.'' He shook his head sadly. "I no understand, but I say *hasta la vista,* not goodbye. That means until I see you again. It's better, no?''

"Yes, much better. *Hasta la vista,* Antonio. Take care of them all for me, will you?''

He nodded solemnly then turned back to his pile of potatoes.

The familiar ride into Rifle was excruciating. So was the drive through town, past the Western Mercantile, Zimmerman's Drug Store, the Winchester Hotel, the First National Bank. Will tied the team outside the Rio Grande depot and came around the rig to help her down. His hands on her waist made Emily suck in her breath in agony and close her eyes.

He bought her a ticket at the window, one-way to Denver. That's all she needed, she'd told him. No sense in him wasting his money.

"Here it is, Emily, your ticket," Will said, coming back to her.

"Thank you," she replied, her eyes downcast, her heart thudding in a horrible, slow cadence.

"And here, take this." Will handed her a roll of greenbacks, pressing them into her hand.

She looked up, startled. "But, I don't need...I..."

"Take it. Remember what happened last time in Denver City. I don't want you to go through that again. I wouldn't like to think..." He looked away, and she could see him swallow convulsively.

"Will," she said softly.

"Take it," he said. "You're always jawing about money. If that's what's important to you..."

"No," she said, "it isn't, not really. And I don't need it where I'm going."

He looked at her sharply.

"I...I mean, I'm going home, so I won't need it, Will."

"Keep it," he said harshly.

They stood there, looking at each other. Around them, passengers milled, children bawled, men smoked cigars and women fussed.

"Take care of the children," she said.

"I did it before you came, and I'll do it now. Don't worry your head about us," Will said.

"Don't hate me, Will."

He took his hat off and ran a hand through his hair. "Damn it, Emily, I wish I could hate you. It'd be a sight easier."

"Oh, Will..."

"Don't, Emily, just let it lay."

"Will you miss me?"

"Almighty God, woman..." His dark blue eyes bored into hers. "Yes, I'll miss you."

"I love you, Will. I'll always love you."

He came to her then, right there in front of everyone inside the depot. He put his arms around her and, in the sudden, shocked hush, he kissed her long and lingeringly, full on the lips.

"Go now," Emily said, her mouth branded with his, her eyes swimming with tears.

"I'll wait till the train comes," he said.

"No. Leave me here. Don't wait. I don't want you to wait."

"Is that your last order, Emily?"

"Yes, Will," she said soberly. "Go home now."

He went. He put his hat on, turned and strode away from her, his back straight and proud, his shoulders broad, his boot heels tapping on the wooden floor. He walked away and never looked back, and then he was out the door, gone, and Emily put her hand to her mouth to stifle a sob.

She sat in a corner, her carpetbag at her feet, waiting until she knew he was safely away. Leaning over, she carefully put the roll of greenbacks into the bag. The stationmaster would return it to him when he found the bag sitting there, abandoned.

She stood. She was ready now. It was time. She walked out of the depot, across the platform and onto the tracks. She paid no attention to the people who might have been watching, puzzling over her behavior. It didn't matter. She walked east, along the tracks, her skirt dragging in the dust.

This time it would work. Her mind was focused, firm. There was no one to pull her back.

She walked on under the hot sun. It wasn't long before she peeled off her kid gloves and dropped her velvet drawstring purse. She didn't need them. She unpinned her hat, the one with the ostrich feathers, and threw it aside. She shrugged out of her dove gray jacket and dropped it behind her. She walked on, feeling light and free, different somehow. She'd done what she had to do. She'd saved Will's ranch. She'd loved and been loved in return. She'd learned what truly mattered. She'd survived.

Emily strode down the tracks, suddenly without regrets. She saw the broad Colorado River to her right, winking at her in the sun, and felt the hot rays on her head. Reaching up, she pulled out the pins in her hair, tossed them aside and shook her hair out.

She walked faster. Yes, there was the wreckage, the rusted cars of the train wreck. Tall green grass had grown up around them, through gaping holes in the sides of the cars, through empty windows. She kept going, not pausing. Her vision began fading at the edges, the sun was so hot. She reached up and undid the buttons at her throat, feeling a little nauseous. The tracks led her on, meeting ahead, in front of her. Her head hurt, and she was dizzy. But she couldn't stop now. She knew what she was going for. Strong in purpose, she strode on to where the tracks met. She reached the confluence of the two endless bands of steel and kept going.

CHAPTER SEVENTEEN

EMILY TRIED TO SWIM UP from the murky waters surrounding her. There was something she had to do, something . . . a task so hard she felt discouraged, weary. What was it? What did she have to do?

She was exhausted, held by a lethargy too powerful to leave, dreaming. She knew she was dreaming, aware of some deep, still-awake part of her brain that commanded her to wake, to remember.

A scent wafted past her nostrils, a sweet, familiar scent, and it dragged at her senses, tugging. There was something . . . something . . .

A voice called to her, a soft, feminine voice, and somehow she knew this voice had spoken her name before, many times before. Who?

"Miss Jacoby," the voice said with absolute patience. "Emily, can you hear me?"

Another voice, male. "She moved. I saw her eyelids move. I tell you . . ." A familiar voice this time.

She tried very hard to answer, but her throat didn't seem to work. It was so difficult, and she was confused. Why was it so hard to talk? Why wouldn't they just let her sleep?

"Emily. Emily Jacoby, can you hear me?" A hand was on her arm, pressing, and she knew she wasn't asleep anymore. "Emily, if you can't say anything, move your hand. Can you move your hand, Emily?"

With a determination she didn't know she had, she forced her eyes open. Light. Glaring brightness that hurt. She closed them again.

"My God," the male voice said, then a hand was on her arm, a heavier hand, gripping her.

"Excuse me," the other one said, "I'll ring for Dr. Stinson."

"Emily. Emily Jacoby. Open your eyes, Emily," the male voice said.

She tried, squinted, felt the painful rush of light explode against her eyes, but she withstood it.

"Emily," he said.

A face swam into view, blurred, sharpened, blurred again. She blinked. The face coalesced in front of her eyes.

Will. It was Will. Of course. She tried to smile, tried to move her hand. Her lips moved, and a small sound came out, but it exhausted her so, she let herself sink back toward sleep. Will was there. It was all right. He'd take care of her. . . .

She woke again later, and things began to make some sense. Some, but not very much.

Her nurse was named Dorothy. "You were in that train wreck a week ago," she told her. "You have a bad concussion. You've been in a coma for a week. Do you understand what I'm saying, Miss Jacoby?"

"Yes," Emily whispered.

"Oh, you're doing very well. We're never sure with a head injury, you know."

"I've been here unconscious for a week?" Emily managed.

"There was a bad storm. Do you remember that? A blizzard. If you don't remember, don't worry. Temporary amnesia is very common. It'll all come back."

"A storm," Emily said haltingly. "Last winter. The train."

Dorothy smiled reassuringly. "It wasn't last winter. It was a week ago. This winter. It's just turned into March. But don't worry, that'll all come back to you."

It came back over the next day. The snowstorm, the train wreck. Small and large details fit themselves together into a picture, still with gaps here and there. But she remembered Will Dutcher and the three kids, Shep the dog, Rifle, all the rest. It came back to her, a sweet, sweet memory.

A dream.

Confused, amnesia. Hadn't Doc Tichenor said the same thing?

But now Emily knew where she was. She was in a hospital in Rifle, Colorado. It was March 8, 1993. She knew. She'd asked.

It came to her that evening after supper. When Dorothy went on duty.

"Was there a man here the first time I woke up?" she asked carefully. "I seem to remember . . ."

"Oh, you do remember? That's good," Dorothy said cheerfully. "Yes, that was Will Dutcher."

She felt the blood leave her head, felt the awful cold sweat and nausea. Everything receded sickeningly and her ears rang.

"Miss Jacoby? Are you all right?" Dorothy asked. "Emily, can you hear me?"

She fought the blackness off. She closed her eyes and willed it to go away. She gritted her teeth and clenched her fists, weak as they were. "Yes," she whispered, "just a little faint."

"That's better," her nurse said.

"Tell me," Emily croaked. "Will Dutcher. Who...who is he?"

"Will? Oh, he was one of the volunteers who helped with the train wreck. He's had some first-aid training, and they needed everybody they could get. Apparently, he helped get you out. He's been visiting you to see how you're doing. Sort of took an interest."

"Is he from here?" Emily asked.

"Yes, he lives on a ranch a few miles out of town. Quiet fellow."

"And his name is Will Dutcher?"

"Yes," Dorothy said, puzzled. "I told you that. See, he brought these flowers for you."

Emily turned her head. A vase of flowers sat on her nightstand. The smell, yes, she remembered, in her dream, only those had been lilacs, and these were hothouse flowers because it was still winter.

Dorothy bustled around, changing Emily's bed position, checking her IV. "Oh, yes, Will Dutcher is a bit of a loner, a bachelor. He's had troubles, too. His brother and sister-in-law died last year and left him with three kids, three little kids. He works hard, but he takes real good care of those kids...."

"Mary...is one of them named Mary?"

"Well, I'll be. Yes, his niece. Common name, though. Then there's Jesse and the little one...what's his name? I never can remember."

"Burke," Emily breathed.

"Yes, well, for goodness' sakes!" Dorothy looked at her in amazement.

"I . . . I, ah, guess I must have overheard Will, Mr. Dutcher, that is, talking in my room or something," Emily said, fumbling.

Dorothy went out of the room then, turned out the light and left her in the semidark hospital room with her IV and the lights of the monitor.

She was weak and confused. There was a bandage on her head, and she hurt all over. But she remembered. Oh yes, she remembered.

Will Dutcher was alive in 1993. Was it the same Will Dutcher? Did he know her? Or had she dreamed the whole thing in her coma, dreamed the whole four months of her life in the past? Had she dreamed the love she felt, the smells and sights and sounds? How could she possibly have known all those details?

Will Dutcher was alive, a living, breathing man. She'd seen his face, and it was him. She'd heard his voice. Will's voice. He was there, and she'd see him again. She closed her eyes and whispered up a prayer. And then she slept.

He came the following evening, knocking softly at the door, then stepped inside.

Emily had been dozing, but she awakened instantly. Her heart gave a leap, blood pounded in her ears. She felt frightened, relieved, full of joy and sadness all at once. Will was there, in her room, in front of her.

"Hello," she said.

"Miss Jacoby?" he asked carefully.

"Emily. I'm Emily. You called me Emily that night . . ." she said, then fell silent.

It was Will. The same blue eyes and dark curling hair, the same nose and mouth. The same mustache, but it was smaller, trimmed closer. His hair was parted on the side instead of the middle, and he held his Stetson in both hands, nervously.

"Okay. *Emily.* I just thought I'd stop in to see how you were. Do you mind? Or should I come back some other time?"

"No, no, please, come in. Sit down."

He pulled a chair over to her bed, sat, crossed one booted foot over the other knee and balanced his hat on it. "So," he ventured, "you're better."

"Better. Not great, though. Not yet. But they tell me I'll recover." She couldn't take her eyes off him. His mouth. It had kissed her. His hands had caressed her.

"Well, you were out for a long time. You're lucky," he said.

"Yes, I'm lucky," she echoed. "Will, you don't mind if I call you that? Thanks for the flowers. They're lovely."

"Oh, you're welcome. No big deal."

"Dorothy told me you rescued me from the train wreck. I guess I need to thank you for that, too," she said shyly. She was talking to Will, face-to-face, but he was a stranger. He was . . . and he wasn't.

"I'm glad I could help. It was a bad wreck, a snowslide over the track. Just knocked the engine right off the rails," he said.

It couldn't be true. It was crazy. She knew him, knew this man sitting by her hospital bed. And he didn't know her.

"I . . . ah . . . hear you have your brother's children," she said.

"Three." He caught her gaze with his and held it. "It was the least I could do after my brother and his wife were killed in a car accident."

"I'm sorry," Emily murmured.

"So am I. But it's over, and we make do." He paused and cleared his throat. "Do you have a family? Someone you'd like notified?"

She thought for a minute, then shook her head. "No, not really. I...my parents are...not well, and I hate to worry them. I have no other family. I should call my friend Judy, but I'll wait till I feel a little better."

A pregnant silence fell between them for a time. "Well," Will said, "I'd best be getting home." He rose and put his hat on his head, tilted it just so in that familiar way. It made Emily's heart stop. This wasn't possible....

"Thank you for coming. I appreciate it." She looked up at him, caught him fixing her with a peculiar, questioning look. "Would you...could you come again sometime?"

"Sure can," he said.

"Only if it's no trouble," she said. "And, do you, do you think you could bring the children? I'd love to see them." She stopped and caught her breath, felt her heart hammering too hard.

"The kids?"

"I love children," she said, wondering how odd her request sounded.

"I guess so."

"Only if they want to."

When he was gone, she lay back and closed her eyes, exhausted. It was Will, her Will, here and now, alone

with three children. But how could that be? Even if she
had traveled through time, spent months in the past
but come back to the present at the very instant the
train had hit that snowslide, how could Will be here,
too?

Emily racked her brain, consumed by the problem.
Had she really been in the past or had it all been a
dream? She rubbed her hand over her face, trying to
think, to make sense of the situation, and then it came
to her.

Slowly, deliberately, she drew her hand from her
face and held it, shaking, in front of her eyes. Oh,
God, yes, it was there! The scar, the faded brown scar
of the burn where she'd grabbed that pot. *It was there.*

She let her hand drop, closed her eyes and drew in a
quavering breath. She *had* traveled through time, then.
It was true.

And yet, this time, when she'd come back...they'd
found her a week ago in the train wreck. So she must
have come back through the same doorway at the
same instant that she left. Yes, that would explain it
all . . . even wearing her own clothes this time.

It would explain everything but the existence of Will
Dutcher. He was here, in 1993, but he couldn't be, not
unless a person believed in reincarnation. Well, she
didn't, but then again, she'd never believed in time
travel, either.

Will came the next evening, too. He brought her a
box of candy.

"Here," he said, "you look a little thin. Hope you
like it."

"I *was* on quite a diet for the past week," she replied. "And I do love chocolates. I'll bet I look like death warmed over."

He studied her soberly, his eyes traveling from her stringy blond hair to the gaping gray hospital gown to the IV in her arm. "Yup," he said, "I'll bet you've looked better." He pulled the chair up and sat down. "I didn't haul the kids along. I figured I'd wait till you're stronger. They're noisy little buggers. The boys, anyway."

"I guess I'll be here another week or so," she said, "so there'll be time. Dorothy said they'll take the IV out tomorrow."

"That's good."

"I got up today," she offered.

"How was it?"

"I was pretty shaky. Ridiculous."

He studied her again in that intense, disconcerting way he had. "You ever been in Rifle before?" he asked abruptly.

"No, never." Her heart flew up into her throat, lodging there. She glanced away, fumbling with the wrapping on the box of candy.

"It's just that you look familiar. I thought..." He shook his head. "One of those crazy déjà vu things, you know?"

"Yes, I know," she murmured.

He leaned back in the chair and fiddled with the leather band on his hat. "So, tell me, Emily Jacoby, where were you heading on that train?"

"I was going to Seattle to visit a friend. I was thinking about moving there."

"And you're from...?"

"Philadelphia." She looked down at her hands. "I was a loan officer in a bank there."

"But you left," he said.

"I was tired of the rat race. Too much stress. The usual," she said.

"Looks like you're having a good rest here then."

She gave a short laugh. "Enforced rest."

"Maybe you needed it," he said cryptically.

He came almost every evening. They talked about nothing and everything. One night he pushed her wheelchair down the hall to the gift shop so she could buy some things, and on another he held her arm as she took her first shaky walk to the cafeteria for coffee and dessert.

When he couldn't make it, he phoned her, and they'd talk, hungry for the contact, and when he wasn't there, Emily craved his presence with such yearning that she couldn't bear it.

She was falling in love all over again with Will Dutcher. And it was doubly sweet this time, because she knew what could be. And doubly wretched because of what might not be.

The idea came to her on a quiet Saturday morning and she called Will at his ranch. "I hate to impose," Emily said, "but could you possibly stop by the library and bring me a few books on the history of Rifle?"

"Sure, no problem."

That night, when Will had gone home, Emily opened the first book with trembling fingers. *Rifle Shots,* it was titled, and it was a more complete history—photos and all—than she could have dreamed for. By midnight she had her answers, no explanation

for them, but Emily knew now for a certainty she'd
met Will Dutcher and his family in 1893. There was no
more doubt. The only trouble was that there wasn't
too much mention of Will Dutcher in his latter years.

Sunday morning she telephoned him again and
carefully asked a few questions.

"So it was your great-grandfather and his brother
who started the ranch?" she asked. "And his name
was Will, too?"

"That's right," he told her. "My father was also a
Will."

"Then your great-grandfather was married?"

"I suppose he must have been," Will replied,
laughing a little over the phone, "or I wouldn't be sitting here on the telephone talking to you, Emily."

"Of course not," she said. So Will—the Will of
1893, that was—had indeed gotten married. But to
whom? "What was his wife's name?" she asked.
"The book never said."

"Oh, Lord," Will said, "I'm not sure. I know she
was a schoolteacher, though."

Emily's heart raced. *Well, I'll be darned,* she
thought. *Violet Lindley.*

"Why are you so interested?" he asked then.

"Oh," Emily said, trying to focus her spinning
thoughts, "I just am. I . . . I like the area, I guess, and
history's so interesting."

She thought about it all day and half the night. Will
had told her also that the family tended to keep the
same names down through the generations. That, of
course, explained some things, such as the children's
names and their father's name, Jesse. But the paral-
lels were still bizarre, and the only thing Emily could

conclude was that she'd been sent back in time to meet Will Dutcher, and somehow set the pattern for the future. But why? Did she dare believe that she'd be a continuing part of the Dutcher history or the family's future?

It was just too crazy. And yet . . .

A couple days later Will finally brought the children. They were so similar to their forebears that Emily should have been shocked once more, yet she wasn't. There was a scheme to this madness, something so right in its impossibility that she no longer questioned it. A scheme, she thought again, yes, just like in some of the Eastern philosophies she'd studied in college . . . rebirth, karma, all that. *Could* Will have been born again, born into her world because their lives together had been unfulfilled?

Crazy, crazy, but then so was this whole situation.

The children stood in her room, three blond heads in order. They wore ski parkas over jeans and sweatshirts and little Sorel winter boots. Mary's hair was pulled back in a ponytail, but otherwise they were so much the same . . . Emily couldn't talk for a minute, and her eyes burned with unshed tears.

"It's nice to meet you all," she finally managed. "I've heard so much about you."

"You're Emily," Burke said.

"You were in the train wreck," Jesse added. "Uncle Will told us."

"You look okay," Mary said.

"I'm better, thank you, Mary. I'll be going home in a few days."

She walked down the hall with them to the cafeteria. She still moved very slowly, and she held on to

Will's arm. The children ran ahead, the boys scampering, Mary skipping, her blond ponytail bouncing up and down.

"They're adorable," Emily said to him.

"They're good kids," he said, shrugging.

They ate ice cream, and Burke smeared himself with chocolate sauce.

"Don't be such a slob," Mary told him. "You'll make a bad impression."

Emily smiled to herself. Had Will told them to make a good impression?

The next day was Thursday, and he came in the afternoon.

"I left the kids with Antonio," he explained. "Enough is enough."

"Antonio?" she had to ask.

"He's my, well, sort of cook and handyman and baby-sitter. He's been with me for years. In fact his own grandfather..."

"The old family retainer," she said thoughtfully, interrupting.

"I suppose so." Will hesitated then, put a hand up to smooth his mustache. "Look, Emily...I thought about what you said yesterday, that you'd be going home in a few days. I, uh, wondered where you meant. Where's home, Emily, back in Philadelphia?"

She swung her legs over the side of the bed and sat there for a moment, her pulse pounding in her veins. "I don't know," she whispered.

"You don't know where you're going?"

"I don't know where my home is."

"Will you go to your friend in Seattle then?" he asked slowly.

They were playing an elaborate game, not looking at each other, mouthing phrases, and she had to wait for him to ask.

"I don't know. I haven't thought that far," she said breathlessly.

"Emily, it's not *that* far off."

She couldn't answer. She sat there, looking at her hands, turning one over then the other. She was thin; her bones showed through her skin.

"Emily," he said again.

"Yes, Will?"

"Could I . . . say, get you a plane ticket from Denver? Rent you a car? So you don't have to worry about it," he said.

Her heart fell. He wasn't going to ask. He had no intention of asking. He was only being friendly. If she wasn't supposed to end up in Rifle—with Will—then why had she been sent to the past to set all this up? My God, Emily thought, *why?*

"That would be nice," she heard herself saying.

"A plane ticket then? To where?" he asked.

She raised her eyes then. "I don't know," she said.

He returned her gaze, his dark brows drawn. "You're not well enough yet."

"I'm fine. I'll be all right."

He stood abruptly, restless, a big man in jeans and scuffed boots and a plaid shirt. He turned his back to her, and the movement was so familiar her bones melted in her body.

"Look, Emily," he said, not facing her, "I know this is a crazy idea. Tell me if I'm out of line."

Her breath stopped in her lungs.

He spun around. "Stay with me," he said. "Till you're all better. I have room." He walked up close and stood in front of her, tilted her face up with a hand. "Just until you're better, Emily. I can't...I hate to think of you traveling like this. You need some time to rest."

"Will?"

"Am I out of line? Tell me."

She looked up at him, and a smile trembled on her lips. "You'd have me at your home? I'm a stranger, someone you pulled out of a train wreck."

His gaze never wavered, that dark blue gaze with the heavy brows above. "You're no stranger, Emily."

"You want me to come, really?"

"The kids will be a pain. They'll pester the bejesus out of you."

"I love your kids," she said.

"You're a...a good woman," Will got out, embarrassed.

"Thank you," Emily managed.

He cleared his throat. "You'll, ah, stay then?"

"I'll stay as long as you'll have me," she whispered.

He took her hand in his, carefully, tentatively, and she knew this was her Will Dutcher, the very same man she'd loved a century before, the man she'd always love.

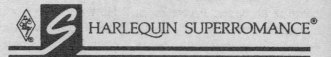

HARLEQUIN SUPERROMANCE®

COMING NEXT MONTH

#550 TWIN OAKS • Anne Logan

Dillon Reynolds had been summoned home to help save the family business—Twin Oaks Country Club. Jobs were on the line, but Dillon was finding that firing people was not as easy as he thought. Especially when he met Adrienne Hamilton, whose career was now in his hands.

#551 ONCE UPON A CRIME • Dawn Stewardson

A long, long time ago, Abby Northberry and Ryan Vaughn were teenagers in love. And then someone robbed her father's jewelry store. Ryan spent six years in jail for a crime he didn't commit and when he returned to Cedar Rapids, he swore he'd find whoever had framed him and stolen his life. But the closer he got to the truth, the closer he and Abby came to losing each other all over again....

#552 EYE OF THE JAGUAR • Jane Silverwood

Eve Gardiner's government grant to seek out rare medicinal plants in the Yucatán jungle came with a price tag—she was to keep an eye on Simon Mercier, her host at the El Gato del Sol ranch. The ex-agent turned international businessman made the feds uneasy. Before too long Eve could sense the danger in the air, but the undeniable magnetism of a man who could capture her soul was too potent to escape.

#553 LATE BLOOMER • Peg Sutherland

Women Who Dare, Book 6

Rose Finley was warm, funny and very restless. On the eve of her fortieth birthday, a stranger arrived in Sweetbranch, Alabama, and promised to turn her whole life upside down. He and his small daughter were on the run—but from what? Rose wondered if she should run herself, but vowed that this time life was definitely not going to pass her by.

AVAILABLE THIS MONTH:

#546 AFTER THE PROMISE
Debbi Bedford

#547 SHENANIGANS
Casey Roberts

#548 THE MODEL BRIDE
Pamela Bauer

#549 PARADOX
Lynn Erickson

Take 4 bestselling love stories FREE

Plus get a FREE surprise gift!

Special Limited-time Offer

Mail to Harlequin Reader Service®

3010 Walden Avenue
P.O. Box 1867
Buffalo, N.Y. 14269-1867

YES! Please send me 4 free Harlequin Superromance® novels and my free surprise gift. Then send me 4 brand-new novels every month, which I will receive before they appear in bookstores. Bill me at the low price of $2.71 each plus 25¢ delivery and applicable sales tax, if any.* I understand that accepting the books and gift places me under no obligation ever to buy any books. I can always return a shipment and cancel at any time. Even if I never buy another book from Harlequin, the 4 free books and the surprise gift are mine to keep forever.

134 BPA AJHT

Name	(PLEASE PRINT)	
Address	Apt. No.	
City	State	Zip

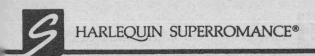

HARLEQUIN SUPERROMANCE®

WOMEN WHO DARE DRIVE RACE CARS?!

During 1993, each Harlequin Superromance **WOMEN WHO DARE** title will have a single italicized letter on the Women Who Dare back-page ads. Collect the letters, spell D A R E and you can receive a free copy of **RACE FOR TOMORROW**, written by popular author Elaine Barbieri. This is an exciting novel about a female race-car driver, **WHO DARES ANYTHING . . . FOR LOVE!**

Mail this certificate, designated letters spelling DARE, and check or money order for postage and handling to: In the U.S.—WOMEN WHO DARE, P.O. Box 9057, Buffalo, NY 14269-9057; In Canada—WOMEN WHO DARE, P.O. Box 622, Fort Erie, Ontario L2A 5X3.

Requests must be received by January 31, 1994.
Allow 4-6 weeks after receipt of order for delivery.   R-O85-KAT

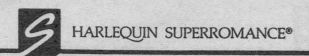

HARLEQUIN SUPERROMANCE®